Rexanne Becnel

Rexanne Becnel, the author of twenty novels and two novellas, swears she could not be a writer if it weren't for New Orleans's many coffeehouses. She does all her work longhand, with a mug of coffee at her side. She is a charter member of the Southern Louisiana Chapter of Romance Writers of America, and founded the New Orleans Popular Fiction Conference.

Rexanne's novels regularly appear on bestseller lists such as *USA TODAY*, *Amazon.com*, Waldenbooks, Ingrams and Barnes and Noble. She has been nominated for and received awards from *Romantic Times BOOKclub*, Waldenbooks, The Holt Committee, the *Atlanta Journal/Atlanta Constitution* and the National Readers' Choice Awards.

The Payback Club

Rexanne Becnel

A girl's got to have friends,
and I'm blessed with a lot of them.

So this book is dedicated to all my volleyball pals
from the Fit With Finn League, Gernon Brown
Gym, Harahan Gym and the Little Farms Gym.

And especially to Brand X, the Mardi Gras Mamas,
True G.R.I.T.S. and Louisiana Spice.

CHAPTER 1

JOAN

It all started up again because of the society page.

I was sitting in my breakfast room, minding my own business, reading the newspaper and eating my bowl of Total with a half-cup of skim milk and a slice of cantaloupe. My trainer would be so proud. Then I opened the Living section, and whom do I see laughing up at me? Ed, my ex-husband, and Barracuda Woman, his much younger new wife. It's a photo of them at the YMCA's annual fundraiser ball.

I stared at them, trying to ignore the sudden pounding of my heart. I shouldn't be surprised. She'd already stolen my husband; why wouldn't she steal my charity too? And yet despite my noble attempt at logic, I felt the little hairs on the back of my neck lift. No, my hackles lifted. "Hackles" sounds more visceral, more primitive. I spy my enemy and my hackles lift.

In the wild, animals have two choices when faced with an enemy: fight or flight. But we humans work so hard to be civilized. Someone carves the heart out of your chest, and all you do is smile and put on the false front of civility so the rest of the world can't see that your life's blood is dripping away, drop by bitter drop.

Even now, at home all by myself, all I did was turn to page four of the Living section and take another bite of cereal. First Ed had ruined our family with that woman; now they were horning in on my favorite charity. But there was nothing I could do about it. Nothing. So I finished my cereal, got up to dress, and, since my heart was already pumping faster than normal, I went to the gym.

That's the day I met Liz.

I was hunched over the handlebars of the stationary bike, depressed and brooding over that damned society page photo, when I heard, "I want to wreck his life."

Had I said that out loud?

Embarrassed, I peered cautiously around the workout room. It was one thing to daydream about wrecking Ed's life, about ruining him socially, financially and maybe physically too. But now I was talking to myself?

Then I heard it again. "I want to wreck his life like he's wrecked mine." It came from a pretty strawberry-blond woman on the ab machine two rows over. Thank God I'm not crazy. My thoughts, but her words.

Trying to concentrate, I gripped the molded plastic handgrips and pedaled. But it was weird how she felt just like I did, as if I were projecting my frustration onto her, except that I'm not the woo-woo E.S.P. horoscope type.

Then again, there are a lot of jerks in the world. She probably had her own version of Ed, and just like me, I wanted to even the score. It wasn't complicated.

Most of the time I got along fine. I was building a new

life without Ed, and it wasn't all bad. But some days the realization of all I'd lost was harder to bear. Like today. On those days, all I wanted was to strangle Ed, to leave him gasping for breath and trying to survive in a world suddenly gone crazy.

I pedaled even faster. And to sweeten the deal, I wanted to yank that blond barracuda he'd married bald-headed.

"Whoa, Joan," Nita, the fitness trainer, called out to me. "Slow down. You won't last five minutes at that pace."

"Interval training," I muttered. "Isn't that what you're always preaching? Sprints get my heart rate up." *So do thoughts of revenge.*

"Well, yeah. But you just got on that bike. What happened to two minutes of warm ups, then one-minute intervals of increasing speed?" She strolled over from where she'd been helping the other woman with her form. "You went from cold to sprint in forty-five seconds flat."

I frowned at her, but I was too winded to argue. Anyway, she was right. You only have to look at her perfectly taut, spandex-clad body to know that when it comes to fitness, Nita Alvarez is always right. The whirring of the going-nowhere wheels eased as I began to slow down.

"And you're gripping too tight." Nita tapped my left knuckle. "Had a bad day?"

I huffed out a frustrated breath. "No more than usual." I took another harsh breath, then exhaled. "I guess I overheard what she said." I gestured with my head to her new client, a plump version of Pamela Anderson, who was scowling with every stomach crunch.

At Nita's questioning look I explained. "About wrecking some guy's life. I was thinking the very same thing."

"Oh." Nita's perfectly waxed brows went up in understanding. "She's in the beginning stages of a divorce."

"So I figured."

"Liz," Nita said, turning to the woman who was focused with pink-faced concentration on her abs. "Liz Savoie, this is Joan Hoffman. She's been coming here for about a year now."

Liz paused, breathing hard from her exertions. "Hi," she said in a sweet, little girl's voice. "I'm new at the Oasis. You look great."

I shrugged, pleased despite my nonchalant response. "Thanks, but Nita gets all the credit. She's a regular drill sergeant."

Liz wiped her damp brow with the back of her wrist. "I'm beginning to see that."

"But only within reason," Nita said. "There's a method to my madness." She sent me a cheeky grin. "Joan was overdoing it just now. She heard you say you want to wreck *his* life and it reminded her of *her* ex, and all of a sudden she was pedaling a hundred miles an hour."

From across the room the owner of the Oasis Spa and Body Works signaled to Nita. "Looks like I have to go," she said. "Keep to your program, okay, Joan? As for you," she added to Liz, "I'll be back to start you on the next machine in five minutes."

With a nod to Liz, I settled into a steady pace on the bike. Liz went back to her ab work. The erratic thunk of the weight machines and soft grunts from several other members were the only interruption to the soothing New Age music piped in to the serene aqua and cream training room.

I did four miles on the bike. Then I planned to swim my usual twenty laps. After that I wasn't sure how I was going to spend the rest of the day. I mean, I had work to do. A new brochure to design for the Louisiana Optical Society, as well as their quarterly newsletter. But it was solitary work, just me in my home office with H.C.—Hunk of Crap—my computer. To tell the truth, I'd rather exercise. At least at Oasis there were other people around.

The fact is, I'm in the best shape of my life these days, and it's mainly due to loneliness. My old life, the one with kids to ferry around town, a husband to keep happy, and all sorts of social and community activities demanding my time no longer exists. Despite my thriving new home business, there are still days when I feel like my life is filled with nothing.

First Pearl went off to college. Two years later Ronnie did the same. Bittersweet, but to be expected. Then a week after that, completely out of the blue, Ed filed for divorce.

Despite Nita's orders, I began to pedal faster.

Divorce! No one in my family had ever been divorced. Even my crazy sister Margie, the South Florida apartment manager, had managed to remain tethered to the same man.

But not me. I'd reached high when I married Edward St. Romaine the Third, and together we'd flown higher still. He was a partner in a top law firm, and I was active in the Junior League, the Preservation Resource Center, and literacy programs at S.T.A.I.R. and the YMCA. Pretty good for a girl from Mid City whose dad made his living driving streetcars.

But at least my blue-collar parents had stayed married.

"How long have you been divorced?"

I blinked at the unexpected question, then twisted my head toward the voice. Liz, the strawberry blonde, was rubbing her sore stomach muscles while she waited for Nita to start her on the next machine.

"Sorry," she muttered when I didn't answer right away. Her flushed cheeks grew even pinker. "I'm being nosy, aren't I? I just thought…well, what Nita said."

I shook my head. "It's all right. I've been officially divorced for almost a year."

"And you still want to wreck his life?" Blowing out a frustrated breath, she sat on the bench in front of my bike. She wore a loose gray T-shirt over her spandex outfit, the sure sign of a newbie trying to hide that extra ten or twenty pounds. "Do you think that kind of anger ever goes away? I mean, my divorce isn't close to being final, but I was hoping that once it was I'd stop being so royally pissed off at Dennis."

"Oh, honey, you have no idea," I said, unable to hide my cynicism. I patted my face with the towel I kept draped on the handlebars. "It seems like your anger and hurt go away. You get through a week, even two, without letting what *he* did be the center of your world anymore. And then he does something else—"

I stopped mid-sentence. I don't like airing my personal

life to strangers. I don't even like talking about Ed with women I've known twenty years. My marriage is the biggest failure of my life. I couldn't keep my own husband interested in me, and he split the first moment he could. Why would I want to admit that to anybody?

But today I was more pissed off at Ed than I'd been in a long time. First the picture in the paper. Then not ten minutes later, Pearl had called from school, complaining that her father hadn't returned her calls in two days. She was worried that he might be sick. As if. Her father wasn't sick; he was just selfish. Too busy screwing Barb the Barracuda to call his own daughter. Of course, I would never say that to Pearl.

I shouldn't even be saying these things to Liz.

I stood up to head for the pool and the anonymity of cleaving through the cold, unforgiving water. My mistake was when I looked at Liz. Moisture glinted beneath her pale lashes, tears held back by rapid blinking. And her Kewpie-doll lips trembled ever so slightly.

This was one of those days when I didn't think I could keep my own spirits up. How could I possibly help anyone else? But I remembered too clearly feeling exactly the way she did now.

"Don't waste any tears on your ex." I draped my towel around the back of my neck. "I don't know why your marriage fell apart, Liz. But I do know that crying only proves he's won."

From across the room Nita started our way. Good. Maybe I could ease out of this conversation. But when she saw us talking, she gave me a thumbs-up and veered in another direction. I let out a sigh. So much for a quick escape.

"But I can't seem to stop crying." Liz stared down at her knotted hands. Then, as if to prove the point, she burst into noisy sobs.

Fifteen minutes and as many tissues later, I had somehow agreed to have lunch with Liz. But as I swam my laps, I fumed. At myself for succumbing to Liz's neediness; at Nita for setting me up; and at Ed—always at Ed—for putting me in this god-awful situation in the first place.

Most of the time I reminded myself that my divorce could have been worse. It could have been one of those slash-and-burn, take-no-prisoners kind of divorces that made *The War of the Roses* look like a skirmish. At least Ed and I could be civil with each other, and going back to work had helped my self-esteem enormously.

But then there were days like today when I felt every one of my forty-six years, like I was skidding—despite my fingernails futilely screeching protest—toward fifty and all the gloomy, twilight years stretching beyond like an endless nightmare. Did I mention that I'm terrified of growing old?

No. That's not precisely true. What I'm afraid of is growing old alone—and of always being as lonely as I've been lately.

I'm used to spending time alone. That's not the problem. Ed's legal practice often took him to Atlanta, to Chicago, to Washington. And as the children had grown, they'd gone off to summer camps and junior years abroad. Through it all I'd never felt lonely.

But I'm lonely now.

Sometimes this awful hollowness made me feel like an empty shell, like I'd crack and shatter if someone bumped into me in just the wrong way. And now I'd gotten involved with Liz and her philandering husband. God, I did not want to hear the details of her divorce. Already they sounded depressingly similar to my own. But Liz needed to vent and I just couldn't abandon the poor thing. So I swam twenty hard-driving laps.

Usually I start with breaststroke, progress to freestyle, and then finish with a slow, cooling-down backstroke. But today I drove myself through the cold, indifferent water. Lap after lap of freestyle, a thousand yards, more than half a mile.

The cool water sluiced off my body as I climbed from the pool; my shoulders and thighs twitched and trembled from exertion. I'd earned dessert today. Pecan pie à la mode. Or maybe bread pudding with hard sauce. Or I could splurge on New Orleans's official lunch order: an oyster po'boy dressed, swimming in mayo.

Once I reached the locker room I stood reveling in the needling heat of the shower. I'd only lost ten pounds since I started at Oasis, but it looked like twenty. That's because I'd firmed up, toning my jiggly thighs, my mushy stomach, and the loose underarms that had appeared right after my fortieth birthday. I hadn't looked this good in twenty years, since before Pearl was born.

But what was the point? To attract a man? The very thought makes me shudder. I'm not in the mood for men these days, and any guy who comes near doesn't stay near.

Probably because don't-touch-me vibes radiate off me like tsunami waves.

But as I toweled dry, I admitted that some part of me wants men's attention. I like it when their eyes follow me. It proves I'm not old. I haven't entered the crone years yet.

Only I don't want those men to talk to me or call me or, God forbid, touch me. Another sin to lay at Ed's door.

I used to like sex. As in, I have my own French maid's costume. But now just thinking about it makes me gag. All those nights together in the Mallard bed he'd inherited from his *grandmère*—on the double mattress that he said he preferred to a new king-sized one because it kept me closer to him—that had all been a farce. The happy marriage, with two happy, healthy children and no blips on the radar to indicate any threat, had all been an illusion.

No, not an illusion. A *de*lusion. I reached for the hair dryer and turned it on. There had been signs. Warnings of trouble. But I hadn't wanted to see them.

Twenty-one months ago Ed floored me when he said he wanted a divorce. A month later I'd discovered why. He'd been having an affair with a thirty-year-old chippy, a media consultant for one of his law firm's clients. It had been going on for a year.

On the surface our divorce was an easy one. No custody issues, just property to divide. He'd agreed to a modest alimony, to deed the house to me plus half of our joint investments. We each kept our own retirement accounts. His was much larger than mine, but he agreed to pay all of Pearl and Ronnie's college expenses.

Then, two weeks after I signed the divorce papers, his

firm settled a huge lawsuit that I hadn't heard anything about. His bonus alone had been in the mid six-figures.

"The rat," I muttered as I opened my locker. The thing is, it wasn't the loss of money that infuriated me most. It was his duplicity, his willingness to cheat on me, first with that woman, and then with money. All those years, he'd let me think he was a good husband. Then he'd let me believe he was a fair—even generous—ex-husband. Now on top of everything else, he'd stolen my favorite charity.

Was it any wonder I sometimes dreamed about wrecking his life?

Liz and I drove separately to Café Degas, a dollhouse of a restaurant built like a cozy porch around a tree. It had drop-down awnings for rainy weather, but on a beautiful spring day like today, the dining was strictly alfresco.

She was waiting at a table overlooking oak-lined Esplanade Avenue. "I just love eating here." She smiled as I sat down across from her. Even with a little leftover puffiness from crying, she was still pretty.

Ed would probably love her.

"It's kind of expensive," she went on. "I hope you don't mind. But I need a treat sometimes. That's what my therapist told me. Actually, she's a friend of mine from high school. I do her hair and she gives me advice."

The waiter appeared with menus and recited the daily specials. We ordered salads, of course. So much for an oyster po'boy. That's the thing about going to lunch with another member of the Oasis: you have to eat right or it gets back to Nita.

Once the waiter departed, we smiled awkwardly at each other. "So, Joan," Liz said, slowly turning her water goblet in a circle. "Who does your hair?"

"My hair?" I put a hand to my auburn, chin-length bob. "I go to Phil. At Lalique's."

"Dr. Phil." Liz nodded. "That's what all the other stylists call him, Dr. Phil. He has a really nice place there, right on St. Charles Avenue and all. Very nice. Very classy." Without warning her blue eyes filled with tears. "I had a nice salon, you know. Before…before…"

I stifled a groan. This was turning into an *I Love Lucy* episode. It took her napkin and mine to staunch the flow this time.

"I'm sorry." Liz choked the words out between noisy sobs. "I'm so sorry."

A young couple at the next table looked over at us. From across the tiny dining area a trio of smartly dressed women stared. No one I knew, but I knew the type. Ladies who lunch. Well-to-do. Smug in their position as the wives of rich lawyers or doctors. Or oil men. I know, because I used to *be* them.

I glared at them until they turned away and bent their heads together. Then I turned back to Liz.

A part of me wanted to throw down my drenched napkin and run away from her. My life was messy enough. I didn't know if I could handle someone else's pain.

But I couldn't abandon Liz, not when I knew exactly how the poor girl felt. Catching the waiter's eye, I said. "Make our lunches to go. Pack two forks with it and deliver everything to the white Avalon on Mystery Street.

Here." I shoved two twenties at him. "This should cover it. And lots of napkins," I added as I guided the still sobbing Liz out of the rapidly filling restaurant.

We ate on an isolated bench in City Park. Or rather, I ate while Liz spilled out the sordid details of her unhappy marriage and even worse divorce. "It was my salon," Liz said, mopping her eyes with the last of the napkins. "I'm the stylist. He's a Volkswagen salesman. But the loans were in my name, and the lease was in his. I couldn't afford to fight him, so he ended up with Shear Delight and I ended up having to lease a chair at a new place on Carrollton Avenue."

"I think it must be a part of our DNA," I said, poking at a kalamata olive in my spinach salad. There isn't a chef alive whose talent can overcome the depressing effects of eating out of a plastic, throwaway container. "Men always come out ahead in divorce settlements. They make us trust them so that, even though we know they've been cheating on us during the marriage, we stupidly believe they'll somehow treat us fairly in the divorce. As if the guilt they haven't felt before will suddenly appear and force them to be fair now."

Liz sniffed and stared at me with reddened eyes. "What did your husband do?"

I laughed, but it wasn't funny. "My story is so much like yours it's pathetic. He cheated on me with a much younger woman his law firm did work for. The only difference is that I was too stupid to catch him at it. I thought we were happily married, heading for the next phase of our lives. You know, empty nesters, still young enough to enjoy our lives together. Then after Ronnie left for college—he's our youngest—Ed told me he wanted a divorce."

I shuddered. I hated to even think about those first bleak, surreal days, let alone talk about them. I'd only gotten through them by keeping my chin up and a smile in place, no matter how much it hurt.

Liz's therapist friend would probably call it denial. But in my circle everyone called me brave. And strong. They didn't know how close I'd come to my breaking point.

But look at me now, blurting out the most humiliating part of my life to this woman I barely knew. On the other hand, we had an awful lot in common. We were two of a kind, two hurt, betrayed women. Ex-wives.

So I swallowed the lump in my throat, shrugged and tried to smile. "At least you were smart enough to catch the slimy worm. I was too dumb to figure it out." I paused, and then made myself go on. "He had to tell me himself. I asked him why he wanted a divorce, and he told me he was in love with someone else. In love with her! And I never had a clue."

Liz gazed down at the uneaten salad in her lap. "My therapist says I'm in the mourning phase, that it's like my marriage died and I have to go through all the crying and the sadness. Then I'll have to go through the anger phase before I can finally get to acceptance. But really, I keep bouncing around from feeling like my heart is broken to feeling like I want to claw him to pieces." She looked up. "You know what I mean?"

"I know exactly what you mean." I picked up a soggy crouton and tossed it to a hopeful squirrel. At once three additional squirrels scampered up. "But I don't cry anymore over Ed." My voice hardened. "Sometimes, though, I sure would like some sort of payback."

The truth was, in the early days of our divorce I'd actually plotted murdering Ed. Not that I'd ever do such a thing. But there was a weird sort of comfort in imagining that I *could* do it. Sometimes I wanted to kill only him; other times I included Barracuda Woman. His condo would blow up like in some James Bond movie; or they'd be broadsided in his new BMW convertible by a runaway eighteen-wheeler full of gasoline. In a funnier version I had him choking on a fishbone while Barb panicked, threw her hands up in despair, and forgot how to dial 911.

I looked up as a woman rode by on a bicycle with her little girl strapped into a child seat behind her. They both wore helmets, matching pink ones. These days, no respectable parent lets her kids ride bikes or skateboards or scooters without a helmet. Protect their heads; protect their knees and wrists and every other bone that a fall could fracture.

But as for their hearts, forget it. Get divorced; find yourself. The kids will understand. No fractures on their innocent little souls. They'll grow up to love stepmom and stepdad and all the stepsisters and stepbrothers, and stepaunts and stepuncles, and stepgrandparents—

The plastic fork in my hand snapped. I looked up sheepishly and dropped the pieces of fork in my tray.

"Are you okay?" Liz stared at me, her eyes huge.

I ran a hand through my hair. "I'm fine. I guess talking to you has dredged up a lot of old feelings."

"I'm sorry."

"It's not your fault I married a charming snake."

Liz nodded. "That's Dennis Savoie too. A charming snake, so cool butter wouldn't melt in his mouth."

Depressed, I closed the plastic lid on the remains of my wilted salad. "Well. I guess I should be going. Will you be all right?"

"Oh, sure. I'll be fine. Eventually. Thanks so much for letting me cry all over you, Joan. I'm not usually such a big baby."

I smiled at her. "Don't worry about it."

I waved as Liz drove off in her bright yellow Volkswagen Beetle. Notwithstanding her copious tears, the Beetle suited her, a cheerful putt-putt of a car for someone who, beneath her current crisis, was basically the sparkly cheerleader type.

I turned the key to my Avalon and felt the solid engine thrum to life. Am I like my car, solid and reliable, elegant and smooth? I've sure worked hard to be. But lately I feel anything but. I feel more like the old Pinto my Dad used to drive, rusty and squeaky, as liable to stall as to get up and go.

I gunned the engine, once, then again. The squirrels scattered. A trio of pigeons fluttered away. Maybe I should get a Volkswagen Beetle. Or a convertible BMW.

Or a classic Corvette.

I gunned the engine once more, then slipped the car into Reverse and with a satisfying shower of gravel and shells shot backward in the parking area. When I put the car in Drive, however, and pulled onto the roadway, I turned back into my old self, driving the three miles home, obeying every traffic light, and using my turn signals, even when there were no cars around to see.

The mail had already come—three catalogues, my cell phone bill and the May issue of *Verandah*. So I was surprised when the mail carrier rang the doorbell.

"A registered letter for you, Mrs. St. Romaine."

When I arched a disapproving brow at him, he laughed. "Sorry. I mean, Ms. Hoffman."

"That's all right, Clinton. Sometimes I forget too."

I signed the green receipt, and then sat in a porch rocker to open it. It was a notice from the Civil Sheriff's Office. A cold chill slid down my spine. The Civil Sheriff's Office?

I had to read the terse missive twice, and even then I didn't entirely understand what it said. A Sheriff's sale of my house? And for non-payment of my mortgage. What mortgage? They had to have the wrong address.

"This is my house," I muttered, shaking the offensive letter. "Mine." And there was no mortgage on it. Ed had ceded it to me in the divorce in exchange for other more liquid assets. I guess to buy that condo he'd just moved into. After all, he couldn't touch our retirement accounts. As for the trust funds his father's will had set up for Ronnie and Pearl, we'd agreed to leave that money where it was for the sole use of the children.

I stood up and folded the letter. But I wanted to wad it up and throw it at the wall. This was a load of bull, and somebody was going to get an earful from me. This was my home, owned free and clear.

Ed and I had purchased the Greek Revival cottage in the Garden District when I was pregnant with Pearl. I paused in the wide center hall and stared into the front parlor. Over the black marble mantel was an original Audubon print Ed had given me for our twentieth anniversary. In the second parlor hung a trio of early nineteenth century landscapes he'd inherited from an uncle.

Slowly I turned on my heel, really looking at the home I usually took for granted. The center hall and stairwell housed the family portraits we'd commissioned. Upstairs were the twentieth-century works we'd collected, the two Picasso pencil sketches Ed had invested in, and my own early George Rodrigue collection—before that stupid Blue Dog was stuck in all his paintings.

I scanned the parlors I'd lived half my life in. Someone thought they could take this away from me?

Like hell.

This time I did crush the letter. Then I snatched up the phone and dialed Ed's number. The best way to get to the bottom of this was to go straight to the source of all my problems: Edward Ronald St. Romaine, the Third.

A woman answered on the fourth ring, not his regular secretary. "This is Joan Hoffman; please connect me to Ed St. Romaine."

"I'm sorry, Ms. Hoffman, but Mr. St. Romaine is not available. Would you like to leave a message?"

I wanted to leave a message all right. "Where's Olivia?"

"Excuse me?"

"Olivia Freeman, Ed's regular secretary."

"Oh, yes. I understand she retired."

First he replaces his wife, then his secretary. I wanted to ask the chirpy voice on the other end how old she was. But I restrained myself. "Tell Ed that his ex-wife called regarding a court matter and that he needs to call me at once."

I hung up without saying good-bye, then immediately felt guilty. None of this mess was the new secretary's fault. If anything, I ought to feel sorry for the poor girl, dependent upon Ed St. Romaine for her livelihood.

I punched in Ed's home number and immediately reached his voice mail. That meant he was on the line, so I waited a few minutes, then dialed again. This time it rang five times before reverting to his voice mail.

I slammed the phone down without leaving a message. The bastard knew I'd called and he was avoiding me— probably because he had something to do with this ridiculous letter. Well, he couldn't avoid me forever.

Snatching up my purse along with the damning letter, I stormed out of the house. But I came to an abrupt stop at the edge of the porch. Across the street Penny Calhoun was unloading her three-year-old twins from her forest-green Suburban. Next door Mildred DeMontluzin, elegant with her straw hat, garden gloves and a French watering bucket was clipping roses from her carefully coddled cutting bed.

Like the bookends of gracious Southern womanhood, the two women stood sentinel over the life I had once thought of as mine. Young wife guiding her children's lives and supporting her husband's career, and white-haired widow still tending the home she'd kept for almost sixty years.

But for me, that life had been derailed.

I swallowed hard and waved when Mildred looked up, and again when Penny saw me. Did they have any idea how swiftly life could change? Was Penny's husband already cheating on her? Had Mildred's husband ever been unfaithful?

Taking a steadying breath, I walked to the car, climbed in, and with a short toot at my sweet but clueless neighbors, I drove down Prytania Street, taking a route I'd vowed never to take: to Palmer Avenue and the outrageously expensive condo Ed had bought for himself and his sharp-toothed new wife.

Up to now my divorce from Ed had been civil, at least superficially. But I knew Ed had something to do with that damned letter. And I planned to get to the bottom of it, even if it meant confronting him in his own den of iniquity.

CHAPTER 2

LIZ

I couldn't help myself. After my lunch with that nice Joan Hoffman, I just had to drive by Shear Delight.

It's hard to explain, but oh, do I love that shop. I planned so long and worked so hard to one day have a beauty parlor of my own, and it had come out exactly like I pictured it: a long red-and-white-striped awning across the front, white benches on the sidewalk under the windows, and a big pot of red geraniums on each side of the door.

I slowed my yellow Beetle as I drew even with the shop. The geraniums looked kind of wilted. Wasn't anybody watering them? And the sidewalk hadn't been hosed down in days.

This part of Magazine Street is yuppie heaven, loads of cute shops that cater to Uptown's well-to-do. You can shop at the Whole Foods Market; pick up the latest best-seller at Beaucoup Books; buy a new dress at Mimi's; get a massage at Earthsaver's. And don't forget to have your hair cut, colored and styled at Shear Delight.

Dennis had been positive the sky-high rent would be

worth it. And I'd believed him. I still do. Only I'm not there anymore to benefit from all my hard work.

All I ever wanted was a two- or three-chair shop of my own, maybe on Hampson Street or Maple Street. But Dennis had dreamed big.

That's what he'd said during one of our last fights. He dreamed big, but he accused me of having no vision. No ambition. "You're ready to ruin everything before the salon is even launched. And for what? A baby? Are you totally insane?"

"A baby won't ruin anything," I'd argued. "And I'm not saying I want to get pregnant today. But soon. Before I'm too old. I'll be thirty-nine next March, Dennis. By then the salon will be up and well on its way. That's when I want to get pregnant."

"Next spring? Fine—"

"Fine?" My heart had leaped for joy.

"Yeah, fine. That's what, eight months from now? That means we don't have to talk about this for eight more months."

"Wait a minute. Are you saying we can start *trying* next spring? Or that we'll *talk* about it next spring?"

"Damn it to hell! You'd better back off, woman!"

"But I can't back off. Don't you see? I'm running out of time, pushing the limits of—"

"You're pushing my limits too! And if you're not careful, you'll push me right out the door."

Like a slap across the face, his threat had left me speechless. Even now my stomach knotted up to remember. The thing was, I got married the first time when I was twenty-one. I was divorced by twenty-four. I waited twelve long years before I got married again, and I really believed Dennis was my forever guy. That's why his threat shook me so badly.

For three weeks I tiptoed around him, scared and resentful. But it didn't change my mind. I went off the pill and prayed every night for his condom to fail. Once I even found one of his used condoms and pressed it inside out up into my womb. Pathetic, I know. But all I needed was one persistent sperm, one tenacious little swimmer. After I was pregnant I was pretty sure Dennis would get used to the idea.

But it turned out he'd had something else up his sleeve—or rather, in his bed. I started getting suspicious when he decided we didn't both have to be in the salon at the same time. While I was there he would disappear. So one day when one of my clients cancelled her appointment, I went looking for him.

That's when I met Cora Lee.

Pretty, redheaded Cora Lee, naked as a jaybird in my guestroom bed with my equally naked husband.

I'd been way too numb to react. But Dennis hadn't. He'd screamed at me for following him, for nagging him, for ruining everything: our marriage, our business.

Later that night he'd begged my forgiveness and I'd given it—but only if we went to marriage counseling. I didn't think he'd agree, so when he did, I actually thought we had a chance.

We started couple's therapy. The first session was awful: he'd cheated on me, yet somehow it was all my fault.

The second session was better, though. It seemed like Dennis was taking it seriously, really hearing me. Then the next day he filed for divorce.

That's when I discovered the true depths of his betrayal. The therapy was all an act, a way to buy time while he and his lawyer plotted against me. And it worked. Because it turned out that I was the one who had signed for all the business loans through my business corporation, which I'd created before I ever met Dennis. That meant I was the one who owed all the banks.

Meanwhile, Dennis held the lease to the salon in his name alone. Which left me with nothing. Even worse than nothing, it left me deep in the hole while he went on like nothing had ever happened.

My hands tightened on the steering wheel as I watched a pair of tan, model-perfect Tulane students waltz into the salon. I'd cut the brunette's hair twice. What was her name?

When a car horn behind me blared, I jumped and my car lurched forward. "Idiot," I muttered, but at myself, not the other driver. When was I going to stop driving past the salon? It only tortured me and made me miserable. I needed to be like Joan, cool and collected, moving on with my life. That's why I'd joined the Oasis Spa and Body Works. My therapist friend Beth had told me to embrace this time of transition in my life, to work on my emotional health and my physical health.

But it was so hard.

At first after Dennis had moved out I'd eaten myself sick, gaining almost twenty pounds. But I was determined to lose that weight. And I wasn't going to work at Archibald's salon forever. Somehow I would start another salon of my own. But first I had to get out from under the mountain of debt Dennis had dumped on me.

On the corner of Bellecastle I saw a mother pushing a stroller, and it brought back the old, familiar ache that had ruined my marriage. One day I *would* have a baby of my own, if not with Dennis, then with someone else. But the ticking of my biological clock was getting louder every day.

At home my ancient orange-striped tabby, Pumpkin, greeted me. I fed him and then poured myself a glass of ice water. I get Sundays and Mondays off, but with no money to spare, my activities are limited. No shopping; no expensive, first-run movies. My six-month membership at Oasis is my only luxury these days. I shouldn't even have eaten out today with Joan.

"Oh, damn." I hadn't paid for my lunch. I'd have to reimburse her. Meanwhile I had the rest of the day to get through.

I was relieved when I heard the mailman on the porch. Maybe there would be an interesting magazine to read or a catalogue to window-shop through. Instead there was a bill from my divorce attorney, a late notice from the Whitney Bank's Commercial Loan Department and a postcard from my mom.

I stuffed the unopened bills under a knitting pattern book on the kitchen table. Reading the card, I meandered into the living room.

Mom and her third husband are the quintessential sunbirds. They always wintered in Tucson, Arizona. This year they, along with some of their motor home pals, planned a caravan to the Smoky Mountains where they would settle in for the summer. She would write again when she had a firm address. As always, she signed it Susu.

I smiled and reread the choppily written note. "It's not like I can't find her if I need her," I said to Pumpkin, who only blinked. Mom has a cell phone with unlimited long distance. But my eternally suntanned mother treats long distance as if it still costs thirty-five cents a minute.

I propped the postcard up against a cinnamon-scented pillar candle on the coffee table and sighed. If only I could get up and drive away from my messy life. Just turn the key and leave, carrying my entire household with me. But I'm stuck in New Orleans, at least until my divorce is final and my finances are straight.

Bored, I flipped on the television and scrolled through the listings. I had the whole afternoon ahead of me. And the evening too. But lately nothing appeals to me. The Lifetime Channel is too weepy. HGTV is too cheerful. PAX is too syrupy.

I paused when an old black-and-white image filled the screen. "Farley Granger," I told Pumpkin. I knew this movie. *Strangers on a Train*.

Climbing onto the pink floral love seat, I settled down cross-legged with a chenille pillow behind my back and another on my lap.

And as the other guy made his twisted proposal to Farley—that they each do away with the other's unwanted family member—I got the most devious, wonderful, vengeful idea of my life.

JOAN

I sat in my car across the street from Ed's magnificent new condo.

Condo. The very idea of purchasing only a portion of a building, of trusting your neighbors to be decent, fair co-owners of your home, makes my stomach turn over. If your lifelong husband isn't trustworthy, how can you rely on perfect strangers?

"Not your problem," I muttered as I exited my car. Ed was home—at least his BMW was there. Why wasn't he at work?

I rang the bell, girding for a confrontation with the Barracuda. But it was Ed's voice that came through the speaker. "Who is it?"

"It's me. Joan. I need to speak to you."

"Now?"

"Yes, now. Since you won't answer your phone I had no choice but to—"

"Not here, Joan. Not now."

"Then when?" God! I wanted to reach through the speaker, grab him by the throat and strangle him!

"We can meet at…at P.J.'s. On Maple Street," his disembodied voice said.

"When?" I repeated, then winced. Once again I was ceding all the choices to him, and it irritated the hell out of me. That's what had gotten me into this black hole: forty-six years old, divorced, and apparently with no control over her finances.

"An hour from now. Four o'clock, sharp. Look, I can't talk anymore. I'll see you at four."

Of course he arrived fifteen minutes late. Another power play. When he finally breezed into the coffee shop, looking crisp and tan, like he'd just returned from a Caribbean vacation, he bought a tall cup of iced coffee, added Splenda, and then took a chair opposite me.

He kept his Ralph Lauren sunglasses in place, a ploy I recognized from the past. Without speaking, I thrust the damning letter at him.

He stared at it a long time, as if studying the language and trying to figure it out. I knew he was just formulating his excuse.

"Well?" I snapped when I couldn't stand one more second of silence.

He looked up and smiled. "It's…a mistake."

"I know it's a mistake, Ed. What I want to know is *whose* mistake. Why would this mortgage company think I owe them money?"

"Right. Well, you see, I had to make a loan some time back and I listed the house on the asset sheet. But they should never have sent you this notice."

"It's from the Civil Sheriff's office," I hissed. "Not the loan company, the Sheriff's office!"

"That's the part that's a mistake," he said.

I gave him a cold look. "A mistake."

"Yes, a mistake. I overlooked a couple of payments and what with moving around, first to that apartment—"

"You mean the Barracuda's fish tank?" I shouldn't have said that, but I was feeling mean. Considering Pearl's description of the woman's place as a glass, chrome, and leather loft, fish tank seemed appropriate. The fact that he didn't react to the insult only made me more suspicious.

"—and then to the condo, a few things got lost in the shuffle. Anyway, I sent them a check last week. It must have crossed in the mail with this notice." He ripped the letter in half. "Just ignore it."

"Don't!" I lurched forward and snatched the letter from him before he could rip it into fourths. A pair of nerdy-looking students at the next table peered up from their glowing laptop screens, but I was way past caring what anyone else thought.

I folded the torn letter and slid it into my purse. "I don't believe you, Ed. And even if it is the truth, you have no business listing my house as one of your assets."

"I told you. It was last year."

"We've been divorced for over a year."

He shrugged. "I don't remember the exact date."

In exasperation I threw my hands up in the air. "If you took the loan *before* we were divorced, it should have been listed as a liability in the property settlement. And if you took it *after* the divorce, then you lied to get a loan." I paused. "Isn't that considered fraud?"

It felt good to watch that patronizing smile of his fade. Real good. He removed his sunglasses and slid them to the top of his head. "Come on, Joan. Isn't it time you got over your anger at me?"

"Get over it? I'm trying like hell to get over it. But it's things like this letter that make it impossible." I tilted my head and stared at him. "What did you do to yourself?"

He grinned and smoothed a finger alongside his right eye. "You like it? Barb says I look ten years younger."

He'd had an eyelid job.

There was no logical reason for that to affect me so profoundly, but as Ed grinned at me, looking young and fit and utterly content with his new life, I felt betrayed all over again. I didn't want him back. God forbid! I hadn't wanted him back since the minute I'd learned about Barracuda Woman. But his ability to dump our old life and move on so easily felt like one more knife in my back. An eyelift, of all things.

Trying to swallow an ugly clot of emotions, I pushed to my feet. "If this is fraud, you'll be hearing from my attorney."

"It's not fraud, Joan. Until our property settlement is official, it's just a tiff between divorcing partners. No judge in this town will go after me for a fraud charge, especially since I've already resolved the situation."

I jerked my purse onto my shoulder. The fact that he was a well-respected attorney and probably right about this made me blind with fury. "We'll just see about that."

"Bye, babe," he called out in an amused tone to my retreating back.

Babe!

My hands were shaking as I dug in my purse for my keys. This was why people murdered their exes: that amused, taunting tone; that twist of the knife for no other reason that pure meanness. How dare that lying, two-faced bastard call me babe!

I slammed the car door, then sat there, strangling the

leather-wrapped steering wheel until my knuckles hurt. First the BMW sports car, then the condo. Now the plastic surgery. Ed's fascination with James Bond had obviously gotten the best of him. Was that what the loan against the house had been for, to keep him looking good for his waxed, botoxed, blond-streaked trophy wife?

I'm not sure how I made it home, maybe autopilot. It was too late to call Doyle Carmadelle, my divorce attorney. I'd do it first thing in the morning. Better yet, I'd set up a meeting and go over everything face-to-face. It was long past time for us to finalize the property settlement. I was an idiot to have let it drag out so long.

But that was for tomorrow. I still had work to do. *The Topical Optical* beckoned from my computer. Except that I was too upset to concentrate on the latest news in opthalmology.

I picked up the phone to call my mother, but then put it down. The last thing my ailing mother needed to hear was how badly Ed St. Romaine was treating her daughter. Losing her own husband four years ago had been a staggering enough blow. Realizing her favorite son-in-law was a low-down snake in the grass had shaken her further. At the moment Mom was content living at Chateau de Notre Dame with all the other uptown Catholic widows. She didn't need to hear about Ed and his shady loans and his eyelid surgery.

So I dialed my sister in Coral Gables instead.

"You've reached Margie and Hamm Foster," the familiar smoker's rasp began. I hung up before the announcement ended.

It was too early for dinner and for turning on the television, but I did both anyway. Another exciting evening on Prytania Street with a turkey sandwich and a movie from our video collection. My video collection.

I settled on an old favorite, one I'd watched so many times I knew the lines by heart: *The First Wives Club*. I'd read the book too.

The telephone rang, but I let the answering machine take it. It was only Rebecca, one of my nosy friends from Junior League. The next time it rang, the First Wives were just getting revenge on their exes as they opened their women's center. How I envied them.

It was Ronnie calling from LSU. "Ronnie, I'm here." I punched the off button of the answering machine.

"Mom?"

"Hey, sweetheart. How nice to hear from you."

"Yeah, well, maybe not," he muttered in a voice even deeper than his father's.

"What do you mean? What's wrong?"

"I hurt my knee."

"Oh no. How bad?"

"Pretty bad." His voice wavered, and a frisson of fear pushed my adrenaline to high. "The thing is," he went on, "the team doctor says I need surgery. That I'll have to sit out the whole season."

I sank onto one of the bronzed breakfast room chairs. "Oh, honey. I'm so sorry. What happened? Where are you now?"

"At Lady of the Lake Hospital. I was warming up with one of the guys. It wasn't even a hot match. I just stopped short and something gave out."

"Well, don't worry. We'll get it taken care of. I'll come right away to get you. And I'll call Dr. Kokemor to let him know what's going on. I'm sure he knows a good orthopedic surgeon."

"Coach thinks I should have the surgery here."

"In Baton Rouge? Why not here where I can take care of you?"

"He says Dr. Healon's the best knee guy in the South."

"Oh."

"After that I'll be sent home to recuperate. But I'll lose the rest of the semester."

"I'm sure the Athletic Department has a program to help athletes who get sidelined by injury. Don't worry. We'll get tutors, whatever you need to salvage the semester."

"It's not school I'm worried about, Mom. It's the tennis season. I'll never be able to make up the lost time."

For a long moment neither of us spoke. Pearl is my scholar; Ronnie is the jock. He'd been hard-pressed to choose between a swimming or a tennis scholarship. In the end he'd gone for the money. He wanted to turn pro someday. But if his knee didn't fully recover…

I wanted to cry for his disappointment. I wanted to blink my eyes and be instantly at his side to somehow take away all his pain. He might be six feet of solid muscle and only a year shy of being of legal age, but he's still my baby, my youngest, and I wanted to protect him.

"So tell me exactly what the doctors have planned. But first, do you have your cell phone with you?"

"Yeah, I have it."

"Have you called your father yet?"

"No, not yet."

"I'll take care of that if you want. Now give me your room number."

After we hung up, I called Ed. Considering our earlier confrontation, he was the last person I wanted to talk to. But Ronnie was hurt and he needed both his parents there for him.

Naturally I got Ed's voice mail. "Your son is in the hospital. Call me." That's all I said. Then I went upstairs to pack an overnight bag.

It was three days before I finally got around to calling my attorney, three days spent in Baton Rouge shuttling between Ronnie's side and the room I'd taken in the nearby Sheraton.

I only saw Ed twice.

He didn't return my call until the next day when Ronnie was already in surgery. When he showed up at the recovery room that afternoon, the picture of fatherly concern, with the Barracuda plastered loyally to his side, I left. It was either that or throw up.

Why had *she* come? This had nothing to do with her.

An hour later when I returned to the recovery room, they were gone. But when Ronnie was wheeled down to his private room, Ed was already there with a grocery bag full of chips and nuts and candy bars.

"Thanks, Dad," Ronnie mumbled, still a little woozy from the anesthesia. What they'd hoped would only be arthroscopic surgery had turned into a more complex operation. Not only had his tendon snapped, they'd found fragments of deteriorating bone floating beneath his kneecap. As a result, the initial prediction of a six-week recovery had turned into six months.

But now Ronnie and I were back home in New Orleans. I'd moved my computer out of the downstairs library and turned it into a temporary bedroom for Ronnie. I'd rented a hospital bed and moved a television and stereo in. I'd also arranged for a home health nurse named Ned to come twice a day to help him bathe and learn to get around.

"I can do it myself," Ronnie snapped when I started to adjust his bed.

"You don't have to be so nasty about it," I snapped right back.

We stared at one another. Glared, actually. Then I relented. "You know what? We're obviously getting on each other's nerves. A little too much togetherness. Why don't I let you and Ned get acquainted, and I'll just...back off."

He gave me an apologetic smile. "Yeah. That's probably a good thing." He paused. "Thanks, Mom."

"Sure thing, sweetheart." I resisted the urge to smother him in a hug. "I'll be back before you leave," I told Ned.

Though I should have closed myself up in the upstairs study with H.C., instead I set up an afternoon meeting with Doyle. Then I changed and went to the gym.

"Where've you been?" Nita asked when she spied me huffing to nowhere on the sadistic stair climber.

"My son needed emergency surgery." I went on to explain the nature of Ronnie's injury.

"You know what," Nita said. "Once the surgical site is

completely healed, he might want to start swim therapy with us. We can coordinate therapy with his doctor. We do that kind of thing all the time."

I slowed my climbing. "That's a great idea."

"By the way, Liz asked about you."

"Oh?" My climbing speeded up. "How's she doing?"

"Up and down. But I think your talk helped."

Nita moved on, and I focused on my workout. I'd eaten nothing but carbohydrates, sugar and fat the last three days, and hadn't exercised beyond pushing elevator buttons. It was the tension, however—the stress of Ronnie's pain—that was the worst. I had kinks in my back, knots in my neck and a nagging headache that wouldn't go away.

That was probably Ed's fault, though. I wouldn't feel at ease again until this business of our property settlement was finalized.

I climbed and spun until my heart rate had reached its optimum speed. But no swimming today. There wasn't time. I'd just started for the locker room when Liz walked in.

"Joan! Oh, am I glad to see you. I've got the absolutely best idea for us!"

I dabbed my face with my towel. At least she wasn't as down in the doldrums as before. "An idea?" I said, continuing on into the locker room. "About what?"

Like an overeager puppy, she trailed behind me. "Well, it has to do with what we were talking about the other day."

I stopped at my locker. Today was not the day for me

to get involved with Liz and her problems. I had more than enough of my own. But she was feeling much better, and I didn't want to hurt her feelings. "We talked about our divorces," I said.

"And our exes."

"Yes."

"And what low-down, cheating, thieving bastards they were."

"And still are," I muttered.

"Has he done something else?"

I shrugged. "Just more of the same." I turned, holding my towel and shower gear. "So what's this idea?"

"Well." Liz glanced around, and then lowered her voice. "I saw this movie the other night, an old black-and-white. Maybe you've heard of it? *Strangers on a Train.*"

I thought a moment. "Is that the one where these two men make this murder pact? One guy kills the other guy's wife, and the other one is supposed to kill the first guy's dad? Something like that, right?"

"That's the one. Well, I was thinking that you and I might do something like that with each other's exes—"

"What?" I took a quick step backward. She *looked* perfectly normal, but this woman must be seriously unhinged.

"Not kill them." She gave me an exasperated look. "Not *kill* them. What kind of person do you think I am? There are other ways of getting even with those weasels for how they hurt us. For how they cheated us. They're still cheating us. At least Dennis is. He stole my business, everything I worked for since I first got out of beauty college."

For a moment I hesitated. There was something seductive about her words. I didn't know what Ed was up to with his creative financial shenanigans, but I knew it was designed to benefit him at my expense. Still, even though I sometimes daydream about being like *The First Wives Club* and getting even with him, it's only wishful thinking. I know nothing can ever change things back to how they were before he betrayed us. It's too late for that.

Unfortunately, that's all I really want.

Beating back a fresh wave of sadness I said, "It's tempting, Liz, but I don't think so."

"Wait. Just listen," she persisted. "I really think we could do this. In a way it's for their own good."

"Quite frankly, I don't want to do anything for Ed's good."

"Don't worry, he won't like it."

Frowning, I turned away and started for the shower room. "Look, I understand why you want to get even with your ex-husband. I felt the very same way in the beginning. Sometimes I still do. But revenge won't change anything. It won't get him back."

"You think I want that snake back? Anything but!"

"So you just want revenge." I looked over my shoulder at her. "Why? To give him a taste of his own medicine? To teach him a lesson?"

"Well, yeah. What's wrong with that?"

"Because he won't learn anything. Trust me. He's going to continue on his way, wreaking havoc in the lives of everyone who gets too close." I put a hand on her arm. "Listen, Liz. You really are better off without him. Just be glad you don't have children together."

Foot-in-mouth disease. I knew I shouldn't have said that even before Liz's eyes filled up with tears.

"That's easy for you to say. You *have* children. But I don't, and it's all I really want."

"I'm sorry." Feeling like an insensitive jerk, I patted her shaking shoulder. "I'm sorry. That was thoughtless of me. But really, Liz, trying to get even with him—"

"I *hate* him."

"Yes, but trying to get even with Dennis—even if you succeed—is not going to solve anything."

"Yeah? Well, it'll sure make me feel better." She sniffed, then wiped her eyes with the hem of her T-shirt. "And it'll be doing a favor for that stupid girl he's roped in."

"As far as I'm concerned, any woman who takes up with a married man deserves exactly what she gets. A cheat and a liar."

"I don't think Cora Lee knew he was married in the beginning. Like me, she was taken in by his charm."

I shook my head. "That's awfully generous of you. I'm afraid I'm not that magnanimous. As far as I'm concerned, Ed and Barracuda Woman deserve each other. Look, Liz. I understand how you feel. Really, I do. But I'm trying to move past this divorce and get on with my life, and I suggest you do the same. I'm sorry I can't talk any longer, but I really have to leave. I have an appointment with my lawyer and I don't want to be late."

On the way downtown I tried hard not to feel bad about cutting Liz off. Yes, I wanted revenge on Ed—now more than ever. But it was wasted effort, a pipe dream, fun to imagine, but pointless to pursue. Ed was the Teflon man. Nothing stuck to him: not guilt over his betrayal of our vows; not guilt over his neglectful attitude toward our children; and apparently not guilt over his abuse of our financial situation.

I arrived at Doyle's office—in Ed's building but on a different floor—five minutes early, and was escorted into Doyle's private office precisely at three o'clock. That was one thing I've always liked about Doyle Carmadelle. He's a punctilious, detail-oriented attorney, the managing partner at Dreyfous, Landry and McCoy.

He'd agreed to represent me in the divorce only because Ed and I had already worked the big issues out with a mediator.

"Hello, my dear." He gave me a kiss, poured me a cup of coffee, and sat beside me on his Natuzzi leather sofa. "So, what's all this about, Joan? Is Ed behaving badly?"

"No more than usual. I want the property settlement finalized, Doyle. The divorce is done; there's no need to drag our feet on the property settlement."

"Fine. No problem. I'll check our files and see where we are and get right on it."

"Good. Because it turns out that Ed has been playing fast and loose with the facts about ownership of my house—and God knows what else." I explained about the fraudulent mortgage and the notice from the Civil Sheriff's Office, growing angrier at every word. Doyle sat there, smiling and nodding and making comforting clucks of reassurance. Except that I wasn't feeling particularly reassured.

"You need to understand," he said when I finished. "Just because Ed has agreed to the division of property as you two worked it out, that does not preclude him from challenging that initial agreement."

"What do you mean? How can he do that?"

"If he wants, he can delay the finalization of the property settlement. He can question the manner in which properties were valued. You know how real estate values have been growing. He can also ask the judge for extensions of time. Things like that."

"But why would he do that at this late date?"

"I'm not saying he will, Joan. I'm saying he could. Of course, I'll try to convince him otherwise."

I stared at Doyle's smooth cheeks, almost boyish in their lack of hair. Whether delivering good news or bad, his expression never changed. I set my cup of coffee down. "How long can he drag this out?"

Doyle made a face. "I know one case that's dragged on five years now. Of course I'm not saying that will happen here. Let me talk to Ed, okay? I'll call you once he and I talk."

He stood up, signaling my time was up. But I refused to take the hint. "Does Ed still have legal access to my stock accounts? And my retirement account?"

"Legally, yes. Remember, until the court finalizes the property settlement, most of it remains in community ownership. However, anything he's taken for his personal use since you filed for divorce would have to be repaid in the final settlement. Not that I'm saying he's taken anything out," he added when my brows rose in alarm.

Slowly I stood, but an ugly new fear had begun to grow in the pit of my stomach. If Ed could list my home as collateral for some shady business purposes, he could just as easily list my stock accounts as part of his assets, or worse yet, dip into them.

Instead of feeling better as Doyle ushered me out, I felt ten times worse. Doyle was too unconcerned for comfort. While I trusted him to pursue the legal aspects of finalizing the property settlement, I don't think he understood the urgency of the situation. Nor did I trust him to keep my feelings confidential. Maybe it hadn't been such a good idea to use a company attorney after all.

"Good-bye, my dear," he said, kissing me on the cheek as the elevator opened.

"Bye." I finger-waved as the door closed. But instead of pressing the down button, I pressed up. The personnel office for the firm was two floors up. That's where the retirement files were kept, and that was where I went.

It took only five minutes for the accounts secretary to pull my investment files, and only two minutes for me to find the three withdrawals—one each from the portfolios belonging to Pearl, Ronnie, and myself. I noticed also that he'd switched the mailing address for each of the accounts to his condo. The unmitigated gall of the man! That rat was hoping I wouldn't miss getting the notices, and discover what he'd done!

I smiled at the girl—she was new to the company—and asked her to copy the three pertinent documents. But behind the politely automatic smile, a new rage burned in my heart. That despicable piece of manure! That vile, lying, son-of-a-bitch!

It was bad enough that he'd screwed around with *my* money. But his own children's? The money that had accumulated in the trust funds his father had set up and that we'd faithfully added to through the years?

I thanked the helpful young woman, and neatly folded the damning financial statements into the six-by-nine manila envelope she gave me. But I was barely out of the elevator before I snapped open my phone and dialed the Oasis Spa. It didn't take long to convince the receptionist there to give me the phone number I really wanted.

I was cool and my hand didn't shake at all as I punched in the number and listened to the mechanical ring.

"Hello, Liz?" I said when she picked up. "This is Joan Hoffman. I've been thinking about what you said today—about getting revenge on each other's exes—and I've changed my mind. Count me in. Count me *way* in."

CHAPTER 3

LIZ

I couldn't wait to get to the spa. Not to exercise, though. I was dying to talk to Joan.

"Hey there, Nita," I said, practically skipping through the door. "Have you seen Joan yet?"

Nita looked up from checking the schedule on the front desk. "Not yet." She tilted her head back to the schedule book, then stopped and gave me a probing look. "You're looking a lot better. What's up?"

I grinned. "This is the first day I haven't cried in, what, over six months. I guess you've just never seen me when my eyes weren't puffy and my nose wasn't red."

"Well, it looks good on you, girl. I guess talking to Joan has been a big help."

"And how." Then I immediately shut my mouth. I have a bad tendency to run my mouth about everything going on in my life, to anyone who wants to listen. Probably a side effect of working in salons for so many years. But Joan and I had agreed to keep this plan just between us. "Well, I'd better get going." I gestured to the locker room. "See you."

I changed into my new pink-and-black spandex work-out suit and was pulling a baggy black Trashy Diva T-shirt over it when Joan arrived.

As usual she looked fabulous. If I hadn't known how furious she was, how hungry for revenge on her lying, thieving ex-husband, I would never have suspected a thing. In her taupe linen slacks and cream-colored sweater set she looked the image of I've-got-it-all-together seren-ity. A single strand of pearls nestled at her throat, a trio of gold bangles swung at her wrist, and not one hair of her carefully highlighted auburn bob was out of place.

But her eyes told a different story. I hadn't really no-ticed Joan's eyes before, probably because they were an un-remarkable hazel color. But today they glittered with a hard green light. A hot emerald fire.

Whatever her ex had done, he was about to pay for it in spades. Which only increased my enthusiasm for our plan.

"So," Joan said, dropping her Coach bag on the bench as casually as if it were a canvas tote bag from Kmart. "We start today."

"Today," I echoed "While we work out we'll prep each other on the other guy's peculiarities."

Joan stripped out of her clothes and pulled on a pair of gray knit shorts and a gray-and-white tank top over her La Perla bra and panties. I would kill to be able to afford lingerie like that. The woman was expensive down to the skin. Even beneath the skin. She probably slathered on exclusive European lotions that cost more than my monthly rent.

"I've been thinking," Joan went on as she pulled on her socks and spotless workout shoes. "We probably shouldn't be seen together anywhere but here. If Barracuda Woman ever catches a glimpse of us together she'll figure everything out."

I pursed my lips. "You're right. Same with Cora Lee. So no more lunches? Stuff like that?"

"Right. We'll talk on the phone, work out, and if we have to meet we can do it somewhere in Metairie. No, let's make it Chalmette. Barracuda Woman wouldn't be caught dead in Chalmette."

"Hey now. No Chalmatian jokes in front of me. When I was little I used to spend my summers at my Grammy's house in Chalmette, and we always had a great time."

Joan smiled. "No jokes. The point is, we need to keep our plan a secret. Did you bring a photo of your ex?"

We were sitting side by side on the bench, swapping photos and murmuring comments when the locker room door swung open. Joan shoved the photo of Dennis into her Coach bag. I pulled a towel over the one of her ex, Ed.

"What's taking y'all so long?" Nita called as she made her way to her own locker.

"We're just…chatting," Joan said.

"Yeah," I said, meeting Joan's gaze. "I was telling her how I've already lost three pounds."

"That's great." Nita's voice came from the next row of locker over. "Exactly what I like to hear." When the locker door clanged shut she came around the corner, a Power-Bar in her hand. "You ready to burn off another couple hundred calories today?"

"I sure am," I said, tucking my towel and Ed's photo inside my locker.

"Right. Let's go," Joan said.

"How's your son doing?" Nita asked Joan as the three of us left the locker room.

"Grumpy and out of sorts. And in pain," Joan said. "But his therapist already has him up and on his feet."

"Great. Just let me know if we can help, okay?"

"Sure thing. Thanks, Nita."

Joan and I shared a glance as Nita headed to the office. By mutual consent we settled on side-by-side ab machines, across the room from any other spa members. "Okay," I began. "It'll be easy for you to meet Dennis. You can just go to Shear Delight and get your hair done. You can meet Cora Lee too. I hear she works there now."

"My hair?" Joan put a hand to her sleek chin-length hair. "But Phil will have a conniption fit if I let anyone else touch his work."

"Well, how else are you going to meet Dennis? We do good work at Shear Delight," I added a little defensively.

"I'm sure you do. Well, I'm sure *you* do. I'm not so certain I want Dennis's little girlfriend touching one hair on my head."

"I can't blame you for that," I admitted. For a moment we both concentrated on our abs.

"Okay," Joan conceded. "I'll let them do my hair." When I didn't respond she glanced at me. "Did you hear me?"

"Yes, I did. But…I was thinking." I stopped and looked at her. Studied her. "You need to already look like Dennis's kind of woman when you first meet him."

"What do you mean, Dennis's kind of woman?" She stared at me, then went on. "I'm not going strawberry blond. I mean, it looks nice on you. And I guess it must look okay on Cora Lee, but it's not for me."

I shook my head. "You don't have to go strawberry blond. But you do need to look…younger. Not that you look old," I added when she drew back. "But you need to update your look. You know, not so classy and elegant. More with it."

Joan frowned and concentrated again on her abs. "Maybe I should just pierce my belly button."

"Or your tongue."

"What?"

She looked so stunned I started laughing. After a moment, so did she. "I draw the line at piercings or tattoos," Joan said. "But when it comes to Dennis Savoie I'll bow to your expertise on my hair."

"And makeup," I said.

"Fine."

"And clothes."

Joan pause mid-stomach crunch and fixed me with a stern gaze. "You do know that what goes around comes around?"

Despite the grimness of our plan, I couldn't help feeling a little excited, even a little giddy about it all. "Are you kidding? Do whatever you want to me. I can hardly wait. Me dressed up like a grand society lady. It's like Halloween and Mardi Gras all in one."

Despite her natural reserve, Joan laughed. "Okay. You turn me into Dennis's kind of woman and I'll turn you into Ed's type."

"Great. So, how am I going to meet up with him?"

"You want Liz to meet Ed?"

We both jumped at the unexpected question. Just behind us stood Nita, her hands on her hips and her brows arched in surprise. "Why would you want her to meet him?"

When neither of us could come up with an answer, Nita came around to face us. Her gaze moved from Joan to me, and back to Joan. She pursed her lips. "You two are up to something, aren't you?"

Joan tried to brazen it out. "What do you mean, *up to something?*"

"Give it up, girl," Nita said, shaking her head. "You two are plotting something. I can smell it. So 'fess up. I'm not letting either of you go until you fill me in on all the details."

Joan would have held out. I could tell. But not me. "Come on, Joan," I pleaded.

"Yeah. *Come on, Joan,*" Nita said, squatting in front of us, laughter brimming in her dark eyes. "I can keep a secret." With one finger she made a cross over her heart.

Joan let out a disgusted groan. "Oh, all right. But I swear, Nita, if you say a thing—"

"Don't worry. I don't even know your exes. Even if I did, I'm on your side. We girls have to stick together. After all, it's not like I haven't been screwed over by a guy before. I know what it feels like to want to get even." She paused. "That *is* what this is about, right? So. What's the plan?"

Joan leaned forward. "We're each going to go after each other's ex—just to break up their current romances. We want them to know what it's like to be betrayed and dumped."

Nita nodded. "Okay. I see what's going on. Liz goes after your ex and you go after hers?"

"Right," I said. "Dennis won't know what hit him."

"Damn." Nita set back on her heels grinning at us. "That is truly inspired. The Payback Club. And the guys will never realize that you two even know each other."

"Right," Joan said.

"Hey, I like that, Nita. The Payback Club. That's us all right."

"So how are you putting all this into motion?" Nita asked.

"Makeovers," Joan and I said in unison.

"Way cool." Her eyes glittered with excitement. "Can I be made over too?"

JOAN

The next few days were frantic for me. Liz and Nita lived alone and could come and go as they pleased. But since Ronnie was home with me, I had to juggle taking care of him with carving out time for my fellow conspirators. To make matters crazier, I took on another client. My contact with the Topical Optical had asked me to design a new logo and pamphlet for his ophthalmology practice, and the daughter of my mother's best friend asked me to submit a proposal to edit a quarterly newsletter for a local businesswomen's group.

At least I had some money coming in. But I was worried. According to the Civil Sheriff's Office, the so-called mortgage holder on my house had received sufficient payment, and my house was no longer destined for the auction block. Until Doyle finalized my property settlement with Ed, however, I couldn't rest easy.

That's why I felt no guilt about this payback stuff. But I was nervous about my makeover.

On Wednesday evening after closing hours, Nita and I went to the salon where Liz worked. Nita was all prepared, with magazine photos and a print-out of her face with various celebrities' hairstyles superimposed over it.

"This is me as Halle Berry," she said, holding up one picture. "But I'm not sure I want short hair again. This is me as Catherine Zeta-Jones. But it's a lot of work for me to keep my hair that straight."

"How long do the cornrows last?" I asked.

"Several months. It's an easy look for what I do. And this," she said, holding up the final picture, "Is me as Lucille Ball."

We burst out laughing at the olive-skinned, dark-eyed Nita as a redhead with a bouffant style. Nita grinned. "Okay, Joan. You next."

I poured each of them a glass of Pinot Noir and passed the glasses around. "I don't know. I think I'm just going to trust Liz on this. So be gentle with me, okay?"

I cringed when Liz held up her scissors and clicked them several voracious times. "Just promise me you won't make me look like Susan Sarandon in *The Banger Sisters*."

One very long hour later I stared at the new me. It was shorter, but not much. "Dennis likes long hair," Liz had explained. Mainly Liz had layered it, then using a volumizing mousse, had blown it into a full shaggy style.

"Very sharp," Nita said. "Now you need an outfit like this to go with it." She thrust a Tommy Hilfiger ad from *Elle* at me—a snug-fitting turquoise dress with black ribbon edging its mid-thigh hemline.

I rolled my eyes. "Maybe if I was nineteen and trying to lose my virginity."

Liz cocked her head to one side. "I don't know. Dennis would love it. And you've got the legs for a skirt like that."

"No way," I swore. "No way." When Liz and Nita held their ground, however I snatched up the magazine and stared at the ad. "Okay. I could wear this if—only if—the skirt was six inches longer."

"Just so it's above your knees," Liz said.

"Right," Nita agreed. "Besides, when she sits it'll ride up higher on her thighs. Especially if she crosses her legs."

"Sexy, but without being trashy. By the way," Liz added, "you need to invest in some push-up bras."

"The Wonderbra, " Nita said. "Go from a B-cup to a C for just $34.99."

"Fine," I conceded. "Just so long as I don't have to wear one of those pumped-up-with-air-bras."

"Okay, Nita," Liz said. "You next."

Liz and I worked together to undo all her cornrows. At first Nita's head was a cloud of dark-brown, shoulder-length crimps. But once washed and defrizzed, trimmed and flat-ironed, it became a thick swinging fall of gleaming silk.

"Wow!" Nita exclaimed.

"Yeah, wow," I echoed. "Move over, Catherine Zeta-Jones."

Nita grinned. "You think so?"

"Oh, yes." I looked over at Liz. "You are really good."

"Why, thank you," Liz murmured.

"No, I mean it. I underestimated you, Liz. You are *really* good."

Our eyes met and held, and a slow glimmer of moisture rose in her blue eyes. She swallowed hard. "Thanks, Joan. I needed to hear that."

"Man, I'll be sending everybody I know to you," Nita said, admiring herself in the mirror as she experimented with swishing her hair back and forth. "Damn, I look like a TV ad for hair products. I can hardly wait to run into that jerk Tim Carlson."

"Tim Carlson?" I said. "From the six o'clock news?"

"You know Tim Carlson?" Liz asked.

Nita shrugged.

I had never seen Miss Cool-as-a-Cucumber blush before. "A former boyfriend, I take it."

Then Liz said out loud what I was thinking. "But isn't he married?"

Nita averted her gaze. "Not my finest hour, okay?"

In the uncomfortable silence my eyes met Liz's. Neither of us knew Tim Carlson's wife, but we felt an immediate bond with her. We'd been cheated on by our husbands—and by younger women just like Nita.

"Did you feel guilty?" I finally asked.

Nita sighed and turned to face us. "Yes, a little. But the truth is, I got swept away in the glamour of it all. I wasn't really thinking about her." She spread her hands, then let them fall. "It wasn't about her. It was about me—and him," she added when I turned away.

"I don't care," I said, shaking my head. "I don't see how you can do that to another woman."

"I wasn't thinking about her—"

"Well, maybe you should be."

"Please don't be mad, Joan. Believe me, I swore off married men after him."

Inside I was shaking with rage. I knew my fury was better focused on Barracuda Woman. But Nita had played the same role for another obtuse wife, and Nita was right here in all her toned and vibrant youth.

I snatched up my purse to leave, but Liz caught me by the arm. "Wait, Joan. We've all made mistakes in our lives. I read this thing once. It said, making good decisions comes from experience, and experience comes from making bad decisions."

It was exactly the sort of unemotional logic I usually subscribe to. But I didn't want to hear it today, especially not from someone I'd initially pegged as a silly, bubble-headed cheerleader type.

Only Liz wasn't silly or bubble-headed. Nor was Nita a man-eating monster.

That fast my anger subsided. Reluctantly I smiled at Liz. "You're right." I turned to face Nita. "I'm sorry. I over-reacted. How you live your life is your business."

"Lived," Nita said. "How I lived it."

"Right. Okay." I took a deep, calming breath. "Okay. Now, what about Liz's hair?"

Liz gave a relieved smile. "One of the guys at the salon is really good. I thought I'd ask him."

"Or I could ask Phil to fit you in."

"Dr. Phil? But won't he be mad at you for letting someone else cut your hair?"

I laughed. "I won't tell him. I'll make the arrangements on the phone. What do you say?"

"I say yes! That would be so great! Except that, well, he's kind of expensive and I—"

"My treat. And don't argue." I smiled at myself in the mirror and ran my fingers through my sexy new hairdo. "It's the least I can do."

CHAPTER 4

LIZ

I stepped into Lalique's, then paused. Joan must have incredible pull to get an appointment for me on just two days' notice. I rubbed the goose bumps on my arms as I stared around the impressive foyer. Phil Deslonde's St. Charles Avenue salon was not the largest salon in town. And it sure wasn't the trendiest. But it was by far the most exclusive.

I breathed deep, appreciating the clear, familiar aroma of hair products. But Dr. Phil's had something else, a hint of lemon oil and the unique ambience of authentic 150-year-old architecture. The soaring Greek Revival ceilings, curving mahogany stair, and gleaming ebony-stained floors were the real deal. No one could duplicate it—not that I'd ever try. In New Orleans, Dr. Phil was the God of Stylists. Like everyone else in the profession, I was in awe of him. But I knew better than to try and imitate him.

Still, I meant to learn everything I could in the hour or so I would have in his chair.

"May I help you, madame?" the receptionist asked.

Madame. I blinked and prayed the woman didn't sniff

me out as a fraud and therefore an undesirable. "Yes, thank you. I'm Liz Savoie. I have an appointment with Dr. Phil—I mean, Mr. Deslonde."

The woman smiled. "Don't worry, we call him Dr. Phil too. But only behind his back." She stood, a tall, slender model of a woman. "Come along. I'll show you to his office."

I felt like a gauche girl being led into the presence of royalty. Dr. Phil's office occupied a large sunny room. A trio of Eames chairs sat on an oriental rug in the bay window, sheltered by a huge variegated ficus tree. A collection of white potted orchids was arranged on glass shelves in the windows. All in all, a photo op for any upscale decorating magazine.

Then the man himself appeared, dapper and simply dressed, but oozing class and good taste. He had to be close to seventy, but he looked twenty years younger. He welcomed me, and sat me down, then began to play with my hair.

"Nice texture, and a lot to work with." His head bobbed up and down with approval. "Joan tells me you're looking for a new elegant look."

"Yes. Elegant and grown-up."

"Very well then." He clapped and immediately another young woman appeared. No chubbies allowed to work here, I guess. In swift fashion I was colored, highlighted, rinsed, conditioned, and settled in the styling chair opposite the bay.

I wasn't allowed to look in the mirror while he worked. Nor did he speak much. I would never have the nerve to assume such a godlike attitude with one of my clients. Yet once he was finished and spun me around to view what he'd done, I had to concede that he deserved his reputation.

You'd think with over fifteen years in the business that I would be used to this kind of transformation. After all, that's what I'd come here for. But I was still shocked at the woman I saw in the mirror. He'd kept me as a strawberry blonde, but with less gold in it. And the highlights were incredibly natural, as if streaked by a week on the sunny French Riviera. The cut was shorter and sleeker, but it managed to look even sexier.

It was like I was looking at an older, prettier version of myself. Not older as in old. But older, as in grown-up. Scary, but good.

"Very nice," he murmured, more to himself.

"It's better than nice," I replied in a hushed, reverent voice.

He dipped his head in acknowledgment, royalty receiving its due. At the same time another of his pretty assistants appeared to escort me out. I thanked him again. I would have tipped him, but Joan had strictly warned me against it. Dr. Phil abhorred tips. Then again, at two hundred dollars a cut plus God only knew what for color, he didn't need tips.

Once in my car I punched Joan's number into my phone. "Oh, Joan. You will absolutely be blown away when—" I broke off when I realized it wasn't her on the line.

"Hi," the man said. "I guess you want my mom."

"Oh. You must be Ronnie. I'm your mom's friend, Liz."

As soon as I said my name, I knew it was a mistake. We weren't supposed to know each other.

"Hey, Mom. It's for you."

"I'm sorry, Joan," I said once he handed over the phone. "I think I just messed up. I told your son my name. I was just so excited about my hair that I forgot."

"It's too late to worry about it now. There's nothing we can do. Besides, he probably won't remember you. And anyway, maybe we're being a little paranoid about secrecy."

"Maybe. Anyway, I just wanted to tell you that Dr. Phil is incredible! Omigod, you will not recognize me!"

She laughed. "That good, huh? I guess that means it's time for us to go shopping."

The three of us met at the Esplanade Mall, as far from uptown New Orleans as you can get and yet still be in greater New Orleans. Joan used the wardrobe planning guide she'd gotten twenty years before from Chameleon Image Consultants: two main colors, three accent colors and a total of eleven items of clothing.

Nita and I were amazed. "Fifty combinations from eleven pieces? You've got to be kidding," I said.

"Let me see that." Nita took the chart from her. "Only eleven pieces? No way."

Joan nodded. "It works. And the beauty of it is, when you buy fewer clothes, you can afford to buy better quality. Or maybe that luxury item you might normally pass up."

"Luxury item," I scoffed. "I can't afford to buy eleven new pieces of clothing even at Wal-Mart prices."

"You probably have several items that you can use."

"We could go to the Junior League Thrift Store," Nita suggested. "They have great stuff. I bet you donate your old clothes to them," she said to Joan.

"As a matter of fact, I do."

"Would you help me shop there?" I asked Joan.

"I'll help you," Nita said.

"Thanks, but I need Joan too. Remember, I have to dress in a way that will attract Ed."

"Right."

Joan wrinkled her nose. "I thought we were going to be careful about being seen together."

"No problem," Nita said. "Just arrive separately. That way you can each be there, but no one will think you're together."

"But what if one of the women from the Junior League recognizes me?" Joan asked.

Nita shrugged. "Bring donations. Then you have an excuse to poke around in the store."

We went the next day. While Joan slowly picked through the used books, Nita and I tore through the clothing section. I ended up with a feminine Jones New York suit, a navy and white polka-dot Shomi silk dress, a pair of cropped linen slacks, and two summer-weight silk sweaters. Nita bought a black fitted linen cocktail dress, a wonderful cream-colored retro dress with giant black buttons running down the front, and an embroidered two-piece slacks set.

As Nita and I modeled the clothes for each other, Joan would glance our way and give a brief nod or frown. Afterward in the parking lot we swiftly conferred. "Okay, we're ready to move on with our plan," Joan said. "I made an appointment at Shear Delight to have my hair trimmed and my nails done."

"Do you have to let them fool with your hair?" Nita asked. "It's perfect just the way Liz cut it."

"I know," Joan agreed. "I love it. But it's a beauty salon and how else am I going to meet Dennis?"

"Just have them do your nails the first time," I told her. "You can go back another time for your hair. What are you going to wear?"

"The tight white capris and the apple green striped tank top."

"Get a pedicure too," I suggested. "Dennis has a real thing about women's feet."

"Damn," Nita exclaimed. "I wish I had a guy to seduce for nefarious reasons. Y'all are like that spy lady, Mata Hari, scoping out the enemy and taking them down."

"We haven't taken them down yet," Joan pointed out. When a BMW went by she turned her back to the street. "I'd better be on my way. My daughter is arriving from college for the weekend."

"Did you ever decide what to do about her graduation?"

Joan got this pained look on her face. "Ronnie and I are going up together. I understand Ed and the Barracuda are going too. But I'll just ignore them and I'm sure they'll do the same to me. It's not like any of us have much choice about this."

Nita shook her head. "Why doesn't your daughter just tell her dad to leave the bitch behind?"

"Because she loves her dad and doesn't want to alienate him," Joan retorted. "Look, I have to go."

Nita and I watched her drive off. "I'm beginning to see the underside of having it 'all together,'" Nita said. "Joan looks like she's got everything under control, but she is one uptight lady."

"It's hard, you know, when you think your life is going one way, and suddenly it goes off in another direction."

"Yeah. I guess so." Nita ran her fingers through the silky length of her hair. "I don't know why I'm getting so into this makeover stuff. Seeing what you two have gone through with your divorces makes me not want to ever get hooked up with just one guy. And I'm damn sure having second thoughts about actually getting married."

"Not me. I really want to get married again."

"Why?"

"Kids. A family." I opened my car door and put my bag on the seat. "I want it all, Nita. I really do. And someday so will you."

"Hah." She rolled her dark eyes. "If that happens, I'll just get me a puppy or a kitten."

"That's what you say now. But I have a cat and as much as I love her, it's not the same. I want a baby of my own."

"So adopt," Nita said with a shrug.

I shook my head. "If I can't have a baby with a husband, then I'll have a baby without a husband. And if that doesn't work, then I'll go the adoption route."

Nita opened the door to her red Jeep Liberty and

paused, one foot in the cab. "I was adopted and my mom loves me."

"Oh, man, I'm sorry, Nita." I could feel my face turning red. "I didn't mean it like that."

She waved me off. "It's okay, girl. Don't worry about it. My mom couldn't have kids so she adopted me and Raoul. Her husband deserted us when I was seven, and she had to raise us all by herself, but she did a good job." Nita tilted her head and smiled at me. "You'll make a good mom someday, Liz, however you become one."

As I watched her Jeep Liberty pull out into Freret Street, I could only hope that she was right.

JOAN

Two blocks from home my cell phone rang. It was Pearl.

"Mom, I decided to drive home today instead of tomorrow. My friend, Jaycie, came with me."

"Okay. Where are you?"

"Outside of Jackson. We should be home by dark."

"Do I need to make up an extra bedroom?"

"No, she can stay in my room." There was a crackling pause. "Have you talked to Dad?"

"Not lately."

"Can't you just tell him to leave her at home?"

If only it was that easy. "That's between you and your father, Pearl. I told you I can't—"

"Fine! I just won't go to my graduation then!"

"Pearl, please."

"I can't talk. Bye." And that fast she cut me off.

Muffling a swear word, I tossed the phone onto the passenger seat and turned into my driveway. He was ruining what should be a joyous celebration of our daughter's achievement. After sixteen years of schooling, Pearl was finally moving from student to adult. But thanks to Ed and his sick fascination with barracudas, our beautiful daughter had regressed into a petulant junior high kid.

"I hate that selfish bastard," I muttered into the silence of my car. "Him and that icy bitch he married." But I was going to call him. No way around that. My daughter was going to attend her graduation if I had to kidnap the Barracuda and drown her.

Pearl arrived around eight. Ronnie had already eaten and was torturing himself by watching a tennis match on ESPN. It broke my heart to see him rubbing his bandaged knee, twitching his shoulders with every shot he watched back and forth across the net.

"Hey, Mom," Pearl said, tossing me a cool look. She didn't give me either a hug or a kiss. "You remember Jaycie."

"Of course. Nice to see you again." Jaycie was a new addition to Pearl's lengthy roster of friends. Not a sorority girl like all the others. Not a Land's End type either, but nice enough. Arty-looking.

"Ronnie's set up in the library," I said as they headed to her bedroom upstairs.

"We'll go see him before we head out," Pearl said, flinging the words over her shoulder.

Head out? "There's dinner in the kitchen. Crawfish étouffée," I called up as they disappeared from sight. *Your favorite.*

I sat in the kitchen for a half hour, thumbing through an old issue of *Cuisine* magazine, determined not to beg them to eat what I'd prepared. But my feelings were hurt. Ed was the jerk, yet I was the one being punished. And she hadn't even noticed my sexy new hairdo.

I got up and went into Ronnie's room. "Can I get you anything from the kitchen, honey?"

His eyes didn't veer from the video game now on his television screen. "I'm cool."

Thud. Crash. Gunshots and a scream from the game.

"Your sister's here."

"Yeah. Cool." An explosion and more gunshots. "Yes!" He leaned triumphantly toward the screen.

I shifted my weight from one foot to the other. "Well. Okay. Call me if you change your mind."

I was almost out the door before he said, "Wait. Is there any ice cream left?"

It's pathetic how easily such lowly maid duty can make an empty nest mother feel needed again. Fulfilled. Not just a bowl of ice cream for my son. Oh, no. Two giant scoops of Vanilla Swiss Almond with fudge sauce, walnut pieces, and a tower of whipped cream, finished off with strawberry slices cascading over the top.

I was just returning with my creation when the girls clattered down the stairs. Pearl gave me a skeptical look. "I hope you don't intend to eat that. That's got to be over two thousand calories."

"It's for Ronnie. You two look nice," I added. Pearl had on a short black skirt with a snug black and white print blouse, à la 1969. Jaycie wore form-fitting black pants and a pink tank top edged in black.

Jaycie smiled. "Thank you."

"Yeah, thanks," Pearl echoed. "I'll take that to the bro'."

And that fast I was left in the hall while they went in to visit with Ronnie. I could have followed them in, but I decided not to. Pearl was obviously sulking. Until I solved the problem of Barracuda Woman and the graduation, Pearl would take her pique out on me. And to think, in a few weeks she'd be moving back here to live.

Given the choice of dealing with her, dealing with Ed, or dealing with my massive sense of loneliness, I decided to deal with Hunk of Crap instead. I went upstairs and with a determined burst of creativity, finished the layout of The Topical Optical, then sent it off as an e-mail attachment for final okay before production. Next came a proposal letter to a potential new client, and then my e-mail.

Delete all the Viagra offers.
Delete Tiffany the Total Turn-on.
Delete Refinance Your Home in 10 Easy Minutes.

Wait. Maybe I could learn some sleazy lessons in sleazy finance like Ed did. But no. I deleted it. Then I paused, wondering if I ought to communicate with Ed via e-mail. I sure didn't want to talk to the man.

So I did. Ed. *I think you should know that Pearl said she won't be at her own graduation if you decide to bring Barracuda Woman*

Delete the last two words.

...if you decide to bring your wife. The ball's in your court.

Then I turned off the computer, checked on Ronnie, and before going to bed, made myself a big bowl of ice cream with fudge sauce, walnuts, whipped cream and strawberries. Lots of strawberries. After all, they're really good for you: antioxidants *and* vitamin C.

I woke up at five. Five in the morning on a Saturday. You'd think I was seventy-six, not forty-six. My mother was probably up.

And so was my daughter! I heard a giggle, then two sets of feet on the stairs. It took all my willpower not to leap up and confront her. What was she thinking, coming home at this hour?

They were probably drunk.

I pulled the bedspread up to my chin and pressed my lips together. *She's twenty-two, Joan. An adult.*

But she's in my house. My house, my rules.

Except that only worked in theory. They were trying to be quiet but not succeeding. The evening must have turned out all right if they were laughing, I told myself. But that only depressed me further. My children did not need me anymore, at least not in the way I needed to be needed.

Nobody needed me.

To stave off a stupid bout of self-indulgent tears, I got out of bed and went into the bathroom. But the sight in the mirror drew me up. My hair. I lifted a hand up to my newly shaped hairdo. It was messy and cute. Bed head, Nita had called it.

I liked it. Best of all, it reminded me that there was someone who needed me. Liz. Liz needed me to get revenge on Dennis. And I needed her to get revenge on Ed.

I smiled at myself in the mirror, then smiled broader. It was 5:00 a.m.; I was awake; and I had a plan. So I went downstairs to make coffee and turned on NPR. Then with a glance up the stairs I switched the radio to WRNO. We're the Rock of New Orleans. And I turned it up loud.

CHAPTER 5

LIZ

My goodness, but I felt just like a hotshot lady lawyer in my fitted navy suit and my extremely high-heeled, sling-back pumps. But Joan had insisted. Apparently this was Barracuda Woman's look: snug designer suits with lots of leg and even more cleavage.

I'm a frothier sort of girl myself, but I had to admit a lot of necks were craning as I walked by. The ivory blouse had a plunging neckline, and the longest loop of my dou-ble-strand pearl necklace fell right into the deep vee be-tween my powdered, scented, and pushed-up breasts. Plus my hair was soft and swinging, sort of a Michelle Pfeiffer look, only strawberry blonde. Lots of mixed messages: tough; sexy; feminine.

It was like I had masked for Mardi Gras and so was free to be someone else. In this case, Joan's ex's sweetest day-dream—and worst nightmare.

Joan had given me a picture of her ex-husband, and had assured me he was a regular at Mr. B's on Wednesday nights. So I was already sitting at the corner of the bar when I got her call.

"He's on Iberville turning onto Royal Street right now," she said. She'd positioned herself in the window of a little gift shop on Iberville Street. "Charcoal suit with a red tie. He's with two other men and a short woman with black hair in a French twist."

"I see him," I said as they entered the restaurant. My eyes widened a bit. Joan hadn't mentioned how handsome her ex was, and his picture hadn't really done him justice. Think Pierce Brosnan, but a little more rugged. "They're coming toward the bar. Okay. Gotta go."

"Good luck," she said. Then I was on my own.

Okay, Liz, it's really not that different from high school. Just…bump into him. As the four of them headed past me, I swiveled on my stool as if I was going to get down from it. Then just before he reached me, I let my clutch bag slide off my lap.

Let it slide? I shoved it and it fell in front of him spilling keys, lipsticks and my compact.

He stopped. Unfortunately, the guy in front of him bent down first and retrieved everything for me.

I slid down from the stool. "Oh, thank you," I said. I tried to coo, but since I wasn't sure whom to coo to, Ed or his helpful friend, I don't think it came out exactly right.

"My pleasure," his eager friend said. He stuck his hand out. "Larry Foucher."

"Elizabeth Savoie," I said, my heart sinking. Joan's ex had moved on with his entourage. Instead of *him* giving me that 'are you available?' look, it was his helpful young friend Larry Foucher who was doing so.

"Are you waiting for someone?" he asked.

Oh, well, better make the best of it. "Yes," I lied, smiling into his eager face. "One of my girlfriends. But she's late and I'm beginning to think she's not coming."

"Well then, maybe I can buy you a drink."

He was the wrong guy, but what else could I do? Joan was counting on me. "How very nice of you. Shall we join your friends?"

"Uh, okay." He had no choice but to follow me as I headed to the other end of the bar where Ed had stopped to greet another lawyer-looking type. I was not going to fail Joan no matter what.

Larry made the introductions. Margo Taylor, Doyle Carmadelle, and Ed St. Romaine.

St. Romaine, not Hoffman? I shook his hand and smiled up at him. Joan had forgotten to mention that their names were different.

I spent an excruciating forty-five minutes trying to encourage Joan's ex without discouraging Larry, who was my entrée into their little group. I'm not naturally a tease but the Payback Club was my idea, so I had to make it work.

I made sure to lean in Ed's direction, giving him a good view down my blouse. At least he was red-blooded enough to stare, then to grin and give me a wink. But Larry had obviously staked me out as his find, and it seemed like Ed respected that.

Yeah, he respected his awkward, round-faced friend enough not to tread on his turf, but God forbid he respect his wife—the mother of his children—enough to be faithful.

All in all, the whole thing was a disaster. Eventually Ed

got a call and left without even finishing his second drink. Then Larry asked for my phone number, which I did not want to give him. Instead I told him that maybe he could buy me a drink at Rasputin's on Monday after work. I waited ten minutes after Ed left, then told Larry I had to leave. My cell phone rang before I was halfway down the block.

"How did it go?" Joan asked.

"Not too good." I frowned down at the sidewalk as I made my way to the Holiday Inn parking garage just off Canal Street. "I think I impressed his friend Larry more than I did Ed. And why didn't you tell me you and Ed don't have the same last name?"

"Oh, damn. I totally forgot. I took my maiden name back after we got divorced. Did he suspect anything?"

"No, I don't think so."

"So…what's next?"

"I guess I need to run into him some other place. Alone this time. Where else does he like to go?"

She made a rude sound. "How about his plastic surgeon's? Or wait, maybe he goes to a gym or something?"

"Yeah. Can you find out? Maybe from one of your kids? Except that I'll have to lose some more weight before I can attract somebody at a gym." I undid the buttons of my jacket as I slid into my car. "This girdle is absolutely strangling me."

"Shape enhancer," Joan corrected me.

"Yeah, well, whatever you call it, you can't wear one under your exercise clothes."

JOAN

Liz and I hung up after we agreed to meet at Oasis the next morning. She didn't have to be at work until eleven, and I needed a boost of courage for my first meeting with her ex. On impulse I walked to Canal Place, went into Saks, and tried on four outfits better suited to my daughter than to a woman in her mid-forties. *Late* forties. Even my neighbor Penny who was barely thirty didn't dress this young.

But I wasn't dressing to impress the Junior League anymore; I was dressing to attract a car salesman turned salon entrepreneur. I needed to look like a rich, grown-up ex-cheerleader—which in a way I was. Redemptorist High School, junior and senior years. And though I wasn't exactly rich anymore, I knew how to play the part.

So I bought an aqua and black polka-dot sweater with a scoop neck and three-quarter sleeves, and a pair of black capris with decorative turquoise stitching at the slit hems. With my Steve Madden slides and my black straw hand-bag—which I would tie a turquoise chiffon scarf to—Dennis couldn't possibly ignore me.

I was feeling pretty good by the time I got home. If Liz could force an introduction to Ed, surely I could smile and bat my eyelashes at Dennis Savoie while his manicurist did my nails.

I hadn't counted on Pearl.

She and her friend were outside by the pool when I drove up, both lithe and firm as they took in the last rays of the May sunshine.

"Hi, girls," I said, pausing on the patio. "I hope you both applied lots of sunblock."

"The point is to get a tan," Pearl said without opening her eyes.

"I put some on my face," Jaycie said. "Otherwise my upper lip gets dark, like I have a moustache." She glanced at Pearl who remained silent and remote. She obviously was still mad at *me* about her father's insistence on bringing B.W. to her graduation.

Life is so unfair to mothers.

"So," Jaycie went on to break the awkward silence. "You've been shopping?"

"Yes."

She sat up. "What did you get?"

I guess I was so hungry for a girl-to-girl chat with my daughter that I leaped at this admittedly feeble chance. "Well," I said, sitting the bag on the glass-topped patio table. "I got this cute little outfit."

"Ooh, I love polka dots," Jaycie said. "Very cute."

Finally Pearl opened her eyes. I should have known she'd hate it, or at least hate it for me. "Good grief," she scoffed. "All you need is a big wig and you can be a Sweet Potato Queen."

"Oh, c'mon, Pearl," Jaycie protested. "It's cute. I'd wear it."

"Yeah, but you're twenty-two. She's almost fifty."

I wanted to slap her. Me, who had never once succumbed to corporal punishment even when my children were real brats. But I'd never felt this belittled.

"Listen, Pearl," I said, hoping my voice didn't tremble.

"I understand that you're angry with your father over this graduation business. But I don't see why I have to bear the brunt of it."

She sat up. "Did you call him? Did you tell him how I feel?"

"He doesn't answer the phone if it's me. So I left him a message and I also e-mailed him. He still didn't respond." I paused a moment. "Does he return your calls?"

She'd didn't answer, but I saw her throat working, and I knew she was struggling not to cry. I clutched the polka dot outfit to my chest. "I'm sorry, honey—"

"No." She shook her head, then lay back on the chaise, with her eyes once again closed.

Why couldn't I reach out to her, my firstborn, my only daughter? She was so unhappy, so devastated by this divorce. Bad enough that Ed had divorced me. But when he'd married the Barracuda, it was like he'd divorced his children too. It didn't seem to affect Ronnie as much— but then he and his dad still had sports to discuss. But with Pearl there seemed nothing left.

I glanced at Jaycie who gave me a sad smile and a shrug.

"Well," I said, reaching for the shopping bag. "I'll see you two later. Do you have plans for dinner?"

"Yes," Jaycie answered when Pearl didn't. "We're going out to West End for seafood."

I had dinner with Ronnie—calzones and a salad delivered from Roman Pizza—and watched NASCAR racing with him on ESPN. NASCAR wasn't my thing, though I had to admit it was a little more strategic than I thought.

But as I went up to my bedroom I realized that my children no longer fit naturally into my life. They were grown up. It was now up to me to figure out how I was supposed to fit into their lives. One more part of my old life had slipped away.

Or maybe something new had been added. A new opportunity. That's how an optimist would describe it. But I wasn't feeling particularly optimistic these days.

Early the next afternoon when I departed my bedroom in all my polka dot and capri glory, I was even less optimistic. I'd shown Liz the outfit and she'd totally approved. My hair was full and shaggy. It had only taken an hour and a half to perfect the use of dry wax to keep it flipped and texturized and messy looking. The snug sweater made my 34-B's look like C's, and the form-fitting capris made me grateful for every step I'd ever climbed on the hellacious Stair Stepper.

I clipped on a pair of sparkly earrings, totally ignoring the fashion rule about nothing glittery before five o'clock. I was ready. If Dennis Savoie didn't succumb to all these lures, I would slit my wrists. Bad enough my husband had ditched me. I refused to let some horny, indiscriminate car salesman ignore me.

But just for confidence I called Liz. "Can I pass by and get your opinion before I head to Shear Delight?"

"Of course. I'll meet you outside, okay?"

"Perfect. I'll be there in ten minutes." I flipped my phone shut when Pearl wandered out of her room. She'd been out late again and looked groggy. Hung over.

She stopped short when she saw me. "Oh, my God," she muttered. She shook her head in disbelief and ran her puffy eyes over me, top to bottom. Twice. "First Dad. Now you?"

I wanted to pretend I didn't know what she meant, but I couldn't. "You don't understand," I began.

She snorted. "Oh, yes I do. Dad hooks up with some bimbo half his age and now you're gonna show him that you can get a boy toy of your own."

"She's not half his age." *Just two-thirds.* "Look, Pearl, you've got it all wrong."

"Then what's with that…that getup? Why don't you look like my mother anymore?" Without waiting for an answer that I could give anyway, she turned and stalked down the hall to the bathroom, then slammed the door.

I'm not looking for a boy toy, I wanted to shout. *Just a sleazy man I have to make a fool of so that my friend Liz will make a fool of your father.*

But I couldn't say any of that, not to her. So I trudged down the stairs feeling sixty-six instead of forty-six, and doubting I could even attract an octogenarian.

"What's up with all the door slamming?" Ronnie called out from his bedroom.

"Pearl," I said as I braced myself for his reaction.

But though his brows raised when he saw me, he gave me a wry grin. "Do you have a date or something?"

"No. I'm just going out for a manicure."

"A manicure? You dress up when you're just gonna see a bunch of women?"

At least he didn't think I looked ridiculous. "Actually, there's a whole subtext when a woman dresses to go to a salon, especially one she's never been to before."

"Subtext?" He laughed.

"Yes, subtext. These people don't know me, so I have to dress in a way that represents how I want them to view me. I don't want an old lady manicure. I want a young divorcée manicure. And pedicure."

"Because you plan to start dating?" His smile faded.

I paused. "Would that bother you?"

He made a face, then shrugged. "No. I mean, I don't want to think about it in any kind of detail. But yeah, I guess it's only logical that you would."

"Thank you, sweetheart." I kissed him on the top of his head. Dating didn't feel at all logical to me, but it felt good to know he wouldn't object. "Listen, when you see Ned today, ask him what he thinks about you starting swim therapy, okay?"

"Yeah. Great. Man, I can't wait to get out of this house— not that you haven't been really cool, Mom. But I'm going stir-crazy, you know? And I'm getting soft. And fat."

He patted his still-flat stomach. But I knew what he meant. My 175-pound lean-muscled tennis-playing son had always had a healthy appetite. It takes an awful lot of food to fuel all that activity. But sitting all day and eating more than usual, just out of boredom, would ruin anybody's body fat index.

"Well remember, the trainer at my gym says she can work with your physical therapist on a swimming program that won't stress your knee but will let the rest of you exercise."

"Ned started me on weights in the wheelchair," he said. "But it's not enough. Next week I start going to physical therapy at Touro Hospital." He frowned, reached down, and gingerly rubbed his bandaged knee. "I gotta get back on the tennis court."

"You'll get there, sweetheart. You will." But a part of me was scared for him. If his knee went out so easily this time, how could we be sure the other one wouldn't do the same? Or this one again, and even worse? I left him with a plate of fruit next to the bed and a promise to give Nita the phone number of Touro's therapy department.

At least Liz approved of my new look. She gushed over me, giving me the confidence I needed.

Then it was only me and my appointment with Dennis—actually with Mai, the manicurist at Shear Delight. I parked on Octavia Street. Then with my head high, chest out, and an I've-got-more-attitude-than-you smile pasted on my face, I waltzed into Liz's former salon.

There were two stylists at work, one a beautiful young man, too pretty to be straight, and the other a redhead with an amazing figure. The infamous Cora Lee. I tried not to glare. The pretty Asian woman at the counter was probably Mai. But where was Dennis Savoie?

"May I help you?"

"Yes, you may. I'm Joan Hoffman. I have an appointment today for a manicure."

"Oh, yes. Yes." She smiled and nodded. "Hello, Mrs. Hoffman. I am Mai, and I will be taking care of you."

At that moment a man came in from a back room. "Where did you put the rest of the order from Sally's?" He waved a paper at Cora Lee. "We're supposed to have ten bottles of activator and I only see eight."

"I used two yesterday," the redhead said.

"Well, why didn't you note it down on the log?"

Cora Lee paused, scissors and comb poised above her client's head. She gave him an imploring look. "As soon as I finish Jeanne's cut we can go over it, okay?"

Big jerk, I thought. Chastising the hired help in front of paying clients is so lowbrow. What had Liz ever seen in him? For that matter, why was Cora Lee with him?

I let my keys fall noisily onto the glass counter. "So, Mai. Where do you want me?"

"Just sit here. Please sit," she said, gesturing toward two nail stations.

I sauntered—me, sauntering!—over to the farthest one, the one that required that I pass Dennis the Jerk. "Hello," I said, giving him an appraising look. Then I sat, crossed my legs, and with the top leg bouncing up and down, let my sparkly slide dangle from the toes of my right foot.

He perked up like a dog who'd just had a juicy steak waved under his nose. "Well, hello there. I'm Dennis Savoie, owner of Shear Delight." He stuck out his hand and smiled a bleached-white smile. Or were they porcelains? "Welcome to my salon…?"

"Mrs. Hoffman." Mai supplied my name.

"Miss Hoffman," I corrected, giving him my hand. "Joan Hoffman. This is my first time at Shear Delight, Mr. Savoie, and I must say it's a most delightful little place."

I wanted to snatch my hand back from his oily grip. Creep! But I didn't. Instead I slowly slid it free of his. Slowly. Regretfully. I bounced my crossed leg up and down. "How long have y'all been open?"

He would have been an attractive man if the avid light in his blue eyes hadn't burned so hot. Avid for what? Sex? Money? I'd dressed to exude both and I guess it had worked. Now all I had to do was hide my utter distaste for the man.

"Let's see now," he said. "Almost a year."

I smiled. "How could I have overlooked you so long?" *You, Dennis*, my eyes said. *You, not your shop.*

He grinned. "I'm glad you've found us. Can I get you anything? Wine? Coffee?"

Me?

I managed not to shudder. "Coffee, please. Hot and sweet."

Mai had stayed in the background while her boss worked their newest client. At the snap of his fingers, however, she hurried to the refreshment counter along the back wall. I glanced surreptitiously at Cora Lee. She was frowning and concentrating on her client. But she kept glancing up into the mirror at her boyfriend and me.

Enough dissension sown for one day. I turned away from Dennis and began to remove my rings. I'd worn a large aquamarine cocktail ring on my left hand, and my diamond engagement ring on my right. Two diamond tennis bracelets and of course, my dressy Rolex.

Dennis offered me a small milk glass dish for the jewelry, and I noticed his nails were neat and buffed. Too buffed. They shone as if they had clear polish on them.

Buffed nails. Too-white teeth. And one of those tousled and tipped haircuts that were all the rage on television. Like Ed, he was just a little too involved with his appearance.

Were all men like that these days? It had been years since I'd dated. Had men become as vain as women?

"Thank you," I murmured, not looking at him. I wanted him to go away. I'd lured him in, but now I didn't know what to do with him.

Fortunately Mai arrived with my coffee. I turned my attention to her. "I think I'd like to try something new," I told her, waggling my fingertips at her. "Maybe corals instead of pinks."

"A French polish is always a good choice," Dennis said. He hadn't taken the hint.

I glanced up at him. "Perhaps. But French nails…" I wrinkled my nose. "It's more of a Metairie look, if you know what I mean."

He obviously did. Shear Delight was situated in the middle of Uptown New Orleans, the most desirable real estate in Greater New Orleans. Metairie was merely a suburb, and even Old Metairie didn't have the same cachet. I'd just pronounced myself to be a true Uptown snob. Would that insult the man or excite him?

He took the coffee cup from Mai and sat it in front of me. Leaning closer, he said, "I'm sure we can provide you with whatever you like. I personally guarantee your satisfaction."

I gave him a half smile, then slid my gaze away before he could read the disgust in my eyes. Thank God for jealousy in the form of Cora Lee.

"Excuse me, Dennis," she said in this almost pleading tone. "Jeanne and I were talking about highlights, just around her face. What do you think?"

He turned away from me, and like a swimmer finally coming up for air, I took a deep, grateful breath. I felt dirty, like I'd just wallowed in nastiness. What had seemed easy, almost a lark, and certainly justified, had somehow turned ugly and more than difficult. But it was still justified. I glanced at Cora Lee, who at the moment didn't look very happy with the boyfriend she'd stolen from Liz. Yes, entirely justified.

I opted for a bright coral polish and kept my nails longer than usual. I had my toes done too, and though I didn't talk to Dennis again, I arched my feet and wiggled my freshly buffed and polished toes whenever I thought he might be looking.

"Thank you, Mai," I said, giving her a twenty-dollar tip for a forty-dollar service. Of course Dennis made a point of being at the front counter when I went to pay.

"Can we put you on our mailing list?" he asked with his sleazy, too white smile.

"Certainly," I replied, knowing he'd be impressed with my Garden District address.

"Perhaps we can lure you back to us for your next cut and style."

"Don't you like my hair?" I asked, all wide-eyed innocence.

He grinned. "You would make any hairstyle look good, Joan. But it's always fun to shake up the status quo. Try something new." *Someone new* was the implication.

I gave him a half smile and a half promise. "Perhaps." Then with a finger wave I sauntered out of the salon, uncomfortably aware that his eyes were glued to my butt.

"Ick," I muttered once the door closed behind me. But despite the ick factor, I was elated. I'd done it. I'd pulled off the first step in my half of our payback scheme. Dennis was interested. More important, Cora Lee was upset.

I found my car, slid in, and called Liz though I knew she was probably busy with a client.

"Mission accomplished," I said to her voice mail. Then I drove home. I needed a shower in the worst way.

CHAPTER 6

LIZ

I wanted revenge on Dennis, and I wanted it fast, especially when Joan told me how well she'd done with him at their first meeting. It depressed me to think how much I'd loved him—such a selfish, disloyal man. But it made me mad too. Joan, however, refused to rush things.

"I can't be too obvious, Liz. I need to wait at least a week for another appointment."

"No, you don't. Go have your hair done this time. Get highlights or a trim. Something."

"I don't want highlights and I don't want to go any shorter. And anyway, I don't want to look like I'm chasing him." Joan adjusted the speed of her treadmill and started to jog. So did I.

"Are you kidding? He'd love it if you chased him. But okay," I conceded. "We'll follow your schedule."

We jogged in sync for a minute. Then she said, "I have an idea. I could call him and ask him if he'd contribute a gift certificate for salon services to the Junior League. We could use it at one of our fundraisers. It would be good publicity for the salon."

"Ooh, just the ritzy kind of clientele he's after. I guarantee, Dennis will jump at that."

"He'll jump at what?" Nita said, coming up between us from behind. "Oh, let me guess. That payback thing, right? So, what happened?"

Joan filled her in on her success with Dennis. I had to tell her about my difficulties with Ed.

Nita laughed. "Sounds like Dennis is ready to snap at the bait. But where's Liz going to run into Ed next?"

Joan sent me a sly look. "Ronnie happened to mention that his dad jogs now. In Audubon Park."

I groaned. "But I hate jogging."

Nita gave me an outraged look. "Bite your tongue. Besides, you're jogging right now."

"Yeah. In air conditioning, with friends to talk to."

"So you'll talk to Ed," Joan pointed out. "You've got to find him someplace when good old Larry is nowhere around."

So Joan staked out Ed's condo. Two mornings he went straight to work. One afternoon he came straight home from work; the other he met his wife at Emeril's for dinner. But on Friday around five Joan called me at work. "He just left his house in jogging clothes, heading toward the park. How soon can you get there?"

Fortunately I was just cleaning up my station. With a darling new jogging outfit in my trunk, it took me twelve minutes to change and make it to the park. "I see the BMW," I whispered to Joan on my phone. Why was I whispering?

"Okay. Be sure to park where he can't see your car."

"Why? Doesn't he like Volkswagen Bugs?"

"It's not that. But think. Your yellow bug is very recognizable. Right now that doesn't matter, but later on we don't want him to figure anything out. I'm just being cautious."

"Good thinking. You know, you'd probably make a good detective in real life."

"Oh, and this isn't real life?" She laughed. "Just go do your stretches near his car until he gets back."

"Where will you be?"

"At home, I guess. Call me, okay?"

"Will do."

Then it was just me, the squirrels, and every other jogger who lives uptown. Cute Tulane coeds; gray-haired lifetime runners; middle-aged overweight matrons like me.

No, not like me. I wasn't a matron because I wasn't a mother. Yet. But I wasn't going to think about that today, otherwise I might start crying. I concentrated on my legs, touching my toes, stretching my hamstrings and my quadriceps.

I was as limber as an acrobat by the time I spied one Edward St. Romaine, cheater extraordinaire. He was jogging my way, tall, fit, with that I've-got-money aura that defies explanation. A babe magnet for women from twenty to sixty. Why should he look twice at me? Still, I had to try.

But before he reached me, he sprinted forward, running past without even glancing my way.

Was he going around again? Should I try to catch up with him? Like I could ever do that.

Then just before he reached the old Golf Club site, he stopped and turned back, jogging slowly again toward his car.

Okay, you can do this. I renewed my stretching, holding in my stomach for all I was worth. *Long, lean muscles,* I repeated like a mantra. I had on a cute aqua jogging suit: snug up top, more forgiving on the bottom. I could do this.

I straightened as he got closer, stretching my back out by reaching my arms one at a time over my head.

The boobs caught his eyes first. *Good girls.* It took him a full ten seconds before he looked at my face. He grinned at me, but I could tell he didn't recognize me. I was just some cute chick with a big chest.

"Ed?" I paused as if surprised by his presence. Gosh, I wish Joan could see me. I was getting awfully good at this acting stuff. "Oh, I'm sorry, I thought you were someone else."

"No, I'm Ed," he said, pausing. "And you're…" I saw recognition dawn on his face. "From Mr. B's, right?"

"Right. Liz Savoie. I've never seen you here before."

"I run a couple of times a week. How about you?"

"I used to be a walker, but I decided to step it up a notch. I want to lose another ten pounds."

"Another ten?"

"I've already lost ten." *Eight.* "But I'm all fired up to lose ten more."

"Well, good. That's a good goal." He nodded and glanced around, and I thought he was going to say something else. But instead he nodded again, then said, "I guess I'll see you around."

I watched him leave in disbelief. *Strike two*. What was wrong with me? Then feeling like a fat, almost forty-year-old, I started running. It was either that or start crying. Joan had my ex panting after her while I couldn't get more than a casual glance from her ex.

I ran—not jogged, ran—until my side hurt so badly I thought I'd keel over. But I refused to stop moving. I was a middle-aged nobody who couldn't get a man to give her the time of day. I walked as fast as I could manage until the stitch in my side eased up. Then I started running again. I'd get rid of these ten pounds if it killed me. And then another ten pounds for good measure.

But none of that changed the fact that I would have to call Joan and tell her I'd failed. First with Dennis. Now with Ed.

JOAN

The minute I walked into the house, Ronnie called out, "There's a message from Dad. You're not going to like it."

"Now what? And be careful," I added as he swung into the foyer on his crutches. Less than a week and he was already a pro.

"He wants Barb at the graduation and thinks Pearl's just being a brat, throwing a tantrum over nothing."

"Did he tell Pearl that?"

Ronnie made a wry face. "You know Dad. He's leaving that ugly job to you."

"Great. So she can scream at me instead of him. Did you tell him she's refusing to participate if Barracuda Woman is there?"

"Barracuda Woman?" He laughed. "Good one, Mom. But no, I didn't tell him anything. Pearl can fight her own battles."

It was good advice for me as well as Pearl. But I just hated how her father's selfish decisions tortured her. On the other hand, it had been mighty peaceful around here since she'd gone back to school. Unfortunately she'd be back in one short week with all her belongings. And all her anger and histrionics.

I tried not to sigh.

"So," I said. "Tomorrow's your first day in the pool?"

"Yeah. I can hardly wait. Ned's taking me the first time, to start me out and to coordinate with that trainer you talked about."

"Nita."

"Yeah. After tomorrow I can go without Ned."

"That's so great, honey. Just set up a schedule and I'll get you there."

"Dad said I could come to his club sometime too." He watched me, waiting for my reaction.

I swallowed and forced myself to smile. "Good. That's good." But as I went upstairs to wait for Liz's call, I was furious. Ed hadn't come once to see his injured son. And the only reason he'd called here was to relay his unpleasant message to Pearl through Ronnie or me. Now he was offering his club as a place for Ronnie to strengthen his knee?

I threw my purse on the bed. Then I caught a glimpse of my scowl in the mirror on the armoire door. Suddenly I felt ashamed of myself. I might hate Ed for what he'd done to our family and me. But he was still my children's father. If Ronnie wanted to exercise at his dad's club, I had to be supportive. I had to. And if Pearl ever got past her rage at her dad, I had to support that, too.

And if Pearl and the Barracuda ever became friendly?

I closed my eyes and groaned. If that unlikely event ever took place I would shut my mouth and be supportive then, too. Even if I strangled on my repressed bile.

I changed into a pair of knit pants and a scoop-neck T-shirt, and was staring at the computer screen, waiting for Hunk of Crap to connect to the Internet when my phone rang. But it wasn't Liz.

"Ms. Hoffman, this is Linda from Smythe, Colton. Ms. Purvis can work you in next Tuesday at eleven."

"Perfect."

"Be sure to bring any pertinent financial paperwork."

I glanced at the file I'd assembled, the taped together letter for that mortgage company, the copies of my and the children's investment account statements. "Don't worry, I will." I no longer trusted Ed's firm to handle my divorce, though I hadn't told Doyle that. On Tuesday I would pow-wow with Ms. Andrea Purvis. On Wednesday...well, we would just see.

Fifteen minutes later Liz called. I knew from the sound of her subdued, "Hello, Joan?" that Ed had blown her off.

"It's all right, Liz. Really."

"No, it's not. This was all my idea and I'm failing you."

"You're not failing me. He's just…" *In love with his wife?*

I didn't want to think about that. Ed was incapable of really loving anyone. Wasn't I proof of that? He pretended to be in love, but he betrayed the ones he was supposed to care for. He would betray Barb eventually, if not with Liz, then with someone else.

But that was no comfort to poor Liz.

"He's just being careful," I told her. "Because of Larry."

She was quiet a long moment. "I'm going on a diet. A really strict diet. The Atkins."

"Liz, it's not—"

"And I'm going to work out every morning at Oasis. And jog every evening."

"Liz, don't be so hard on yourself."

"No. This is a wake-up call, Joan. I'll be forty next year. And if I'm not careful, I'll be fat and forty. And I'll never find anyone to love me, and I'll never have a baby, and… and…I'll die all alone. Just this…this lonely, miserable, lonely old woman. With a bunch of cats." She burst into tears, and nothing I said could console her.

"I'm coming over to your house."

"No." Her breath caught on a sob. "You don't have to do that. I'll be okay."

"I'm coming over."

"You don't know where I live."

"You're in the new phone book. I looked you up. I'm on my way, Liz."

Ten minutes later I parked behind her VW in front of an unobtrusive shotgun double on Valmont Street. It was dark, but a light shone on her side of the front porch, and in the front window I saw her silhouette waiting for me.

"I'm sorry," she said as she opened the door. "I know you have better things to do than come hold my hand."

I gave her a hug. "Actually, I don't."

It was true. Ronnie had friends coming over. I was relatively caught up with my work, and I wasn't in the mood for either television or a book. "I know we said we need to be careful about being seen together, but, what the hell. We're in this together, aren't we? So we have to support one another."

She gave me a watery smile. "I'm so glad I met you, Joan, even though my great idea isn't working out so good."

"But it *is* working out. I'm going to wreck Dennis and Cora Lee's romance, and as for Ed, well, I'm meeting with a new lawyer and if Ed's done anything illegal, I'm suing him. I'm betting the Barracuda won't stick around long if Ed has to pay me and the kids back everything he's stolen from us."

"Yeah. But that could take a long time. I'm supposed to be breaking up him and his wife now."

My hands tightened on my purse strap. "I know that was our plan. But lately I've been wondering how much good that will really do. Dennis and Ed—they'll never lack for women. Even if Cora Lee and the Barracuda ditch them, some other foolish women will fall for their b.s. So what are we really accomplishing?"

"How about personal satisfaction?" Liz asked.

"Revenge just for revenge's sake?" I stared at her a long moment. Then I grinned. "You're right. I forgot about that. Personal satisfaction does count for something."

"Right." She pushed her hair back from her face, sniffed, and then smiled. "Okay, it worked. Now that you're here I feel a lot better. Would you like a cup of tea?"

"I'd love some. But first show me your apartment. Oh, and this must be Pumpkin."

* * *

I called Dennis Savoie's salon the next morning.

"Shear Delight, Cora Lee speaking. How may I help you?"

What luck. Just the person I wanted to torture. "Hello, dear," I said, trying to channel Barracuda Woman and her bitchy, superior attitude. "This is Joan Hoffman. I was in a couple of days ago."

"Oh, yes. Ms. Hoffman." I could feel the chill through the phone line. "What can I do for you?"

"Actually, I'd like to speak to Dennis. Could you be a dear and put him on?"

I could feel her animosity and her fear, and I felt weird about it. A part of me felt good and powerful. After all, she deserved the same sort of heartbreak she'd given Liz. But another part of me felt small and mean. Two wrongs don't make a right.

She didn't respond, but after a muffled exchange, Dennis came on the line. "Joan Hoffman. So good to hear from you. What can I do for you?"

"You can do all sorts of good things for me if you'll just say yes." *Good grief! Who was this throaty seductress?*

"Yes," he said. "Yes, yes, yes."

What a jerk. I hoped Cora Lee was listening. "Down, boy," I purred. "I have a little favor to ask of you—or maybe I should call it a little proposition."

"A little proposition?" he echoed. "I can hardly wait to hear the details."

I laughed as if he were the wittiest man alive. Poor Cora Lee. "A business proposition, you naughty thing." Ugh. I hated myself. "You see. I'm a past board member of the Preservation Resource Center, so I'm always eager to lure new businesses into our circle of supporters."

"Lure away," he said.

This time my laugh was sincere. What a predictable buffoon. I made my pitch for the gift certificates; naturally he agreed. In fact he offered two gift certificates, one for a manicure/pedicure and the other for a cut, highlights and styling.

"You are so generous, Dennis."

"Anything for one of my best clients," he said. "You are going to become my new best client, aren't you, Joan?"

His voice had become low and intimate, and a part of me actually felt sorry for Cora Lee. "Of course," I answered. "Meanwhile, however, I have other calls to make."

"Wait. Where should I deliver the gift certificates?"

"I'll pick them up the next time I come in."

"And when will that be?"

"Actually…" Gritting my teeth, I took the plunge. "How about Thursday?"

"Perfect. Nails again, or are you ready for a cut?"

"A cut," I forced myself to say. Would Dr. Phil ever forgive me? "Who's your best stylist?"

"That would be Cora Lee. She's the best of the best."

Perfect. I'd already sown the seeds of jealousy. On Wednesday I could fertilize them like crazy.

Unfortunately, she would be the one holding the scissors. I stared in the mirror above the front parlor mantel. I'd just begun to love the look Liz had given me. Even if

Cora Lee was the best, could professional pride trump jealousy and the chance for revenge?

I turned away from my reflection and reminded myself that no matter what happened, my hair would eventually grow back.

Besides, Cloris Leachman and Kathy Bates looked great with their heads practically shaved. Maybe I would too.

CHAPTER 7

JOAN

I'd never seen a woman as determined as Liz. We met at eight every morning at Oasis, but while I kept to my toning and aerobic workout routine, Liz was focused on radical change with a capital *R*.

"You've got great musculature and proportions," Nita told her as she watched Liz's form on overhead chestcrunches. "Who knows? If you like weight lifting and the results it gives, you might want to move on to competition."

"Competition?" Liz asked, struggling for breath.

"Yeah. You know, body-building contests."

Liz burst out laughing, and the weights fell with a clang. "Body-building contests? You've got to be kidding!"

"Liz Savoie, Miss Body-Builder U.S.A.," I said, keeping a steady pace on the stair-stepper.

"She could do it," Nita said. "Look." She picked up Liz's left arm. "Tighten it up. Now look at that definition."

Liz rolled her eyes. "That doesn't count. I've never had fat arms. What I'm waiting for is muscle definition on my stomach. And my butt."

"Give it a month," Nita said. "You'll see. By the way," she added with a grin. "How's the Payback Club coming along?"

"We're making progress," I said. "I've hired a new lawyer and had my investment accounts frozen. Ed's going to have a cow when he gets subpoenaed for his financial records." I wiped my neck with my towel. "I'm going to screw that man to the wall."

"How much did he take?" she asked.

Normally I'm closemouthed about money. But just the thought of how Ed had stolen from me and the kids made me crazy. "Let's just say that we're talking significant six figures."

"Damn!" Nita exclaimed.

"Whoa!" Liz echoed. "But your house is safe, isn't it?"

"Now it is. He repaid the loan he'd taken on it. The illegal loan."

"What about alimony?"

I looked over at Nita. "It's not much. That's why I started working."

"*You* work?"

"Yes." I slowed to a stop. "Yes, I work." I shook my head. "You think I'm just some rich bitch, don't you? Somebody living the easy life while you have to work hard for every dollar. Am I right?"

"I didn't mean it like that, Joan." But her defensive expression told me she did. "It's just that you show up here at all different times of the day. And you never seem like you're in a hurry. So…" She shrugged.

"So I don't have a job and I'm coasting on my ex's coattails, right? And that's why you think this payback stuff is just, what? Funny?"

"C'mon, Joan. You're making this into too big a thing."

Yes, I was. But I couldn't help it. Even if everything she said was true, even if I was collecting a huge alimony check every month, enough to break Ed's back, it still wouldn't make up for what'd he'd done to me—and to his two children. To our family. He'd wrecked it all, and for what? Barracuda Woman?

"You've never been married," I said to Nita. "You've never had a husband betray you."

"No. But I've had lousy boyfriends who cheated on me."

"It's not the same. Not by a long shot." I shook my head and sighed, feeling very old and very wise, but in a used up, jaded way. "You're twenty-eight, and though I wouldn't wish that sort of pain and betrayal on anyone, chances are someday you'll be where Liz and I are now. Payback won't seem so funny then."

I stepped down from the machine. "Look, I have to go check on Ronnie. I'm sorry. I'm not mad at you, Nita. And I hope what I said doesn't make you mad either. I'm just—I don't know—really furious with Ed. Again. I'll see you later."

I walked away, conscious of the deafening silence in my wake. There was no reason for me to go off on Nita like that. Maybe I was getting too wrapped up in this payback business. I pushed open the door to the pool area. Instead of feeling sorry for myself all the time and being so furious at Ed, maybe I should focus outside myself. Do something for someone else.

I'm helping Liz.

Part of payback, I countered the angry little voice of revenge.

I saw Ronnie holding on to the side of the pool, doing slow, even leg-raises in the water. Maybe I should concentrate on my injured son and my poor, tortured daughter.

"How's it going, baby?" I asked when I reached him. "Any pain?"

"Not really. I want to try swimming a couple of laps, but the therapist said not yet and your friend Nita said if I try to cheat she'll kick me out and tell the therapist why."

I glanced toward the bank of windows that separated the workout room from the pool area. "Yes. She's tough. But good," I added, knowing I owed her an apology.

"Are you friends with all the people here?"

I looked back at Ronnie. "Not really. For a long time I just focused on exercising—and staying mad at your father," I added in an impulse of honesty. "I've only started making friends here recently. Why do you ask?"

He shrugged and didn't answer. But I knew my son. There was a reason for his question. "Oh," I said. "You're wondering about guys, if I've met anyone here that I'd like to date."

He laughed. "No, not that." He hesitated. "Her." He gestured with his head to a swimmer two lanes over. It was a young woman swimming an easy paced backstroke. She was slender with pale skin and chocolate-colored hair. Probably a pretty chestnut when it was dry.

I grinned at my handsome son. "Sorry, honey. I don't

know her. But I bet Nita does. Do you want an introduction?"

He laughed. "Thanks, Mom, but I can manage that on my own. I'd look pretty lame if I needed my 'mommy' to introduce me to girls."

I laughed, too. "Tell me, does it hurt when your head swells up that big?"

I was rewarded with a big splash of water.

"Okay, okay." I tried to shield my face from his antics. "I'll do my laps in the far lane while you work up to meeting your pretty little mermaid."

But first I found Nita. "Hey, I'm sorry for being such a bitch. Can you forgive me?"

"It's my fault," she said. "I'm too nosy, asking about things that aren't my business."

"No, I'm way too touchy these days. Just so you know, I work at home designing newsletters, logos, invitations. Things like that. I work directly with clients, but I also freelance for a couple of PR agencies. That's why I have such a flexible schedule."

"Cool," she said. "I'm impressed."

"Thanks." I was relieved to have that done with. "On another subject, I have a question for you." I pointed toward the pool. "Who's the girl swimming in lane four?"

She squinted toward the pool. "Oh, that's Suzanne. Suzanne Kronin. Why do you ask?"

"No special reason."

She arched her brows and grinned. "Ronnie?"

I laughed. "Yes, Ronnie. But don't introduce them. He said he can manage that himself."

"I'm sure he can. That boy has serious heartbreaker potential." Then her face grew serious. "Suzanne's a little older than Ronnie. Not much." She paused. "She broke her back two years ago. A really bad break."

"Poor thing."

"She's doing good now. Really improved a lot. She works hard on her therapy, but she's always going to limp. Her left leg hasn't fully recovered, and after all this time it probably won't get much better. It'll probably do Ronnie a lot of good to get to know her."

Yes it would, I thought as I slipped into lane eight and started my laps. But would it do Suzanne any good to meet my charming Ronnie, who had always demanded perfection from himself and everyone else around him? Especially his girlfriends.

LIZ

For one week all I did was exercise and work. Oasis in the morning; work till six; then jogging in the park. At home I did stomach crunches—a total of three hundred a day in sets of fifty. And all I ate was boiled eggs for breakfast, salad—no dressing—for lunch, and tuna and vegetables for dinner.

I was hungry all the time, and sore too. My hands hurt from strangling the weights and the machine grips; my torso hurt no matter which way I bent; and I had headaches, probably from clenching my teeth so much. Nita told me I was overdoing it and banned me from the weight room for two days. But I just worked harder on the treadmill and stair stepper.

I hated every minute of it. But every time I wanted to quit, I drove down Magazine Street and stared at my pretty little shop. My shop that Dennis had stolen. Joan and I would get even with him, but I had to do my part. Only so far I was failing.

I saw Ed one time at the park. He was jogging in the opposite direction. He gave me a distracted smile. I smiled back, then once he had passed, increased my pace. I hated jogging; I hated sprints even more. But most of all I hated being ignored.

Dennis had ignored me and my feelings, then betrayed me in the worst way. Thanks to my crazy plan, however, Ed had become the focus of my revenge. So I worked out and dieted, and in one week lost three pounds. Not enough to qualify for that TV show, *The Biggest Loser*, but not bad.

So here I was, six-thirty on a workday evening, with the temperature still over eighty, ready to take on Ed one more time. I had on a new lavender-and-aqua jogging suit—my best colors. My hair was up in a bouncy pony-tail. My makeup looked perfect—it had only taken twenty-five minutes to make me look like I had on no makeup at all.

Best of all, my stomach was flat. If he didn't give me a second look, I'd have to slap him.

I saw his BMW on Walnut Street and parked just two cars away. Then I did my stretches, just watching and waiting. He was a counter-clockwise runner. I'd been going clockwise. But not today. I spied him coming around the front of the park and got ready. To my shock—and immense relief—he called out to me. "Hey, Liza. How're you doing?"

Liza. "Fine," I said through gritted teeth. "You?"

"Great. Great."

I fell into step beside him. "How many laps do you do?"

"Two. How about you?"

"I'm working up to two."

"Good."

Ah, the aborted conversations of joggers. It's hard to huff and puff and talk at the same time. Those who converse easily as they run are the elite, and they know it.

He glanced at me, at my perky, aqua-clad breasts. *Hooray!* "Seen Larry lately?"

Larry? Boo. "Nope. How is he?"

"He goes to Mr. B's every day."

Looking for me? I didn't say anything.

"I take it you're not interested."

Okay, Liz. Here's your chance. I looked up at him, stared at him, willing him to get the message. "He's a really sweet guy. You know? But he's not exactly my type—"

"Watch it!"

Too late. I tripped over the toes of my brand new cross trainers and went sprawling. "Ow!"

"Are you all right?"

No, I'm not all right. I'm a spastic idiot who can't walk and chew gum at the same time! "I'm fine," I muttered as I clambered to my feet. The heels of both of my hands were scraped from the asphalt; my left knee hurt like crazy, and I know I heard something rip. "I'm fine." *Ow, ow, ow!*

"Are you bleeding?"

"No." I curled my hands into fists, not wanting him to see.

He obviously didn't want to see, because he was still jogging in place. I guess he didn't want to miss a beat in his exercise routine. God forbid I had broken my leg.

"You go on," I said. "I need to wash my hands."

"There's a bathroom over there." He indicated a picnic shelter back near where we'd parked.

"Thanks," I said. *Thanks? For what?*

"See you around." And he was on his way.

Self-centered jerk! No wonder Joan hated him. But as I limped back to my car, my anger at him couldn't hold. I couldn't blame the man for disappearing as fast as he could. Who wants to be seen in public with a walking disaster like me?

I cried all the way home. Once more I'd failed Joan— and myself. But that wasn't the low point of my day. Oh, no. I had a message from Joan on my cell phone. "I have to talk to you," she said, sounding kind of odd. "Call me right away."

I waited until I was home, in my oldest nightgown, with my wounds washed and covered with gauze, and had a cup of Earl Grey tea with a shot of Southern Comfort in it. "Please don't answer," I prayed as I dialed her number. She answered almost before it rang.

"Are you at home?"

"Yes, but—"

"I'll be right over."

"No—" But she'd hung up.

"Great." I picked Pumpkin up and buried my face in his

thick golden fur. "Now I'll have to describe my disaster with Ed face-to-face."

But Pumpkin didn't care about my agony, neither the physical nor the emotional. He just started purring, kneading his paws against the thin fabric that covered my lap, pricking my skin with his needle-sharp claws. Considering all my other pains, I didn't bother to stop him.

Joan looked all flustered when she arrived. Nervous.

"Is something wrong?" I poured her a cup of tea. When she didn't meet my eyes, my heart began to thud. "We've been found out?"

She shook her head. "No. But—"

"But what?" I picked up Pumpkin from a chair and pulled him against my chest. "You've changed your mind, haven't you? Dennis got to you and you don't want to be mean to him."

"Liz, wait." She reached for my arm, but I backed away. Pumpkin yowled, then leaped out of my arms, leaving more claw marks.

"Please, Joan, just don't tell me you've fallen for his bull. Anything but that."

"Liz, listen to me!"

We faced one another across the width of my crowded kitchen. She slid an agitated hand through her hair. "There's no easy way to tell you this, so…"

I swallowed, waiting for the worst. But I had no idea just how awful the worst could be.

"It turns out," she said, a world of pity in her eyes. "That Cora Lee is pregnant."

I heard her. With my ears I heard her. But the rest of me didn't hear, didn't understand. "What?"

She pressed her lips together. "I went to the salon yesterday to get the gift certificates from Dennis. I was having second thoughts about letting Cora Lee near my head with scissors, so I was relieved that she wasn't there. At the time Mai said she'd gone to the doctor or something. I didn't pay attention," she added with a distracted wave of her hand.

"That doesn't mean she's pregnant." It made me nauseous just to say that word in connection with Cora Lee and Dennis.

"Let me finish. I had pretty much decided I was going to cancel my hair appointment for today. But since I'd missed out on my chance to torture her yesterday, I resigned myself to just go through with it." She ran a hand through her hair. "What the hell, I told myself it would grow back."

I looked at Joan's hair. It was easier than dealing with the subject at hand. "She didn't do much to it."

"I told her just a trim. The thing is, Liz, while I was chatting her up, going on and on about how great Dennis is and all that, I could tell she was getting kind of upset. I don't know why she didn't just come out and tell me up front that he was her man. Not that it would have changed my course of action. It would just have brought everything out into the open sooner, and I—"

"Joan!" I cut her off with the slash of one hand. "How do you know she's pregnant? She could be lying."

"Because…" She took a deep breath. "Because of the

way she looked when she told me. She said, 'You're right, Dennis is a super guy.' Then she put her hand on her stomach and she got this happy glow on her face—I'm so sorry to have to tell you this, Liz. Then she said 'Dennis and I are pregnant.' That's how she said it." Breathing hard, Joan just stared at me.

"But she could still be lying." I didn't want her to be pregnant. Absolutely no way. Not Cora Lee; not with Dennis.

But Joan looked so sorrowful that I knew it was true. "Oh, Liz. I'm afraid she is. Mai already knew and she was all excited about it."

I could not believe this. All I'd wanted was to have a baby with Dennis, to make our marriage solid, to fill in all the holes in our lives. But he'd left me for Cora Lee and now *she* was having his baby.

"That was supposed to be me," I said, trying to swallow down the tidal wave of grief rising in my chest, rising to strangle me, drown me, crush me. "That was supposed to be my baby. Mine and Dennis's."

"I know." Joan came up to me and put her arm around my shoulder. "I know."

"How could she do this to me?" Tears were stinging my eyes. "How could *he?*"

But Joan had no answers. There were no answers. That's when I really started to cry. I'd thought Dennis couldn't hurt me any worse than he already had. Boy, was I wrong.

CHAPTER 8

JOAN

Liz fell off the map. She didn't meet me at Oasis in the morning; she didn't answer her phone. Even when I knocked on her door, she only called through the window that she didn't feel well enough for visitors. She was severely depressed, and I couldn't blame her. But she was still going to work every day. I saw her car one day, parked near Archibald's salon where she worked.

So I made an appointment with her to have my hair cut. Not that there was a lot left to cut.

She washed my hair in silence.

"Liz, please don't be mad at me."

"I'm not mad at you. I'm just…I don't know. Numb." She directed me to her styling chair. "Now. What do you want done?"

She wasn't going to talk to me about it. I shook my head. "Whatever you want."

But as she combed out my hair, playing with it, holding out segments of hair on both sides, in the back, and on top, her face began to crumble. "This is…" She gulped. "This is a good haircut." Then she snatched the towel from my shoulders, buried her face in it, and burst into tears.

Casting an apologetic glance at the other two stylists and their staring clients, I hustled Liz into a back room. "Just cry, honey. Just let it go."

"I don't think I can." She choked the words out. "I feel like…like my heart has been mangled."

"You will have a baby of your own one day," I insisted. "You will."

"How? I'm a mess. I don't have a boyfriend. I can't even get Ed to look twice at me. And…and I owe so much money because of the shop that I'll never get caught up."

It was a long afternoon. I cleaned her up enough to take care of her next client. Then I left and went straight to Shear Delight. I don't know what I hoped to accomplish. My hair had dried naturally with no product on it, so I was a frizzy mess.

"Hi," I said with so much false heartiness I almost gagged. "Cora Lee, do you think you could possibly fit me in, just for a blow out and styling?"

"Okay," she said. But I could tell she was reluctant, and she didn't smile. I couldn't really blame her. Obviously my plan to make her suspicious about my interest in Dennis— and his in me—was working.

I sat down and flipped through a copy of *Elle*, but I kept peeking at her. She was finishing up a cut on an incredibly handsome guy, definitely gay, more's the pity. He was quite the chatterbox, but she seemed kind of somber. Morning sickness?

"Where's Dennis?" I asked Mai when her client left.

She shrugged, then glanced warily at Cora Lee. "He went out."

Out. As in how he used to go out when Liz was here? Maybe Cora Lee was getting a taste of her own medicine.

But it was hard for me to be happy about it. She might deserve it, but now there was a baby involved.

"Are you feeling okay?" I asked once I got in Cora Lee's chair.

"Sure." She faked a smile as she wet my hair down with a spray bottle. "What do you want today?"

"Umm, something nice and…motherly." I blurted out the word. "I'm going to my daughter's graduation tomorrow and I want to look my part."

"Motherly." She repeated the word, her chin trembling.

Oh, my. She looked about ready to cry. Hadn't I just been through this with Liz?

She ducked her head and mumbled, "Excuse me a minute." Then she disappeared into the color room.

I met Mai's gaze in the mirror. "What's wrong?"

Again she shrugged. "I think maybe Mr. Dennis, he not too happy. You know, about the baby."

Now that was interesting, though not at all surprising. Dennis didn't want a baby with Cora Lee any more than he'd wanted one with Liz. Maybe that would make Liz feel a little better. But I doubted it.

Meanwhile, although I wanted to know more about what was going on, I didn't have it in me to torture an unhappy pregnant woman.

Of course, that's when Dennis chose to waltz into the

salon dressed in cream slacks, an apple-green shirt and a totally fake tan. He grinned when he saw me. "Well, if it isn't my favorite customer." Then he actually bent over the chair and kissed my cheek.

It was all I could do not to grimace in disgust and wipe off his slime. When I spied Cora Lee in the doorway, I realized he'd done it on purpose. Kissed me to strike out at her. Her face paled, and I felt like a sleazy lowlife. I needed to get out of here. But how?

To her credit, she somehow pasted a pleasant expression on her face and crossed over to us. "Hi, honey," she said to Dennis.

"Hey," he said without even glancing her way. "Mai, has the mail come yet?"

It probably took less then ten minutes for Cora Lee to blow out my hair and style it with a silicone gel and a light hairspray. It looked very nice, smoother and more sedate than before. Just what I needed to keep Pearl happy. But that ten minutes felt like forever. I practically threw a twenty at her. "Keep the change." And I hurried out.

Once in my car I just sat there trying to calm my shaky nerves. Was every woman's life this awful? Instead of hating Cora Lee for being Liz's Barracuda Woman, all I felt for the girl was pity. She was unmarried and pregnant by an unfeeling oaf who didn't want her to have his baby. Even Liz would feel sorry for her.

What if Barracuda Woman got pregnant?

That hideous thought hit me like a cannonball to my solar plexus. Surely Ed, with his eyelid surgery, wasn't looking to start another family with her.

But they were married. If Barracuda Woman wanted a child, I didn't think for a minute that Ed was man enough to stop her.

Except that Barb was the last woman to want a child. It would ruin her perfect figure and interfere with her perfect career.

But what if she *did* want a baby with Ed? After all, she was in her thirties now, and time was running out—

"No!"

I thrust the key into the ignition and started the car. I had to put that thought out of my mind. I had to. Otherwise I would never make it safely home. Ed with another family? If that didn't send *me* over the edge, it would definitely do in poor Pearl.

The next morning Ronnie and I drove to Lafayette. Prior to Pearl's official graduation from the University of Louisiana we met her for lunch.

She seemed a little calmer, and actually kissed me hello before asking, "Is he bringing her?"

"I don't know."

She switched her gaze to Ronnie.

He shrugged. "Don't look at me. I think you're making a big deal out of nothing."

"Oh, really? Well I think you're making a big deal out of a little knee injury."

"Shut up."

"You shut up." She turned her frosty gaze on me. "Look, Mom, if you see them coming, just head them off. Could you at least do that?"

"Head them off? How am I supposed to—"

"Then at least warn me and I'll split! Geez!"

"Fine. Whatever you want."

She let out a huge breath. "Okay. Thanks. By the way," she said after a moment. "You look nicer today."

"Nicer than what?"

She just made a face at me and didn't reply. But I knew what. With my smooth, shorter version of my old bob, and in my Chanel summer suit, I looked like the mother of her childhood. Betty Crocker in pink with pearls at my throat. Except for the absence of a wedding ring—and a husband—I was the nice reliable mother she still wanted.

It made me a little mad. It was okay for *her* to change, for her to grow up and move away and not need me like she used to. But God forbid I change and adjust to the new life that had been left to me.

"I like your new hairdo better," Ronnie said as Pearl headed off and we went to find seats in the audience.

"Thank you, sweetheart. I do too." The truth? If we should run into Ed and the Barracuda today, I'd much rather have had my new look in place. My new armor. But for today Pearl's needs came first. "Let me know if you spot your father."

"You mean my stepmother, don't you? Barracuda Woman?"

"Yes. Her."

Fortunately the place was so crowded we probably couldn't have found them with binoculars. We could barely locate Pearl in the endless rows of graduates. As the ceremony wound down, however, I began to feel bad for my poor daughter. Her dad should be here to celebrate this milestone in her life. But knowing how self-involved Ed was these days, I suspected he wasn't. He'd probably forgotten, or else was miffed about Pearl's attitude toward his wife.

How I wish that had been true!

Because after the ceremony, when Ronnie and I finally found Pearl in the jam-packed lobby, who was there but Ed in a sharp dove-gray Oleg Cassini sport coat over a black silk T-shirt. Who did he think he was, Warren Beatty?

And there, hanging on his arm in a filmy red sundress and stiletto heels, was the Barracuda.

My gaze went straight to Pearl, who was trapped in the corner by the two of them. My poor baby's eyes were huge and filled with terror, darting around, looking for a way out. Like a fox beset by hounds, she wanted to bolt. But she had nowhere to run.

At once my instincts as a mother surged, a hormonal tsunami of murderous rage and self-sacrificing protective-ness. And when she spied me, I practically heard her kit-ten's mewl of panic and fear.

Like an offensive guard protecting his running back, I thrust myself between Pearl and my insane ex and his wife. "Why are you here?" I hissed at Barracuda Woman. "Haven't you done enough to torture this family? Do you have to ruin this too?"

To my immense satisfaction she cringed back from me. Of course her fear didn't last. "It's not my fault you were a failure as a wife."

I think Pearl's and Ronnie's gasps were even louder than mine.

"Now, now," Ed said in his best mediating attorney's voice. "This is not the time or place."

"That's what Pearl's been trying to tell you," I bit out. "That this was not the time or place for her." I glared at the woman. "This is Pearl's day and she made it clear—"

"Barb is my wife. She goes where I go. Look, Pearl." He turned to his now-weeping daughter. "You've got to let go of all this misguided anger."

"No!" She pushed past him, nearly toppling her brother off his crutches and careening off a portly man behind him. Then she was gone.

Ed whirled on me. "This is your fault, Joan. You hate Barb, so you've made Pearl hate her too!"

"*I* made her hate Barb?" People were beginning to stare. I'd never been so outspoken in a public place. Certainly I'd never created a scene before. But today I didn't care. Ed was an idiot and he'd married a bitch. "I think Barb has managed to make Pearl hate her quite on her own."

But if I wanted to claw Barracuda Woman's unlined face and rip her form-fitting dress to shreds, it was clear she wanted to murder me. To eviscerate me. And it didn't matter if my son—Ed's son—was witness to it.

Eyes glittering with malice, she thrust her chin forward. "You may be the mother of his children, but Ed needs more than a little Suzy Homemaker who's lousy in bed."

"Barb!" Ed yanked her by the arm. But the damage was done. I was lousy in bed? He'd said that to her?

"C'mon, Mom." Ronnie touched my elbow. "Let's go."

Barb shot me a triumphant smile, an evil barracuda grimace of glee over one more foolish foe mortally wounded. Then she turned and, head up, waltzed regally away.

Of course, just like a dog on a leash, Ed followed her. He looked back once, as if he was maybe a little embarrassed by her behavior, but not enough to do anything about it.

As for me, it was all I could do to breathe. Moving was out of the question.

"Mom? You okay?"

I couldn't speak. I was stuck on one thought, like a broken record playing so loud that everyone could hear the flaw over and over. *I was lousy in bed?* Though a part of me knew it wasn't true, what if it was?

"Come on." This time Ronnie grabbed my elbow and pushed me through the crowd. Don't ask me how he managed it on crutches. At the moment, though, I was more crippled than him. No longer a wife; not needed as a mother. Now I wasn't even any good as a woman.

I don't remember how we got out of the building or how we found the car. The worst of it was that Ronnie looked just as devastated as I felt. Neither of us spoke a word as we waited for the parking lot traffic to move, nor while I drove to Pearl's apartment. Of course she wasn't there. But I left a note for her. Then we headed home.

Ronnie slept all the way. At least his eyes were closed. I wasn't brave enough to find out one way or the other. Teenagers do not want to admit their parents have a sex life. I'd learned that the hard way when Pearl interrupted Ed and me one night when she was fourteen years old. She'd avoided both of us for a week, as if we'd committed some crime against nature, which in her world I suppose we had.

Ronnie wasn't a teenager, and though I didn't know any details, I had no doubt he'd lost his virginity long ago. Maybe even in high school. But he might as well have been fourteen today, the way he withdrew from me.

Still, ignoring the great big elephant in our living room wouldn't make it go away. Finally, while we waited for the automatic driveway gate to open, I got up the nerve to bring it up. "About today, sweetheart—"

"He's a bastard!"

I recoiled from the force of his rage. Though I wanted my children on my side, I didn't want them to hate their father. Love me best; hate what he did. But keep on loving him too. It's a difficult, probably impossible equation to balance. Still, I had to try.

"Look, Ronnie. Relationships are complicated. Sometimes people say things just…just to hurt each other." *I'm not lousy in bed.* "And anyway, it wasn't your dad who said it."

"He married her, didn't he? He divorced you and married her." He flung the door open and clambered out, then pulled his crutches from behind his seat. "He didn't have to bring her to Pearl's graduation today."

We stared at each other over the roof of the car. "No. He didn't." I sighed. "I'm going to go call Pearl. Do you want something to eat?"

"I can make myself a sandwich."

At least we were talking again. But as he limped into the house beside me, I felt every bit as wounded as him.

Whether either of us would fully recover from our injuries remained to be seen.

As I started up the stairs he said, "Are you going to the gym before it closes?"

I stopped and looked down at him. "I hadn't thought about it. But if you want to we can."

"Yeah, I think I should. I'm stiff from sitting so long in the car, and I need to work this knee, to get back in shape as fast as I can."

"Okay. Make your sandwich. And one for me too. I'll be ready in a few minutes."

In my bathroom I stripped out of my mommy outfit, then stared honestly at myself. That bitch Ed had married would not sap me of my confidence. I wouldn't let her.

So go to bed with someone.

The very idea made my stomach go queasy. And not in a good way.

"I could date." I stared at my mirror counterpart as if waiting for her response.

Maybe.

Maybe I could date.

I immediately thought of Dennis. I was pretty sure he'd jump at the chance. I shuddered in disgust. No way. But there had to be some decent guys out there. Maybe.

Heaving a sigh, I mussed up my nice neat bob, pulled on my exercise clothes, then reached for the phone. I got Pearl's voice mail. "Hi, honey. It's Mom. I'm so sorry your day was ruined. I hope you know how proud I am of you. And your dad is too. Give me a call and let me know how you are and if you need help with your move. I love you, baby."

I had a broken-hearted daughter and an angry son. And then there was Liz who was depressed, and Cora Lee, who I was beginning to feel sorry for too. Wasn't anybody happy anymore? Weren't any relationships working?

Downstairs Ronnie and I ate our sandwiches. Then we were off to the Oasis where I didn't see anyone I knew. I exercised. He swam.

When I was ready to go, however, I saw him at the side of the pool talking to a pretty young woman. The one Nita had told me about with the back injury and the permanent limp.

Despite the ongoing ugliness of his parents' divorce, Ronnie wasn't giving up on the opposite sex. I saw her laugh and him use his cupped hands to make a towering splash of water.

My son has never had any trouble with girls. From his second-grade girlfriend, Trudy, to whomever the last one at LSU was, I don't recall him suffering very long over any girl's rejection. Though maybe that wasn't such a good thing.

But he was still in the game, and there was no reason why I shouldn't be too.

Heartened, I turned back to the elliptical trainer. I'd give it another fifteen minutes. And when we got home I'd try once more to reach Pearl.

CHAPTER 9

LIZ

I stalked Cora Lee.

It sounds worse than it actually was. First off, I only did it on my days off—and the two days I called in sick. Second, I only wanted to see her, to see how she looked now that she was pregnant with Dennis's baby. The baby I'd wanted to have.

But though I didn't want to hurt her, I still knew it was stalking and that it was wrong—and probably illegal. Otherwise I wouldn't have tried so hard not to be noticed.

That meant I couldn't take my car. A bright yellow VW is hard to overlook. So I parked on Pitt Street and jogged to Magazine Street. Then, with my hair stuffed up in a Zephyrs baseball cap, and a pair of oversized, really dark sunglasses covering the rest of my face, I sat in the front window of P.J.'s Coffee House and watched my old shop.

The geraniums didn't look too good. They needed to have the old blooms pinched off, some fresh fertilizer, and a daily watering. They needed to be healthy to thrive in such a hot, southern exposure. But even though it wasn't summer yet, they were already drooping.

My first day watching Cora Lee, Dennis drove up in his F-150 truck, let her out without even pulling over, then zoomed off. He has these big twin chrome tailpipes on his truck, and they're really loud. She stood there a minute staring after him and I kind of felt sorry for her. Dennis was obviously mad at her. About the pregnancy?

Today they were late. Mai was waiting outside the shop for twenty minutes before they got there, and so was Bitsey Albertson, one of our most faithful customers.

Were they trying to ruin everything I'd worked so hard to build?

Again Dennis roared off. He sure wasn't spending very much time at the shop these days.

I stirred the slushy remains of my granita. Was he cheating on her? Sleeping with somebody else in their bed?

Even though Cora Lee had ruined my life, and the whole point of the Payback Club was to break her and Dennis up, somehow I didn't feel as good about it as I'd expected.

"So here you are."

I jerked and nearly dumped my granita into my lap. "Joan!"

"Oh, so you remember my name. It's been so long I was afraid you'd forgotten me."

"Of course not," I protested, but I knew she had a point. "How did you know where to find me?"

She laughed. "I was visiting my mother at Chateau de Notre Dame. On the way home, I happened to make a detour down Arabella Street, and whose yellow car do I see but yours? Since it was close to your old shop, I was afraid you might be confronting Cora Lee or Dennis. So I came looking for you." She pulled out the chair opposite mine and sat down. Then she peered out the window at Shear Delight. "What are you up to?"

"I'm just…watching." I shrugged and swirled my straw in my granita. "That's all. Just watching."

"Oh, Liz. That's a terrible idea. You're just torturing yourself."

"I know. But it's an even worse idea for you to be seen with me."

"Why? Because it will wreck our plan?" Joan shook her head. "I'm beginning to think our plan is already wrecked."

"Because she's pregnant, right?"

"You have to admit it's a problem."

I nodded. "I know."

Across the street the door to the shop opened, and who should come out but Cora Lee. I squinted to see better. She looked upset, pacing back and forth with her arms crossed like she was trying to hold herself together.

"He's probably not taking the pregnancy very well," I murmured.

"Mai said he wasn't."

I straightened. "When did she say that?"

"I went back there, the day I came to you for a trim. If you would answer your phone, you would know that."

"Sorry about that. Really, Joan, I am. I've just been so…"

"Unhappy?" she threw in. "Depressed? Miserable?"

"Yes." I swallowed hard. "So, what exactly did Mai say?"

"Very little. But between her cryptic remarks and Cora Lee's tears—"

"Cora Lee cried?"

Joan nodded. "She cried."

My heart started to thump, almost like I felt bad for her. "Do you think he's going to dump her?"

Joan frowned at me. "Please tell me you're not thinking of getting back together with that man."

"No way."

"Thank God. You know, the best thing that could happen to Cora Lee would be if he dumps her."

"But what about the baby?"

"I don't know." Joan shook her head and both of us stared out the window at Cora Lee. "They'll have to figure that out."

While we watched, Cora Lee edged away from the shop window. Then sheltering it with her hand, she lit a cigarette.

"Oh, my God, Joan. She's smoking!" I lurched out of my chair. Don't ask me what I intended to do.

"No!" Joan grabbed me and pushed me back. "Stay out of it, Liz. This is between them."

If I'd had reason to hate Cora Lee before, now I positively despised her. Everyone knows pregnant women should never smoke. Never! The fact that Joan was right—that it wasn't my business—only made it worse.

"I'll go over there," Joan said. "I don't want to but…" She fixed me with a stern look. "As soon as I get her inside, you disappear. Understand? I'll call you later. And this time answer your phone."

"Wait!" I caught her wrist. "What are you going to do?"

"Get my bangs trimmed. Buy some new product. Sniff around. I don't know."

"She's not going to be happy to see you."

"So?" Joan finger-combed her hair, then reapplied her lipstick. "What goes around comes around."

It was an unbearably long two hours before Joan called. I'd run to my car, then once home, had fixed myself a smoothie. But my stomach was in knots, and the smoothie made me nauseous. Not pregnant nauseous, but still nauseous.

Life is so not fair.

Added to that, my imagination ran wild with all kind of scenarios. Despite his resistance to fatherhood, I pictured Dennis and Cora Lee happily married, him totally in love with his new baby boy—and with his new wife. I was already grieving, as if their happiness was the exact inverse of my misery when Joan called.

"How could you ever have married that sleazeball?" She didn't even say hello.

"What happened?"

"I'm never going back there."

"What happened!"

She was breathing hard, like she'd just run a 5K. "He's pressuring her to have an abortion."

I swallowed hard. "He told you that?"

"Not him. Her. Well, not in so many words. Mai is pretty upset, and I got it out of her. Apparently Dennis was ranting about Cora Lee ruining everything. Just like he did with you. I think he's going to break it off with her."

It was what I wanted, what our plan was all about. But not like this. "He's dumping her unless she gets rid of the baby?"

"That's how it sounds."

"So, what's she going to do?"

"Mai thinks she's going to keep the baby."

Holy confusion! I was so relieved she was keeping the baby, even though I should have felt just the opposite. I wound a strand of hair around my finger. "Knowing Dennis, he's going to fire her at the same time he dumps her. You know he doesn't want to see her every day at work with her stomach getting bigger and bigger." A shudder of complete revulsion ripped through me. "God, I hate him!"

I paced to the window, then plopped down on the sofa. "We have to help her, Joan."

"Help her? No, Liz. We do not have to help that woman. I mean, I understand you feel bad for her. But there's nothing we can do."

Pumpkin jumped up onto my lap, as if he sensed my agitation. It made no sense, these feelings of mine. I hated Cora Lee, but I wanted to protect her.

No. I wanted to protect her baby.

But a part of me wanted to protect her too. I knew how it felt to be bullied by Dennis. I buried my head in Pumpkin's soft, thick fur.

"When it comes to Dennis, she's on her own," Joan repeated.

My eyes started to water and I sneezed. Cat dander. As if insulted, Pumpkin leaped down from my lap and stalked away. "But that's the problem," I said to Joan. "These guys screw with our emotions as if they don't matter, and we're left to deal with everything all on our own."

"Good grief, Liz. What are you thinking of doing?"

"I'm not thinking of doing anything." *Not yet.*

"I'm glad to hear that. Look, just relax. Okay? And I'll see you tomorrow at Oasis."

"Okay. Wait. I never did ask how Pearl's graduation went. Did Ed bring the Barracuda with him?"

"Oh, yes. It couldn't have been worse if I'd planned it."

JOAN

For some reason I couldn't bring myself to tell Liz the absolute worst part of my run-in with Ed and Barracuda Woman. Bad enough Ronnie had witnessed it. I sure wasn't going to replay it for anyone else. Even so, it replayed over and over in my head every time I closed my eyes. *Lousy in bed. Lousy in bed.*

I wasn't!

But until I could prove it with somebody else, I couldn't erase the thought.

So I glossed over it. "Pearl ran off in tears and she hasn't returned any of my calls. But I'm not too worried. She's furious with her dad and I'm just catching the fallout. She'll call me when she's ready."

I heard her sigh. "Our plan for payback isn't going too well, is it?"

I sighed too. "No. I guess not. On the other hand, Dennis's relationship with Cora Lee is on the rocks. And once

Ed hears from my new divorce lawyer, neither he nor his new wife are going to be very happy."

"Really?"

"I'm suing him for the return of almost half a million dollars."

"A half million dollars!"

"It's my retirement money and the kids' trust funds. None of which was his to take."

"Yeah, but does he have enough money to pay it all back?"

"If he doesn't, he can just sell that overpriced condo of his."

She giggled. "The Barracuda isn't going to like that, is she?"

I grinned. "I certainly hope not."

"But seriously, Joan. What if you can't get it all back from him? What will you do then?"

"The same thing I'm doing now. Work. Maybe I'll have to hustle a little more than I am now. But I can do that. And speaking of which, I've got a pile of work waiting for me."

"I know what you mean. I need to clean up this place and do some laundry."

"But you're going to meet me at that spa tomorrow, right? No more hiding out at home."

"Don't worry. I'll be there."

After I hung up with Liz I went out into the patio, sat in a spot of hot May sunshine, and took stock. Pearl was still missing in action. But Ronnie was progressing well, really working on the rehabilitation of his knee. As for me, I might not succeed in wrecking Ed's marriage, but I was sure going to make his life miserable. Meanwhile I was supposed to meet with that guy from the literacy program about their new brochure and maybe even a monthly newsletter.

Downstairs Ned was putting Ronnie through his daily therapy. I stuck my head in his room. "I'll be gone a couple of hours. How about I bring dinner home?"

"Cool. Sushi? No, make it Mexican."

I laughed. "You would pick the one cuisine with absolutely nothing low calorie."

He grinned at me. He is such a good-looking kid, with Ed's blue eyes and my darker hair. "C'mon, Mom. You don't need lo-cal. I've never seen you looking so good. Right, Ned?"

The therapist nodded. "He's right, Ms. Hoffman. You don't need to lose a pound."

Ronnie was not one to compliment me, and at first I was floored. Then I realized what he was doing, and it brought the sting of tears to my eyes. He'd seen how devastated I was yesterday, and he was trying to build me back up. When had my self-involved jock become so sweet?

"Okay. Tacos and burritos and refried beans it is. Tomorrow I'll just work out for two hours instead of one."

The funny thing about Ronnie's transparent attempt to bolster my self-confidence is that it worked. Then, as if the universe had taken its cue from him, on the car radio WRNO had Gloria Gaynor singing "I Will Survive." To top it off, while I stood in line for café au lait at Rue de la Course, Aretha Franklin belted out "Respect."

I was smiling to myself and humming along, stirring real sugar into my coffee when a man approached me and said, "Excuse me, are you by any chance Joan Hoffman?"

"Yes."

He smiled and stuck out his hand. "I'm Quentin Ledet. From the Literacy League."

Okay. I had cut my hair reluctantly, and doubted my new clothing choices. I'd only done it for the Payback Club, to lure Dennis Savoie into complacency before we ripped the rug out from under him.

But today I was glad for every single change Liz had strong-armed me into. I was glad for Tea Tree Cream in my cute messy hair and for Crystal Shine in my new lipstick. For push up bras and tight Capri pants. Because Quentin Ledet, the man I was meeting with to discuss literacy brochures and newsletters, was gorgeous.

No. Gorgeous is an understatement. He was drop-dead gorgeous, as in I thought I was going to drop dead away.

"Yes. Yes," I repeated, unable to say anything else. I belatedly stuck out my hand to shake his, and then when he took it, nearly melted onto the floor. Oh. My. God!

"I have a table for us over there." He gestured toward the front window.

"Fine. I...I have to put sugar. Sugar," I repeated like I was the stupidest girl in ninth grade and Mr. High School Senior Jock had just singled me out.

"Great." He smiled once more then went back to the table. I fought down an idiotic blush and stirred three heaping tablespoons of sugar into my café au lait—at least that's how it tasted when I finally sat down across from him and took a nervous sip. Ugh.

I cleared my throat and forced myself to get a grip. Quentin Ledet was a client, a paying client in this case, whose money was just as green as any other client's. He was also at least fifteen years younger than I am. Well, at least ten. And he was black with a shaved head and a basketball player's physique. I'd never been attracted to a black man before. Then again, while I was married to Ed I hadn't been attracted to anyone but him, and since my divorce I'd been repulsed by all men.

But I wasn't repulsed anymore.

Struggling to get a grip on this unexpected hormonal surge, I slid a folder across the table. "These are samples of other brochures I've created, to give you an idea of what I've done, and also help you decide what form you want your brochure to take. Tri-fold mailer. Stapled book format. Glossy. Matte. Full color or drop-in color."

I was babbling, and I was avoiding his eyes because of the irrational fear that if he looked into them he might just read my mind: that I'd been celibate for almost two years and content in that state.

But I wasn't content anymore.

Cool your jets, girl, and be reasonable. I was Joan Hoffman, I reminded myself, a respectable uptown matron.

Matron. What an ugly word. Nonetheless that's who I was: a forty-six-year-old matron, not some single twenty-eight-year-old fitness instructor like Nita.

I cleared my throat. "First let's discuss your goals and how you plan to use and distribute the brochures and newsletters."

"Okay. I understand you're already familiar with literacy efforts in New Orleans, so I'll skip my explanation of what we do." He pulled out his own folder and gave me a print-out of distribution numbers spread over a two-year time line.

"We're thinking about three separate items. Bookmarks to be distributed free at every bookstore in greater New Orleans. Brochures to be used primarily at speaking engagements, author appearances, special event mailings—things like that. And newsletters which will go mainly to volunteers, board members, donors, and contributing institutions."

"So the largest printing will be of the bookmarks."

"Right. We'll be working with three different printers, however."

"Three?" Thank goodness I'd beaten my libido down enough that my professional self could function. "Why three?"

"Since we're getting all the printing done at cost, we spread it around so no single printer takes too big a hit."

"That's smart."

He smiled at me. What a great smile. "I was told that you offered to do the design work at half your normal rate."

"Yes, I did." *Gulp.* The man had the most gorgeous amber-brown eyes I'd ever seen. He had to know the effect he had on women, even older women like me.

"That's really generous of you."

I averted my gaze and fiddled with my folder. "Actually, it's good business sense. My logo will appear in the credits portion of every piece that goes out, alongside the printer's. That was part of my agreement."

"Right. I understand your business is pretty new."

"Yes. For years I just did graphic design as part of my volunteer work. But now…"

"But now you're divorced and have turned your volunteer work into a real job."

My gaze shot back up to his. "Is it that obvious?"

He shrugged. "No wedding ring."

"Oh." Feeling self-conscious, I slid my left hand off the table and onto my lap, rubbing the empty place where my ring used to be. I cleared my throat. "Fortunately, it turns out that I like working for myself."

He grinned. "Yeah. Me too."

"I thought you worked for the Literacy League."

"It's a part-time, unpaid gig."

Gig. That's a young person's word, and it made me feel twenty years older than him. "What else do you do?"

"I own a Smoothie Palace with my brother."

"Smoothie Palace. I've been in one of those. They're great. But you still have time to do this? I always heard retail outlets are an around-the-clock commitment. Especially food services."

"Yeah. That's why Darryl and I went in together on it. Between the two of us and his wife, one of us is always there."

He was single. I heard that loud and clear. He was single and I didn't have a husband.

"Well," I said, smiling at him. Flirting, actually. "If you ever need some graphic work for your Smoothie Palace, I hope you'll keep me in mind."

"Absolutely. Do you have a card?"

"Of course."

He was going to call me—and not just for work. Don't ask me how I knew this. But I knew.

And I was going to accept, whatever kind of invitation it was.

Good grief! What would my neighbors think if they saw me going out with a good-looking black man ten years my junior? They'd think I'd totally lost my mind.

Ronnie would probably approve. He'd like Quentin.

But not Pearl.

Of course she'd object whether he was white, black or green. Twenty, fifty or seventy-five.

We spent another thirty minutes discussing content, format, and delivery dates. And when we parted I was in somewhat better control of myself. Quentin Ledet had revived my dormant sexuality, and whether or not anything happened between us, at least I knew I wasn't dead inside.

I arrived home with a spring in my step and a happier outlook on life.

It lasted about an hour and a half. That's when Pearl arrived with her car loaded down, as well as a van driven by a lanky kid with dyed black hair and tattoos across his knuckles that spelled out "love" on one hand and "hate" on the other.

"Hey, Mom," she said as she came up the steps. She had on black jeans, a black tank top with no bra, and a pair of heavy black shoes. My pink-toenail-polish-and-dainty-sandals girl wearing Doc Martens in late May in New Orleans?

The love/hate guy was right behind her carrying a big box. He wore black boots laced halfway up his calves with his black jeans tucked into them.

"This is Stark," she said. "Stark, this is my mom."

"Hi, Mom," he said.

I stiffened. "Call me Joan." Ms. Hoffman, I wanted to say. Or better yet, don't call me anything, just disappear and never come back.

"Okay, Joan."

Pearl held the door open for him. "Upstairs. Last door on the left." She watched him for a moment, then looked at me. "Isn't he great?"

Great for what? "Is he a new friend?"

She laughed. "Yeah. You might say that."

She started inside, but I caught her by the arm. "What are you saying, Pearl? Is he your boyfriend?"

She gave me a challenging look. "Yeah. He is."

Oh, dear. Better yet, oh shit.

I swallowed hard. "He's not your normal type." *Just like Quentin Ledet isn't yours,* a voice in my head said. But I ignored it.

"No, he isn't my normal type," she said. "But then, people change, don't they. First Dad. Now you." Her brittle smile faded. "Be nice to him, Mom. Because if you're not, I'm out of here."

"Out of here? What do you mean? Where would you go?"

"To his place. Stark wants me to live with him, only I think it's a little too soon. But I can always change my mind."

Oh, shit.

I watched her bound up the stairs, my beautiful, unhappy daughter. Her father was going to absolutely hit the ceiling. Then again, that was probably the whole point.

CHAPTER 10

LIZ

I was settled in bed with an apple, a romance novel and Pumpkin purring on my lap when the phone rang. It was Dennis.

I nearly choked on a chunk of Red Delicious.

"You okay?" he asked while I sputtered and coughed and tried to catch my breath.

I hadn't spoken to him except through our lawyers for three months. I didn't want to speak to him now.

Except that I *did* want to talk to him. Some deep-down buried part of me felt that old familiar thrill at the sound of his voice. He has this nice deep voice, you see, with just the right amount of southern drawl. My own Tommy Lee Jones from *The Client*. Slick and self-serving, but sexy as all-get-out.

"I'm fine," I said once I finished hacking out the mangled apple. "What do you want?"

"Can't I just call you to talk?"

"To talk?" Even while my insides were melting from the rumble of his voice, the hair on the back of my neck lifted up in alarm. What was he up to?

"I've been thinking about you lately, Liz. A lot," he added when I didn't respond right away.

Uh-oh.

"That's funny," I said. "'Cause I try not to think about you at all." And I hung up.

I was so proud of myself for that, even though my heart was pounding like the drum section of the St. Augustine High School Marching Band. I stared at the phone. Was he going to call back? Did I want him to?

When it shrilled again, I braced myself. Okay, I could do this. "Hello," I bit out. "What do you want?"

"I want you to come back to Shear Delight."

That knocked all the righteous indignation out of my sails. "What?"

"I want you to come back, babe. Come back."

"But...but..." I had to remind myself to breathe. "But we're getting divorced."

"Yeah, well..." I could picture him running his hand through his thick, spiky hair. "Maybe we should talk about that. Just you and me without the lawyers."

I was on dangerous ground, thick, swampy emotions that could suck me under with one wrong step. "I...I don't think that's a good idea." My left hand hurt from strangling the phone. "I've gotta go—"

"Wait! Wait a minute. Look, Liz, I made a mistake, okay? I screwed up really bad."

"Screw being the operative word." *Good one, Liz!*

"Yeah. But I'm sorry. I'm so sorry, babe. All I want to do now is make it up to you."

Until he said he was sorry, I didn't realize just how

badly I'd wanted to hear those words from him. It was hard to swallow past the big knot of emotions clogging my throat. Anger, pain. Hopefulness. Maybe he really was sorry. Maybe we really could make our marriage work. I didn't want to be twice-divorced before I was even forty.

"What about Cora Lee?"

He was silent a moment. "I fired her."

That's when reality came hurtling back, crashing like a meteor onto my head. "You fired her?"

"Yeah. Today. You see, Liz? I'm serious about this. Serious about you coming back to the shop. To me," he added.

What about her baby? Your baby?

Our baby?

That's what I wanted to ask him. To scream at him. But instead I shoved another piece of apple into my mouth and started chewing. I knew his answers to those questions. He didn't have to say them in his low bedroom voice that muddied up his ugly message.

"Liz?" His voice was a little sharper. "Did you hear me?"

I swallowed the apple and stared at the couple on the cover of my book. The man was cupping the woman's face so tenderly. His face hovered just inches above hers, like they were about to kiss. That's all I'd ever wanted, that tenderness. The sparks and the passion were great, but it was the day in and day out caring that really mattered to me. I reminded myself that despite his charm and his sexy, cajoling tone, Dennis didn't know how to do that.

"I don't think so," I said. "Besides, I already have a job."

"Working at some sweatshop salon isn't the same as owning your own place."

"But it's not my place, is it? You made sure of that."

"Hey. We can work all that out, babe. I promise we can."

I hesitated. Could I really get my shop back? "I don't know."

"Say you'll think about it. Say you'll think about it, Liz, and I'll call you tomorrow."

Ooh, that voice was so smooth, so seductive. If I didn't get off the phone and fast, I'd be saying yes to anything he wanted. "All right. I'll think about it. Look, I have to go."

Afterward I just sat there unable to finish my apple, unable to read my book. Unable to make sense out of any of this. I wanted to call Joan, but I didn't. She hated Dennis, so she'd never understand how tempted I was to go back to him. I didn't understand it myself.

"He's a mean, self-centered jerk," I muttered to Pumpkin as I rubbed behind his ears. He promptly rolled onto his side so I could give him a belly rub. "I should have trusted your good kitty judgment. A man who can't be nice to cats doesn't have it in him to be nice to women either, at least not for long."

Then two things occurred to me. One, Dennis was still officially my husband. And two, his sperm was obviously potent.

Pumpkin let out a discontented yowl and I resumed the tummy rub. But my mind was spinning. I could use Dennis just like he'd used me. He'd used my good credit to build the salon, then stolen it from me. I could do the same to him, make a baby then dump him.

And the irony was that he wouldn't care if I left with his kid. Look what he was doing to Cora Lee.

First thing the next morning—after a night of strange, disconnected dreams of babies forcing me to exercise, faster, faster. Faster!—I was too exhausted to go to Oasis. Instead I did something I knew Joan would be really mad about. I went to Cora Lee's apartment.

I knew where it was because I'd tracked her down the week after Dennis moved out. Despite visions of burning it down, or vandalizing her car—a faded white eight-year-old Neon—I'd never gone back. It was an upstairs apartment in a brick building in mid-city off Canal Street, an ugly no-personality building. It figured. Outside her door two big bags of garbage nearly blocked the balcony walkway. A pair of plastic lawn chairs was stacked on the other side of the door.

When I knocked, my heart was pounding so hard my chest hurt. Why had I come here? What was the point? Did I mean to gloat over her predicament or to sympathize?

I didn't have a chance to decide. Because once Cora Lee opened the door and realized who it was, her eyes got big, her face went sheet-white and she gagged. She slapped a hand over her mouth and gagged again. Then she turned and bolted for the bathroom.

Though she slammed the door in my face, I could still hear those awful retching sounds. They made me want to gag too. They also made me feel sorry for her. Pregnant, dumped *and* fired.

So I went in and closed the front door behind me. While I waited for her to come out, I stared around her living room. There were boxes everywhere, and pictures stacked and leaning against the wall. It wasn't Dennis's stuff. Was she moving?

I heard the toilet flush, and braced myself.

But when Cora Lee came out of the bathroom, peering with frightened, watery eyes, it occurred to me that I had the upper hand. Except that I wasn't interested in using it. I made myself smile at her. "Are you okay?"

She nodded, but her face still looked sickly.

"Can I get you something?" Like this was my house and she was my guest. "A cracker or some toast?"

"No." She took a deep breath through her nose. I saw her nostrils flare. "What do you want?"

Good question.

"Look, Cora Lee, I…I'm not here to attack you, okay? I know Dennis dumped you."

Her already watery eyes overflowed, but she wiped them with the cuff of her shirt.

"And I know he fired you."

She gave a faint nod.

"And…and I know you're pregnant."

It was strange how that started her crying really hard, while it didn't really affect me. I found some tissues for her, and made her sit down. Then I got a damp washcloth for the back of her neck in case she started feeling nauseous again. When she finally seemed all cried out I sat down opposite her. "Are you okay, now?"

She nodded. Then she shook her head. "No. I don't

know what to do. I have to move out of here but…" She trailed off.

"Why are you moving?"

She stared at me, too helpless to care that I was the last person she should reveal her weakness to. "I was moving in with—"

"Dennis." We both said it at the same time.

"Only now you can't," I said. "So why not stay here? You can get another job in another salon."

"This place is already leased to somebody else. They're moving in on Saturday."

A half-grown black-and-white kitten emerged from what must be the bedroom and leaped into her lap. I don't know if it was Cora Lee's desperation, her baby's innocence, or her obvious affection for the kitten. Whatever the reason, I opened up my mouth and the absolutely stupidest words came out. "You can come stay with me."

Stupid. Stupid. Stupid.

Yet I meant every word. I leaned forward. "You can stay with me at least until you find another place."

She hiccupped once, then again. "I can't do that."

"Sure you can."

"But I—Dennis—" She averted her eyes.

"Dennis is a jerk. He screwed both of us over. And I'm sure he'll do it to someone else. But I'm over him." At least I hoped I was. "And one day you will be too."

She wiped her nose. "He wants me to have an abortion."

"That figures."

Then she frowned. "How did you know I was pregnant?"

At least I wasn't stupid enough to blow Joan's cover. "He told me he'd dumped you. And then when you threw up I guess I just put two and two together. He dumped me because I *wanted* to have a baby."

Her eyes got big. "So you have even more reason to hate me."

"Yeah, I do. But…" I shrugged. "But I don't hate you, Cora Lee. Believe it or not, I don't."

JOAN

Liz was late for our date at Oasis, which gave me too much time to think about Quentin Ledet. I'd gone to bed horny, awakened horny, and effectively destroyed the ugly image I had of myself as a dried-up almost-old woman. Screw Barracuda Woman and her accusation that I wasn't any good in bed. Today I was feeling so juicy I practically sloshed. And all because of one tall, dark and handsome younger man.

You'd think a creative person wouldn't deal in such clichéd terms. But clichés are clichés for a reason: they're so damned accurate. So I circulated through the machines at the spa with unusual vigor, fueled by my unreasonable lust for Mr. Tall, Dark and Handsome.

I was overheated—inside and out—and ready for the cold shock of the pool when Liz hurried in.

"Sorry I'm late, but I've got so much to tell you. Some you'll like." She made a face. "Some you probably won't."

"I have something to tell you too."

"About Dennis?"

"No." I fiddled with the controls of the stationary bike.

I wanted to tell her about Quentin, even though it didn't have anything to do with the Payback Club, because I knew she'd be excited for me and would understand what a milestone this was. Certainly I couldn't tell my kids or my mother. And as for my other friends…I realized that most of the friends I'd cultivated as Ed's wife would be horrified.

I looked up at Liz—really looked—and saw her as I hadn't seen her before: a woman who could truly be my friend in the best sense of the word. I stopped pedaling and smiled. "What time do you have to be at work?"

"My first appointment is at noon."

"Okay. It's nine-thirty. Do your routine, but fast, okay? Then we'll go for coffee and fill each other in."

"You're being very mysterious, but from the smile on your face, it's good mysterious."

"Oh, yes."

We went to Little Rue, a funky coffeehouse no one we knew was likely to be in. "You first," I told her. "First the bad, then the good."

"I don't think any of it is bad," Liz said. "Though you might." She took a breath. "Okay, you were right. Dennis dumped Cora Lee."

"Hooray!"

"Well, yes and no. He called me and asked me to come back."

My jaw dropped open like in a campy cartoon. But I couldn't help it. "He what?"

"He fired her and needs me back at the shop. Plus he dangled the possibility of us patching things up."

"The man's a snake, Liz." I frowned and shook my head. "Don't get lured in by him. Don't. Because though he might behave for a little while, eventually it'll be the same old, same old. Plus there's the whole baby thing, you wanting one, and Cora Lee having one."

"I know." Liz paused, her pretty face creased in doubt. "I won't lie. I was tempted at first."

"Oh, God!"

"But then I went to see Cora Lee."

Another shock. "You did?"

"Yes. And here's the part you won't like. I invited her to move in with me."

This time I was too stunned to do anything but listen. "And she actually agreed to it?" I asked after Liz had detailed her discussion with Cora Lee.

"Not yet. But she's practically homeless," Liz said. "Think about it, Joan. She got treated even worse by Dennis than I did."

"Yes, but you didn't deserve it. She does." I shook my head in amazement. "You are either the nicest person I've ever met, or the craziest."

She gave me a self-deprecating smile. "I probably am crazy, but she was so desperate, and when you get to know her, she actually seems sweet."

"I'm sure she is. Dennis only chooses really sweet women. Unlike Ed."

"You're sweet," she pointed out.

"No. I'm stupid."

"You are not. So, tell me your news."

"Okay." I twisted my coffee mug in a circle on the table, then took a deep breath. "I met someone."

She blinked her eyes. "You mean, like, a guy?"

I nodded, and gratified by her happy enthusiasm, I rushed through the story. "I'm meeting him tomorrow to present several layouts for the bookmarks and fliers."

Liz sat back in her chair, smiling. "You know, I *thought* you had an extra sparkle about you today."

She'd noticed? I grinned, almost embarrassed. "I haven't felt this alive in months. In years."

"Well, just be sure to keep some condoms in your purse."

"Liz!" Scandalized, I ducked my head.

"You have to be prepared for anything," she said. "Things have changed since you last dated."

Yes, they had. So on the way home I stopped at Walgreen's and stared at the racks of condoms and other "personal items." Ed and I had never used condoms during our marriage. Not once.

"Hi, Ms. Hoffman," one of the pharmacy clerks said as she walked by. I nodded, then left as fast as I could. If I needed condoms I'd buy them at a pharmacy across town, not here where they knew what shampoo I used and what brand of tampons.

At home I found a note from Ronnie. Ed had picked him up to go to his club to swim. I suppose that was nice, a pleasant father and son outing. I wondered if he'd get as far with Pearl. But why was he doing it on a weekday afternoon when he would normally be at work?

Probably so Barracuda Woman wouldn't know.

I actually felt a little sorry for Ed being married to that woman.

Pearl wasn't home either, but there was no note from her. Naturally. I suppose she was determined to punish everyone for her father's defection. Oh, well.

I settled in with Hunk of Crap, determined to wow Quentin with my designs. Like my other juices, today my creative ones were flowing too. I didn't even know Ronnie had returned until around three when my stomach growled. I went downstairs for food and found him sitting on a bar stool in the kitchen staring out into the backyard.

"Hey, baby. How was swim therapy today?"

"Good. I guess."

"Good, you guess? What, you missed Suzanne?"

He shrugged but didn't meet my eyes.

"It's good to have someone to pace yourself with," I went on. "Maybe she'd like to try out your dad's gym too."

"Maybe," he said, very noncommittal. "The pool's not as big, but they have this smaller resistance pool that really works you hard."

"That's great, honey. How's the leg feeling?"

"Good. Dr. Healon says I can increase my workouts to twice a day. So I thought I'd go with you every morning, then Ned could take me to Dad's gym in the afternoon. In another week or two I should be able to drive myself."

"And Suzanne?"

This time he shot me a grin. "Quit poking around, Mom. She's just a girl I know."

"Yes, she's just a girl," I agreed. But I suddenly felt protective toward her. "She's a disabled girl who's become a real friend when you needed one. But once you're on your feet again, will you still be her friend?"

"Yeah. Of course."

Suddenly there seemed to be an important lesson for him to learn. "You know, Ronnie, you are a handsome, charming young man. You may not understand the effect you have on girls, especially a girl like Suzanne whose physical limitations have probably created limitations in her personal life too." I paused. "Just…don't lead her on, okay?"

I thought he'd get mad at my meddling, or else make a joke of it. Instead his face screwed up in thought. "Okay. But…do you want me to take her to Dad's gym or not?"

"I want you to be her friend and not lead her on, that's all. Unless, of course, you really mean it." I tilted my head and peered at him. "Do you like her? I mean in that way?"

"Geez," he muttered, his ears turning red. "I don't know. When did you start getting all interested in my love life?"

"I've always been interested in everything you do. And Pearl, too. I don't want either of you hurt, but I don't want you to hurt anyone else, either. Especially someone who's already vulnerable."

"Okay. I get the message." He turned on his crutches and, with natural athletic grace, swung out of the kitchen.

I hoped he did get the message. But mainly I hoped I'd raised him to be a better man than his father.

I met Quentin the next afternoon at the coffeehouse. I'd spent two hours getting dressed. Ridiculous. He, of course, looked better than ever in black slacks and a crisp white shirt rolled up to reveal his strong forearms. As before he was friendly. But as he studied the three logo options and the preliminary designs for the bookmark and flier, he was all business.

He pointed to the second option. "This one with the stylized image of the child, and the shadowy images of adolescence and adulthood, it really captures the ongoing problem of illiteracy. If the problem isn't caught early, it becomes a shadow dogging a person his whole life."

"That was my favorite, too. I showed it in shades of blue, but of course it can be done in any color. It would be just as effective in black and white, too, which would save money."

He looked at me with his mesmerizing amber eyes. "You know, Joan, you're really good."

My ego shouldn't have been so affected by his approval, but, oh, it was. "Thank you. It helps working—" *with such a stud as you* "—on a project so dear to my heart."

"Okay. It's agreed then. I'll show these to the committee, but I'm pretty sure they'll go along with our choice. Now, how about I take you to dinner to show my gratitude?"

Dinner? I could practically feel the condoms prancing like little Trojan horses in the bottom of my handbag. It scared me witless.

"You don't have to do that, Quentin."

"I know. But I want to."

And suddenly it was easy. "All right. Dinner." I smiled at him. "I'd like that."

"How about tomorrow?"

Tomorrow, not tonight. Like an idiot I was disappointed. Then again tomorrow was Friday. Date night. I took a deep breath. "Tomorrow would be perfect."

I practically floated home.

I should have known my euphoria wouldn't last. Pearl was in the kitchen making grilled cheese sandwiches for lunch. Lunch at five in the afternoon. Of course when you stay up all night and get up at noon, I guess five o'clock *is* lunchtime.

"So, what are you up to?" I asked, settling across from her at the breakfast bar.

"Not much," she mumbled.

Okay, be that way. When I got up to leave she said, "What's up with Ronnie?"

I turned to face her. "What do you mean?"

"I don't know. I tried to talk to him and he practically snapped my head off."

"When?"

"Just a little while ago. He came back from swim therapy snarling like a bear."

That didn't sound right. Oh no. I hoped my advice about Suzanne hadn't somehow backfired. Maybe he liked her more than she liked him.

I left the kitchen, and knocked on his door. No answer. I knocked again, then cracked it open. "Ronnie? It's me."

He didn't hear that either, because he had headphones on. Even from the doorway I could hear the music, loud enough to make him deaf. He sat hunched in the window bay, frowning morosely, blind to the beautiful day. What had happened?

"Ronnie?"

He started when he saw me, then whipped off the earphones and pasted this totally fake smile on his face. "Hey, Mom. What's up?"

"Are you okay?"

"Sure." He shrugged. "Why shouldn't I be?"

"I don't know. Pearl said you were in a bad mood."

"Like she's ever in a good one?"

He had a point. "How was your swim?"

A pause, then, "Okay."

"You went to Oasis this time?"

He turned away. "No. Ned took me back to Dad's gym. He wanted to see the resistance swimming equipment."

"What did he think?"

"I don't know. I guess he liked it."

I waited a long moment, then asked, "Is something bothering you, honey?"

His Adam's apple bobbled before he said, "No, why should there be?" But that convulsive bobble said otherwise.

"Look, honey, if I was out of line with what I said about Suzanne, I'm sorry. I just—"

"It's not Suzanne!" he shouted, turning to face me. But instead of looking angry, he looked devastated. "It's not Suzanne." He swallowed hard. "It's…Dad."

I drew back. "I'm so sorry, honey. Sometimes he can be really self-centered."

He laughed, this ugly, sarcastic sound. "Yeah. I'll say."

I hated that Ed so carelessly hurt his children. I crossed the room to stand at the end of the bed. "Do you want to tell me what he did today that got you so upset?"

He stared at me, this sad, betrayed expression on his face. Like an old man's. "I don't know if I should tell you. Then again, you might get a big kick out of it. I guess it serves her right. But he's still my dad and—" He broke off, and his head sagged down between his shoulders.

"What, Ronnie? What did he do?"

He lifted his head, looked at me, then blew out a breath. "I think he's cheating on Barb."

I'd expected something truly awful, so I couldn't help it; I started laughing. "Cheating on the Barracuda?"

When he didn't laugh along with me, I tried to calm myself, but it was hard. Ed was cheating on the woman he'd cheated on me with. Somehow it seemed fitting. Payback at last. "What are you saying, that you saw him with someone else? Where? At the gym?"

He nodded, his young face creased in a frown. "I guess he thought I wouldn't be there in the afternoon. I'd told him I was going in the morning. Anyway, I was in the pool and I saw him in the weight room and she was there too."

"Is she younger than Barb?" I shouldn't have asked that, but I couldn't help it.

"Yeah," he answered, slowly, painfully. "I think so. And she's somebody you know."

"Somebody that I know?" I tensed. That changed everything. "Who?"

He hesitated before answering. "Nita."

"Nita." I repeated the name like I'd never heard it before. Like I had no clue who she was.

"Yeah. Your friend, Nita."

I shook my head. " No. Nita works out at Oasis, not at—"

"It was her, Mom. It turns out she moonlights sometimes at Dad's gym."

That's when his words finally sank in. Nita—my Nita who I knew had dated married men in the past—was screwing my ex-husband!

CHAPTER II

LIZ

Cora Lee hadn't said yes about staying with me, but she hadn't said no, either. I worked the whole day in this weird fog, like my hands and mouth were working just fine, but my brain was on disconnect. I did three cuts, two highlights and a blue-hair special on a little old lady who was going to dinner at Commander's Palace for her sixtieth wedding anniversary. Sixty years married to the same man.

She's the only one I really pulled out of my daze for, and she was really happy with her hair when she left, though she only tipped three dollars. But she was raised in the Depression, so…

Anyway, all day I obsessed about Cora Lee, or more precisely, Cora Lee's baby. I did not want her to have an abortion, not because a baby would guarantee her break up with Dennis, but because I wanted that baby to have a chance. And I wanted to hold it, to admire its little round face, its pink, chubby cheeks, and its sweet, gummy smile.

I drove past Shear Pleasure on my way home, telling myself it was stupid. But I couldn't help it. They were already closed. Had he hired someone to replace Cora Lee? Should I call him?

In a way my plans for payback had all come to pass. But it wasn't what I expected. I didn't want my pretty little shop to fail. On the other hand, I didn't want it to succeed without me.

I went home, fed Pumpkin, and called Cora Lee. "So, when are you moving in with me?"

"Are you sure about this?" I could tell she thought I was a little wacko. But she was also desperate.

"I'm absolutely, one hundred percent sure. I told you I have a spare room. It's not huge, and you can't fit all your stuff in it. But I know we can make it comfortable."

I heard her sigh. "Okay. But only till I get settled in a new job and can afford my own place."

"Fine. Perfect."

I wanted to jump for joy. Joan was right: I was crazy.

But I knew this was the right thing to do. "Look, my other line is ringing, so I have to go. But I'll make you a key and drop it by later, okay?"

I took the other call. "Hey, Joan. How's it going?"

"Horrible!"

Not what I expected, and her voice was shaky, like she'd been crying. I was usually the weepy one, not her. "What's wrong?"

"What's wrong? How about Nita, our so-called friend who acted like she was in complete support of our Payback Club. It turns out that she's screwing my ex-husband!"

Holy cow!

I met Joan at the Fly, where the back end of Audubon

Park meets the Mississippi River. The sun was a sizzling red ball that turned the river gold and the trees that lined the far side of the water black. She pulled her Avalon in next to my car, braking hard. She was dressed to kill, in a classy gray linen skirt, a white sweater set, and pearl earrings and necklace. Lauren Bacall in a 1950s movie, only updated. She didn't have to remove her sunglasses for me to know she'd been crying.

We walked to the edge of the levee and looked down at the lapping waters, so deceptively calm. A lot of people had drowned in this mud-colored current.

Joan let out a really unladylike curse. "How could Nita stab me in the back like that?"

I knew I had to step carefully. "Now, what exactly did Ronnie say happened?"

Joan shook her head. "He saw Ed kiss her on the mouth. Ed initiated it and she kissed him back. Not a lot of room for misinterpreting that."

"But Joan, that just doesn't make sense."

Just then her phone rang. She yanked it out of her purse and stared at the screen. "It's Nita again." She tossed the phone back into her purse. "She knows she's been busted. That's why she keeps calling me."

"Maybe you should take her call."

"I'm never talking to that woman again!"

"Okay. But if it was *another* woman with Ed you'd be happy about it, right? He'd be cheating on the Barracuda, just like you wanted."

Her chin trembled until she clenched her jaw. "I know this probably sounds unreasonable, Liz. The whole point of our plan was to break up our exes' relationships, and I guess that's basically what's happened. But I thought Nita was my friend."

"And I thought Cora Lee was my enemy. Only now she's going to be my roommate."

Joan wrapped her arms around her middle. "Oh, Liz. Everything is so messed up."

I rubbed her shoulder. "Yeah, it is. But I still think we should listen to what Nita has to say. Could we at least check to see if she left a message?"

She rolled her eyes, but she didn't object. So I dug in her purse and pulled out the phone. "Please call me," Nita said in the first message. "Right away." The second was more frantic. "I'm guessing you've talked to Ronnie by now. But Joan, you have to believe me. I didn't know he was your ex. Please call me. Please!"

"Maybe it's just a bad coincidence," I said to Joan.

"A coincidence? You know what, Liz. You can invite a snake into your house, but I'm not that naive."

"Hey, there's no need to take this out on me."

"Oh, God!" She pressed the heels of her hands to her temples. "I'm sorry." She heaved a dejected sigh and looked over at me. "I'm sorry."

"Then call her. She really sounded upset, Joan. Let's get to the bottom of this."

She didn't want to do it, but she finally agreed. Nita arrived within fifteen minutes. By then it was almost dark, but there were enough lights and enough people along the river bank to make it safe.

"I am so sorry," Nita said almost before she was out of

her Jeep. "I didn't know he was your husband, Joan. Even when I saw Ronnie, I didn't get the connection."

Joan wasn't buying it. She stared coldly at Nita. "If you didn't date married men, you wouldn't be in this predicament, would you?"

"Teddie never said he was married."

"Teddie?" Joan exclaimed. "He calls himself Teddie?"

"That's right. Teddie St. Romaine."

"Not Ed Hoffman," I chimed in. "No wonder she didn't know who he really was."

Joan didn't want to let go of her anger. "Are you saying I never mentioned that my married name was St. Romaine?"

"Not to me," Nita said.

"Or me," I added. "I figured it out that day at Mr. B's."

Joan looked away, digesting that. "Okay. That part is my fault," she conceded. Then she swung her narrowed gaze back to Nita. "How far did things progress between you two?"

Nita didn't have to answer. We could tell by looking at her guilty expression that she'd slept with the man.

"Oh, my God," Joan choked out, her face sagging with horror. "I…I have to get out of here."

Nita and I stood there in the still, evening heat and watched her leave.

"She hates me, doesn't she?"

Nita was normally so bouncy and cheerful. It was strange to see her so glum.

"It's complicated," I said. "She hates Ed—Teddie—and since we're her friends, we're supposed to hate him too.

Innocent or not, the fact that you were attracted to him makes her feel betrayed, like he's still this great guy." I peered at her stricken face. "What's he like?"

She swallowed. "Charming. Great looking. Rich, and good in bed." She let out a humorless sort of laugh. "The exact kind of guy every woman is searching for."

"Except that he cheats on his wife."

"Yeah." She sighed. "Except for that."

"Look, Nita, don't beat up on yourself. You've been had by a real slick operator. At one time or another we all have." I gave her a hug; she managed a weak smile.

"Well, so much for moonlighting at Taffaro's Gym."

"By the way," I said as we turned for our cars. "You haven't heard the latest about Dennis. And about Cora Lee."

JOAN

I took a forty-five minute shower and only came out when there was no more hot water. Ronnie had friends visiting in his room, and Pearl was gone, which suited me fine.

I'd gotten what I wanted: Ed was already cheating on Barracuda Woman. Even if she didn't know it, I knew, and that was supposed to make me feel vindicated. But it was a hollow victory, because the new woman he was cheating with was Nita. Nita who was supposed to be my friend.

The thing was, on my drive home down Tchoupitoulas Street, I'd reluctantly accepted that the whole situation was a coincidence. A bad coincidence, with a capital B, but nonetheless, not a deliberate betrayal by Nita. What still hurt, however, was that even though Ed had cheated on his new wife, it didn't faze him. Even if—when—Barracuda Woman found out and divorced him, he would just go on his way being the same self-centered bastard he'd always been.

Even the financial judgment I was pursuing against him would only end up a blip on his horizon. The law firm of Dreyfous, Landry, and McCoy was doing very well these days, and Ed was a senior partner. Between his salary and his bonuses, he had to be rolling in money. He might not *want* to reimburse my retirement account and the kids' trust funds, but in the long run it wouldn't really affect his life.

I stared into my closet, trying to decide what to wear. It wasn't fair. Ed had ruined my life, wrecked our family, and now he was cheating on his new wife. Yet he got off scot-free.

If it weren't for my upcoming date with Quentin Ledet, I would have been below-sea-level depressed. One thing I knew, however—I wasn't introducing Quentin to Nita any time soon.

The next day I jogged the path around Audubon Park twice. I was boycotting Oasis Body Works *and* Nita Alvarez. After that, just for spite I paid thirty-five dollars to try out one session of Super Slow, a new exercise trend at a new exercise salon. My muscles, even the cheeks of my behind, were trembling when I left. Thank goodness all I had to do for the next few hours was sit at the computer.

When I got home, however, Ronnie was sitting on the front porch swing. He was obviously waiting for me, and even before I was up the steps he said, "I'm worried about Pearl."

"Worried? What do you mean? What's wrong?"

He stood up from the swing and reached for his crutches. "I thought she was just, like, hung over, you know?"

"Hung over?"

"Yeah. I mean, just 'cause she's a straight-A student doesn't mean she never parties."

"Okay. So why are you worried now?"

"Well…" His face looked as scared as it had when Ed and I had told him we were getting divorced. "I can't get her to wake up."

Every fear I've had was nothing compared to what I felt as I bolted inside and ran up the stairs.

"She's in the TV room," he yelled from the foyer.

I reversed direction, and fueled by panic, flew to the back of the house. So much for aching muscles.

Pearl was sprawled face down on the leather sofa, still dressed in yesterday's clothes, boots and all. I fell onto my knees behind her and grabbing her wrist, searched for a pulse. Slow and steady. Thank God. Finally catching my breath, I looked up at Ronnie. "When did she get in?"

"I don't know. About two hours ago."

My mouth sagged open. "She was out all night? Oh, God. I should have checked her room before I left."

"She got in right after you left."

"Who brought her home? She didn't drive, did she?"

"I don't know, Mom. I don't know."

The door buzzer rang and, as if relieved, Ronnie swung off on his crutches to get it. It was Ned, thank God, and he was trained as a nurse. He hurried in with Ronnie close behind. Nervously I stood up. "Should I take her to the emergency room?"

Frowning, he flipped her over, then angling a lamp toward her face, he gently opened her eyes one at a time. "Yeah, she's out all right," he muttered. "But her pupils react to the light. And her pulse is good."

"So it's nothing dangerous?"

"She smells like a damned barroom—excuse my French. 'Course, that doesn't mean she didn't use the liquor to wash down anything else. I'd say, for now just watch over her. Pinch her good every once in a while to make sure she reacts."

So that's how I spent Friday, pinching my daughter, alternating between wanting her to wake up so I could hug her, or so I could kill her. The only good thing that happened was that I got a call from Andrea, my new lawyer, saying she was sending me copies of her filings regarding Ed's hanky-panky with my money and the kids'.

"I suggest you not discuss it with him should he call. Make him sweat," she said in this take-no-prisoners voice.

My last hope for revenge on Ed was the threat of legal censure. If he'd illegally taken our money, I could fight him in court to get it back. But that wouldn't embarrass him as much as a charge of fraud brought before the Louisiana Attorney Disciplinary Board. If they got involved he could be disciplined to the extent of even losing his law license, though Andrea had told me that wasn't likely since this was personal monies, not client related.

I guess lawyers can steal from the kids and ex-wives, but God forbid they stiff their clients.

Pearl eventually woke up around four in the afternoon. Though it was more like sleepwalking, she staggered to the bathroom, then to her bedroom, where she passed out on the bed. I followed behind her, afraid she'd fall down the stairs, all the while biting my tongue so hard it should have bled. I wanted to scream at her, but I didn't. At least she was going to recover, I reminded myself. I wasn't sure I would.

Then around six as I was stepping out of my bathroom I heard her on the phone.

"…got blasted. Yeah, I know. Who, Stark?"

I strained to listen. I've never been a mother who eavesdrops on her kids. But then, I'd never been the mother of a lush before.

"We could do that," she said. "Yeah, good. Pick me up around ten. But call first."

I could feel my fuse burning shorter and shorter. Sleep until six, then go out at ten so she could come home loaded sometime around noon?

I don't know what came over me. I'm not one to berate my kids. I never really had to. But I'd had a rough couple of days, following on the heels of a rough couple of years. I barged into her room, snatched the phone out of her startled hand, and threw it across the room.

Threw it!

"You will *not* be going out at ten o'clock, young lady!"

Her mouth gaped open in shock. But she recovered fast. "Really? What are you going to do, Mom? Sit on me?"

What *was* I going to do?

"I'm taking away your car." *So there.* All I needed to do was stick out my tongue and I would be five years old again.

She lurched to her feet, this beautiful woman/child of mine who had somehow become a complete stranger. "You can't do that! You *gave* me that car. You and Daddy."

"We gave that car to our daughter who did not come home drunk, who did not pass out, only to get up and go out partying again." I reached out a hand to her. "Listen, Pearl, I know this divorce has been hard on you. It's been hard on Ronnie too. But you've got to get—"

"I'm an adult!" She spat the words at me. "I graduated from college and I'm not a little girl. Face it, Mom, you can't run my life anymore."

"I don't want to run your life. What I want is for you to run it, to make good decisions and—"

"It's *my* car!"

I stepped back from her rage, but I knew I couldn't back down. "The car is in our name, not yours, and we pay the insurance. You know what, Pearl? If you don't like it, go complain to your dad." That would really get her goat.

Her eyes were slits, and her chest heaved with fury. "Why are you being such a bitch?"

"Because...I love you."

"Yeah, right." She glared at me. "Go ahead, do what you want. You still can't control me."

"No?" I braced myself. "If you stay out all night again or come home like you did today, so drunk or high or I don't know what, well...If that happens even one more time, you'll have to move in with your father, because I won't stand for that kind of behavior in my house."

"Fine." She marched to her closet and flung the door open. "I'll just pack and move in with Stark."

Though I knew that's what she'd say, I shuddered at the thought. Had I gone too far? Inside I was shaking and ready to fall down on my knees and beg. *Please don't do that, Pearl. We can work this out. Please, just stay.*

But a part of me must have known better. Instead I said, "If getting loaded every night is that important to you, honey, I doubt anything I say or do can stop you." Then I turned and walked away.

"I hate you!" she shrieked, slamming the door to prove it.

I flinched at the sound, but I didn't turn back. I stalked into my room, closed the door, then burst into tears. This wasn't supposed to be happening, not to our family. Not to our Pearl.

At that moment I wanted so badly to call Ed. But how could I?

And yet, how could I not? He was still her father and despite everything we needed to present a united front when it came to our kids. I sagged down onto my bed and with shaking hands I dialed his number. He picked up on the first ring.

No. The Barracuda picked up. "It's about time," she said in this clipped voice.

I should have just hung up. She obviously was expecting another call. But I needed to speak to Ed. "Hello, Barb. This is Joan. Could I please speak to Ed?"

There was this long pause. Then in a voice that should have struck me dead, she said, "Screw you," and hung up.

I just stared at the phone. Shock, I guess. I dialed his cell number, which is what I should have done in the first place. He didn't pick up. I didn't leave a message. Then I called Liz.

"You did the right thing, Joan. I'm really proud of you. We've both been big pushovers in the past. That's why we're stuck in these awful predicaments. But husbands and money aren't nearly as important as kids. Tough love. That's what you gave Pearl. Tough love. Now you just have to hang tough."

"Yeah." I sniffled and wiped my nose. "I know you're right. But it's going to be hard. What if she *does* move in with that Stark guy? I mean, you should see him, Liz. Pale and skinny and tattooed."

"And Ed and Dennis are so perfect? Face it, Joan, she may just have to learn the hard way. Like we did."

That stopped me cold. Ed had always been any potential mother-in-law's dream. Yet look how he'd turned out. I sighed. "I don't want it to be so hard for her."

"I know. But like she said, she's a grown-up now, and she's in charge of her own life. Maybe she has to screw it up a little bit in order to figure it all out."

"I suppose you're right." I said the words and I knew they were true. But my heart was breaking.

"Now. Don't you have a date tonight?"

I used cucumbers over my eyes, but I'm not sure they helped much. An hour of hard work in front of the mirror with at least five hundred dollars' worth of cosmetics to choose from can't counteract the puffy effects of a furious daughter storming out of the house, then tearing back in to demand I move my car so she can back hers out of the driveway. Of course I refused. This time she left on a wave of curse words far more creative and vitriolic than anything I could have dreamed up.

Ronnie wisely holed up in his room until the crash of the front door signaled her final departure. Even then he only stuck his head out. "What happened to her?"

I was trembling. Nothing had prepared me for such venom, and from my own child. Then again, I hadn't expected betrayal from my husband, either. How had I lived so long as Pollyanna?

"I took her car away from her." I fixed him with an amazingly steady stare. "If I ever discover that you're abusing alcohol or drugs, I'll do the exact same thing to you."

"Hey, Mom, I'm an athlete." He grinned. "My body is my temple."

"I'm not joking, Ronnie."

Now here I sat, puffy eyes and all, waiting for Quentin to arrive, feeling as tired as an old woman. Emotional storms do that to you. If there had been a graceful way to get out of this date, I would have.

But I'd forgotten about that counterbalance to female emotions: female hormones.

Precisely at seven-thirty Quentin drove up in his black Ford Explorer. I watched him walk up the brick walk with his long, relaxed stride, wearing a pale gray sports coat over a black silk T-shirt and black slacks, and my estrogen levels shot up so fast my peri-menopause disappeared. I actually felt blood rush to all the parts of me that counted: cheeks, breasts and somewhere deep south of my belly button.

Then I opened the door for him, he smiled, and my hormone output doubled. Holy cow, what had I gotten myself into?

CHAPTER 12

LIZ

Cora Lee had made three trips to a storage facility by the time she showed up at my apartment. She was drooping with exhaustion, her hair was up in a plastic clip, and she didn't have any makeup on. Not the picture of what you want in a hair stylist.

I, on the other hand, had changed clothes three times and styled my hair four different ways before settling on a casual green-and-white halter dress, a pair of sassy sandals from Feet First and my hair blown out smooth and straight. You'd think I was going on a date, not welcoming my husband's pregnant ex-mistress into my home.

Then again, how *do* you dress for that sort of occasion?

She came in carrying one suitcase, a canvas tote bag, and her cat carrier. Pumpkin immediately began to growl.

Cora Lee looked at me, then at my overfed cat. She shook her head. "This isn't going to work."

"Yes it will. Don't mind him. He'll get used to you and..." I took the cat carrier from her and peered inside.

"Kitty Little."

Kitty Little. How original. I smiled, reassured by the superiority of my looks and my cat. Then I remembered which one of us was expecting a baby, and all that smugness drained away.

"I'll just put the cat carrier down here. Give me that suitcase. Do you have more in your car?"

While Pumpkin serenaded us with unhappy yowls, I got Cora Lee settled in my spare bedroom, the room Dennis had used as his so-called study. And not once, not even when it dawned on me exactly what an insane thing I was doing, did I let my smile slip.

In the end it was okay, because when I made her a cup of green tea and told her she should drink it while she soaked in a warm bubble bath, and she gave me this grateful smile and almost started to cry, I knew I'd made the right decision to invite her to stay with me.

While she was in the bathroom I called Joan, even though I knew she was on her date and wouldn't answer. "Call me as soon as you get in," I told her machine. "Even if it's two in the morning."

My phone rang at twelve-fifteen.

It was Dennis.

"Hey, Babe." He sounded drunk.

For a long moment I couldn't respond. Then I swallowed and said "Wrong number" in a fake Latino accent and hung up.

He called back. I picked up, then hung up without responding.

Five minutes later the phone rang again, and I started to hang up like before. I could last longer than him at this stupid game. Only it wasn't him.

"Joan! Hi! I'm so glad you called." I turned on the bedside lamp and sat up. "How was your date?"

"Oh, Liz. There aren't the right words to describe it. Quentin was just great. Just…wonderful. But first, why'd you call? Is everything okay with your new roommate?"

"Oh, yes. She got moved in just fine. She's asleep, poor baby."

"Poor baby?" I heard her laugh. "I don't know how you do it, how you can be so truly nice to her after everything she did."

"It helps that she's in a lot worse shape than me." I paused. "You know, maybe if you acted a little nicer to Barb she would—"

"She told me to screw myself when I called Ed today."

"Oh."

"She's a horrible human being, Liz. Nothing will ever change that. And I resent the implication that any of this is my fault."

"That's not what I meant, and I'm sorry if it came out that way. I guess I just hoped that she would meet you halfway."

"She won't."

"Okay. Well. So, tell me about Quentin, then."

"Quentin." Her voice changed when she said his name, and I could picture her smiling. "Gosh, I don't know where to begin. I was so scared, Liz. I haven't been on a date in twenty-five years, and I'm sure he could tell. But he was so nice about everything. A perfect gentleman. We had dinner at Figaro's, casual but nice. Then we went to this club I've always heard of but had never been to. Not that

I've been to any music clubs in years. Snug Harbor on Esplanade. Have you ever been?"

"I went once." *With Dennis, of course.* "Who was playing?"

"John Rankin. It was just perfect. Quentin and I talked and listened to music. Did you know he started off as a teacher? But he couldn't make it work financially. His mom and disabled sister live in the other half of his double. So he and his brother bought a smoothie franchise."

"Wow, a man with a real job who's good looking, takes care of his family, and does charity work too."

She laughed. "When you put it like that he really does sound too good to be true."

I stared at where my toes poked up the yellow floral sheets, debating my next words. "You didn't sleep with him, did you?"

I heard the sharp intake of her breath. "Of course not!" Then she added, "But I sure wanted to."

I laughed, relieved. "Yeah. I remember that feeling. Right after I got divorced the first time, I fell in love with the first guy who treated me nice. I went to bed with him on the first date." I sighed. "Not my smartest move."

"How long did you and Dennis date before…?"

I grimaced. "I made him wait until the fourth date. Of course that was only four days. You might say that my judgment about men is not all that good."

"I'm not sure mine is any better."

We were silent a moment. Pumpkin leaped onto the bed and walked in a restless circle over me.

"Here's an idea," I said. "Don't go to bed with anyone

you wouldn't take with you to one of those literacy fund-raisers you used to go to when you were married."

"Hmm. You know, the YMCA's fundraiser for their adult reading program is next month. I could invite Quentin—though I'm not sure I can wait that long," she added in a suggestive voice.

I laughed. "Does Ed go to that?"

"He might. But even if he doesn't, he knows a lot of the people who do. He'd hear about Quentin, that's for sure."

I hesitated, then said, "I hope you aren't dating Quentin just to spite Ed. Because that's not really fair to Quentin."

"Don't worry. I'm dating Quentin because I like him. And because the first time I saw him he reminded me how it felt to be a woman. A whole, complete woman. I just hope he asks me out again."

"Did he kiss you good night?"

"Mmm-hmm."

I grinned. "With tongue?"

She burst out laughing. "I can't believe you asked me that!"

"Well, did he?"

"Yes. And he had a hard-on too!"

We dissolved into laughter. You'd think we were tenth graders, not jaded divorced ladies, the way we carried on.

Later, after we hung up, I thought about that, about how good it felt to be kissed by a man who you could tell wanted more from you. That hardness pressed against your belly might be buffered by your clothes and his, but the rush of desire and the magic of feeling desired weren't muffled at all. Even now, four years after my first kiss with Dennis, I remembered how wonderful it had felt. How powerful and feminine I'd felt.

But those feelings hadn't lasted. And now here I was, alone again, no prospects in sight, with only my cat and my husband's pregnant girlfriend to keep me company. I turned out the light and lay back, but I was awake now and restless. All this talk about men and kissing and hard-ons.

After ten minutes I got up and went to my closet. Up there on the top shelf in a red shoebox was the solution to my itchiness.

I only hoped the batteries were still good.

JOAN

For the three and a half hours I spent with Quentin, I managed not to worry about Pearl. But by 1:00 a.m. in my silent bedroom with my hair scraped back by a headband, and a cleansing mask covering my face, I was regretting the harsh line I'd taken with her. Better she come home drunk to my house than somebody else's. Women got taken advantage of all the time when they were drunk. Raped. Beat up. Murdered.

I reached for the phone to call Ed. He needed to know. But what could he do? Nothing.

I held the phone to my chest. Who could she be with? What friends would put her up, besides the cadaverous-looking Stark?

In the end I hung up the phone, took two Tylenol PM, and prayed she'd come home tomorrow.

Pearl didn't come home or call the next day. I tried to reach Ed at work only to be told he wasn't in. No doubt he'd received the legal papers from my new attorney and was too angry to speak to me. "This is about his daughter," I told his secretary. "It's important."

"Yes, ma'am," she said. "If he calls in I'll be sure to tell him."

I hung up furious, then tried his cell again, to no avail. I left a detailed message. Where was he?

"She's probably fine, Mom," Ronnie said. "You're getting all worked up over nothing."

I settled in with Hunk of Crap, hoping to distract myself with fonts and tab settings and the peculiarities of my balky printer, and actually, I was very productive—until Quentin called.

"The committee loved your designs," he said. "All of them. But they decided the hands motif was the best."

I was smiling from ear to ear as I sat back in my desk chair and with one toe pushed myself in a slow circle. "I'm so pleased." It was always nice to hear that people liked my work, but especially nice to hear it from that sexy, masculine voice of his.

"I really enjoyed last night," he went on.

"So did I." Then afraid I'd chicken out, I added, "Would you like to attend the ABC Ball with me? You know, the YMCA's fundraiser. It's in mid-June—I don't have the exact date in front of me. But I'll find out and call you back as soon as I—"

"Yes."

I halted, mouth open, and took a breath. "Yes?"

"Yes. I was already thinking about going. Now it's definite."

Yes! I had actually asked a man out for the first time in my life, and he'd said yes!

Afterward I somehow managed to e-mail two clients and print out bills to three others. But once the euphoria wore off, hunger set in, and when I went downstairs and Ronnie said none of Pearl's old friends had seen her last night, I sank back into my I'm-a-bad-mother depression. What was I going to do about that girl?

For now, my only choice was to stay busy until she decided to let us know where she was.

"I have to go out to the post office," I told Ronnie. "Can I drop you anywhere?"

"No. Suzanne's coming to pick me up. It's not a date," he added when my brows rose up. "She's showing me her car. It's got all these special hand controls. Then I'm gonna help her with this presentation she does every once in a while at Touro's physical rehab center."

Not a date. Right. I gave him a knowing smile. "That's very nice, honey. Have a good time."

He gave me a sheepish grin as I left, and it filled me with joy. My baby boy was growing up. His injury might have hurt his tennis career but it seemed to have been good for his personal development.

But my happiness didn't last six blocks. As I turned onto Louisiana Avenue and headed for the post office, I knew I had to find Pearl. And I needed her father's help.

After the post office I took Freret Street to Palmer. His car wasn't at the condo. So I took State Street to Magazine and turned for home.

Just as I passed Nashville Avenue, a little white car going the opposite direction slammed on its brakes and swerved abruptly into the Quilt Corner's parking lot. "Idiot driver," I muttered. I glanced at the rear view mirror and saw the same car, a Mercedes sports car, pull back into traffic a few cars behind me. It boldly passed a Ford F-150 on a narrow street where only drunks and cops attempt to pass other cars.

But I was too worried about Pearl to care about another of New Orleans's insane drivers. Where had my little girl disappeared to? And where was her damned father?

I had just passed Louisiana Avenue when I saw Walgreens and remembered that Ronnie's prescription refill should be ready.

Perhaps I did brake too fast. The car behind me—that same white Mercedes—screeched to a halt and the driver laid on the horn. "What's the damned hurry?" I swore under my breath. When the driver again hit the horn, it was the last straw. I'd had a rough day, and I suppose genes really do tell. My dad was famous for giving other drivers the one finger salute. So like him, I flipped off the driver of the Mercedes while I waited for a break in the oncoming traffic.

In hindsight it was the wrong thing to do. Then again, maybe it was inevitable. At any rate, just as I started to turn left, the car behind me rammed into mine. Hard.

"What on earth?" I muttered. The other car had hit

mine hard enough to push me into the opposite lane so that I was blocking both lanes of traffic. Smothering a furious oath, I jumped out. "Where did you learn to drive?" I yelled at the low-slung vehicle.

Who should pop out of that supremely classy little car but the utterly classless Barracuda Woman? Could this day get any worse?

"You bitch!" she screeched.

I was *not* in the mood for her crap. "*You* hit *me!*" I spat right back.

She thrust her face almost into mine. "You're so jealous of us, you're still trying to ruin our lives!"

"I don't give a damn about your stupid lives!"

Cars had begun to back up. One of them honked and on the sidewalk several pedestrians stopped to watch.

She followed me as I examined the spot where the corner of her bumper was buried in mine.

"Why don't you just leave us alone!" she went on.

I whirled around. "Pearl is missing. I thought her father might actually want to know."

"Maybe she's tired of being smothered by you. God knows, Ed certainly was—"

I punched her.

Don't ask me where I got the nerve or even the technique. *Million Dollar Baby* must have had a bigger impact on me than I thought. Whatever, I drew back my arm and let her have it, a straight jab right into her nasty little Michael Jackson nose.

The amount of blood was astounding. And very satisfying.

She started to cry and I…I couldn't help it; I started to laugh—which earned me some rather ugly looks. A woman hurried up to the Barracuda saying, "Sit down and put your head back. I'm a nurse."

Disgusted, I turned back to my car to get my phone. But when a young man fell away from me as if I might deck him next, it occurred to me that despite my satisfaction at having shut Barracuda Woman up, I might have been a little hasty. Especially when a police car drove up on the wrong side of the street with lights flashing and stopped.

Two police officers got out, a stout black woman and a skinny white guy with a huge Adam's apple.

"She deliberately plowed her car into mine." I pointed at the Barracuda who was currently bleeding all over her Donna Karan suit. Seven hundred dollars if it was a dime.

Officer Kirkland questioned me while Adam's Apple called for an ambulance. I thought I was telling my side of the story pretty well. It had to be obvious to Officer Kirkland that the white Mercedes was in the wrong for running into the back of the white Avalon. Barracuda Woman would get a ticket, that was for sure.

But then Officer Adam's Apple joined us. "She's saying that you punched her."

"It was in self-defense. She attacked me with her car."

They shared a look. "She ran into the back of your car. This is a little fender bender and no one was actually hurt—until you punched her."

Uh-oh. "Did she tell you that she's my ex-husband's new wife?"

"Your ex's wife?" As one they swiveled their heads to look over at her.

"That's right," I said. "Like I told you, she rammed into me on purpose. She had stopped her car behind mine. Then out of the blue she starts up again, and bam!"

Officer Kirkland said, "Can you prove that's what happened? Do you have any witnesses?"

"What do you mean, prove it? Look at my car. It's perfectly obvious that she followed me and did this on purpose."

"It's obvious she ran into your car, but was it deliberate?" She shook her head. "That's harder to say."

"Meanwhile," Officer Adam's Apple said, "we have witnesses that say you punched her without any provocation."

"I'm not denying I punched her, but I did have provocation. Look what she did to my car!"

"We'll be writing her a ticket for the accident," he said. "But since you attacked her—"

"Attacked her? I did not!"

"—we have to arrest you."

"Arrest me? Arrest me? But she started it."

"That's not what she's saying."

I could not believe this. "Look at my car." I pointed at it with a hand that shook with rage. "Look!"

"The fact remains, Ms. Hoffman. We have two witnesses that say she never touched you."

"She tried to run me down!"

It was no use. According to police procedures, I'd touched her first, which made me the aggressor. The car accident didn't count. They acted like it never even happened. While Adam's Apple talked to the EMTs, Kirkland sat me in the back of her car.

I guess I was in shock. This couldn't be happening. Not to me. I glared at the Barracuda, who had prostrated herself on the sidewalk. What a fake. I guess since her suit was already ruined, she'd decided to put on a real performance. I'd never wanted to kill someone before, but I desperately wanted to kill someone now.

Kirkland rifled through my purse, looking for weapons, I guess. She handed me my cell phone. "Do you want to call anybody before I confiscate your belongings?"

I grabbed the phone like it was a lifeline. But who to call? Not my mother or Ronnie. Maybe my new lawyer. But her firm didn't practice criminal law. I tried Liz with no success, but I left a message. The ambulance arrived. Adam's Apple turned and started back to me.

Last chance, Joan. Call somebody. Quick!

I called Quentin. He answered on the third ring. "Joan, I was just thinking about you. What's up?"

I took a big gulp of air. "I'm being arrested. Right now."

"What?"

"For slugging my ex's new wife after she rammed her car into mine. They're taking me to jail!" I ended, almost hysterical.

"Where are you? I'm coming right now."

"It's too late. They're taking me away. I don't know where."

Adam's Apple extended his hand. "You have to hang up now, Mrs. Hoffman."

I cringed away from him.

"Probably to Central Lockup," Quentin said. "Don't worry, Joan. I'll get you out."

Kirkland stepped forward too. "I'll need to take your phone, Mrs. Hoffman. Now."

"Bye, Quentin," I said, feeling like I was headed for the guillotine. Kirkland took my phone, put it in my purse, then closed me into the back seat. No door or window handles, and a mesh screen separated me from the front seat. I felt like a poor mutt trapped in the dogcatcher's truck.

Outside, the Barracuda was sitting on the edge of a gurney. She held an ice pack to her nose and she was covered with blood. I'd done all that damage with one little punch? Fastidious and controlling as she was, I knew the woman hated her role as the bloodied victim.

But she wasn't really the innocent put-upon victim. When she glared my way and shot me the finger, it was clear that she was still in charge. She might have lost it for a minute there, but she'd managed to turn everything to her advantage.

If only I hadn't punched her. Maybe then she'd be the one going to jail. Assault with a deadly Mercedes.

I slumped into the cracked upholstery of the back seat. Pearl was still missing; Ronnie was still hobbling around on crutches. And now their mother was going to jail.

We pulled out into traffic heading downtown. Thank God for Quentin. He sounded like he knew someone and could get me out. But after all this, would he still want to go out with me?

Then as we passed my street and kept going, it hit me that this fiasco might get into the newspaper. I could just see the front page of the *Times-Picayune*: "Garden District

Cat Fight." Or "Uptown Socialite Punches Out Ex-husband's Trophy Wife."

I felt nauseous. Even if it didn't come out in the paper, it would still get around. Barracuda Woman would make sure of that.

For the first time I felt the sting of tears. But I held them back. I gritted my teeth and blinked my eyes and swallowed down my fear and rage and helplessness. That woman might have smashed into my car. She might have gotten me arrested. But I'd be damned if I'd let her bring me to tears.

CHAPTER 13

LIZ

I nearly fainted when I listened to Joan's message. Arrested? I called Nita, even though I knew Joan wouldn't want me too. But Nita needed desperately to make up to Joan for her mistake with Ed—Teddie—whoever. So I knew she'd help.

"I don't think it'll do any good to go down there just yet," Nita told me. "A couple of years ago I bailed out one of my boyfriends—one better forgotten—and it took like six or seven hours for him to even get booked. You can't bail out someone until she's been booked and goes before the judge."

"Poor Joan." I paced back and forth through my living room. "How much money do you think we'll need?"

"I don't know. Do you have any?"

"My rent money, which is due next week."

"Don't worry. Joan's good for it."

This I knew. "So how can we find out when she's been booked and everything?"

Nita said she would call the Orleans Parish Criminal Sheriff's Office every half hour until she got a status on

Joan. Meanwhile I went to the bank and pulled out seven hundred dollars. That left me with seventy-six dollars and eighty-two cents.

Not much of a nest egg. But I shook off my panic. This would all turn out okay. It would.

Finally, around 7:30 we got word that Joan was booked and would appear before the judge around ten. After she entered her plea we could bail her out.

Nita and I drove together to Central Lockup. It's not a pretty place under the best of circumstances. But on a dark blustery night it's really creepy. Even Nita looked uneasy.

It didn't help that every single person in uniform treated us like we were criminals. Because we knew someone in jail, I guess they assumed we were the scum of the earth. One of them, a big, flabby, skinhead-in-uniform creep who couldn't chase a real criminal a half a block stared at our chests. Stared. Like we were hookers come to bail our pimp out of jail.

At that point I seriously hated all men.

"Hoffman." Tearing his eyes away from our boobs, he checked the prisoner print-out. Then he lifted his beady eyes up for one last leer. "Looks like your friend's already gone."

"Gone?" Relief felt like a thousand pounds lifted off my back.

"With who?" Nita asked.

He shrugged then leaned forward on the counter. I instinctively stepped back. Nita didn't even flinch. She stared at him. "Does it say there who bailed her out?"

"Signed out on her own recognizance. She must be in tight with one of the judges."

That figured after being married to an attorney for twenty-something years. Whoever had helped her out, Nita and I couldn't leave that place fast enough. "I feel like I need a bath," I muttered.

"I know. Imagine how Joan feels."

Then as we hustled down the steps, who do we see standing on the corner but Joan?

"Oh, my God!" I yelled as I practically tackled her with hugs. "We've been so worried!"

Joan held on to me tightly, like she didn't want to let go. She was really strong; all that weight lifting had paid off. She hugged Nita too.

"What an ordeal," she said when we finally broke apart.

"We came to bail you out," Nita said, "But they told us you were already gone."

"Quentin arranged for it." She reached a hand to the man she'd been talking to.

So this tall, good-looking man was Quentin. I'd assumed he was her lawyer. Nita and I stared at him with new interest.

"One of my cousins is a city attorney," he explained after the introductions were made. "Joan will have to come in day after tomorrow to plead innocent." He gave her this look, very tender, but possessive too. "I don't think the charges are going anywhere."

What a day!

After more hugs Joan left with Quentin. Oh, did I mention, he is one *incredibly* good-looking man? Tall with great shoulders and a really great butt.

Nita drove me home. We were both exhausted, but Nita wanted to come in and check out Cora Lee. Poor Cora Lee had fallen asleep on the couch with Pumpkin and Kitty Little curled up in one furry ball in the curve of her body. Pumpkin had obviously gotten over his jealousy of the newcomer.

She had on a cute yellow-and-white nightgown, and with her hair messy and no makeup on, she looked about fifteen. I looked at Nita. "Now how can you hate a pregnant girl that loves my cat?"

Shrugging, Nita shook her head. "Okay. I don't get it, but if you're happy with the situation, who am I to argue?"

At the sound of our voices, Cora Lee shifted, then blinked and opened her eyes. "Oh, hi, Liz." She sat up, careful not to disrupt the cats. Oh, yes, she was a sweetie. No wonder Dennis had pounced on her.

"Sorry we woke you. This is Nita."

"You had a call," Cora Lee said after they'd exchanged greetings. "From Dennis."

I stiffened. "What did he say?"

"I didn't talk to the jerk. No way. He left a message on your machine."

The three of us circled the answering machine as if it were the villain, not Dennis. It was odd, because when Dennis's voice came on, nothing happened. I didn't get this heartsick feeling like I used to. I didn't even get angry, at least not in the you-bastard-how-could-you-betray-me-like-this way.

I was over him, I realized. Finally, totally over him. I

should have jumped up and down for joy. But what he had to say got me mad on a whole new level.

"Hey, babe. Listen. You get one more chance to come back and keep the shop going. Otherwise I'm selling out. So call me. Soon."

Nita shot me a worried look. "You're not buying that bullshit, are you?"

"No way! Not a chance." I paused. "But I sure wish I had the money to buy out his lease."

Cora Lee picked up Kitty Little and hugged her to her throat. "I'm sorry I caused all this trouble, Liz." She had tears in her eyes.

I shook my head. "Forget it. If he hadn't found you, he would have found somebody else. Don't you see, Cora Lee? Dennis uses people. That's just how he is."

"Why doesn't he just hire some other stylists?" Nita asked.

"I don't know," I muttered. "Probably because that's the kind of stuff I used to handle. Now that he has to do it, running the salon has become too much like a job. Besides, it takes time for a stylist to build up a clientele. I worked myself sick opening that shop. I took out loans in my separate corporation's name because he said he had old credit problems. The lease is in his name, though. His. And now he's going to sell the shop and leave me holding the bag." I grabbed an orange throw pillow and flung it at the door. "Holding forty thousand dollars worth of debt!"

Nita burst out laughing. "Temper, temper. Throwing pillows around."

"Hey, I'm the one that came up with the idea for the Payback Club," I said, scowling at her.

"The Payback Club?" Cora Lee looked at me. "What's that?"

Nita grinned and raised her brows. "Yeah, Liz. Tell her about the Payback Club."

I blew out a frustrated breath. Me and my big mouth. On the other hand, what harm was there in telling Cora Lee the truth?

"Okay. But can we at least sit down?" Once we settled around the kitchen table I began. "You know Joan Hoffman, right?"

"Joan? Joan, our client at the salon?"

I nodded. "She's a friend of mine and we…we plotted to get even with our ex-husbands."

When I paused she asked. "But how?"

"Well, I was supposed to break up her ex's new marriage. Meanwhile she…." I trailed off.

Cora Lee stared at me a long, uncomprehending moment. Then she inhaled a sharp breath and her eyes got big. "And she was supposed to break up Dennis and me?"

I nodded, feeling like the worst kind of bitch. "But we weren't actually going to sleep with each other's ex."

"No," Nita threw in. "I was the idiot who did that. Not Dennis," she hastily added.

Stunned, Cora Lee looked back and forth at us. "So you actually slept with Joan's ex-husband to break up his marriage?"

"No, no," Nita said. "I mean, I slept with him. But it

was like this really bad coincidence. At the time I didn't know he was her ex. I dumped him as soon as I found out."

"Oh. But Joan, she was coming on to Dennis. Only you're telling me that it was all an act?"

I nodded. "Right."

"Huh." Cora Lee sat still a moment. She fixed her blue eyes on me. "So in the end I guess you each got what you wanted. Right?"

I rubbed my left temple, which was starting to throb. "It *looks* like we did. But really, nothing is turning out like we planned. I'm still going to end up with no salon, and deep in debt." *And not pregnant.*

"Why don't you just buy the salon from Dennis?"

"Because I don't have the money. And nobody's going to loan me any, not with all the debt I already have. I can hardly keep up with my bank payments as it is."

Cora grimaced. "Bummer."

"Yeah. Bummer."

Then she giggled. "Dennis is gonna feel like an idiot when he finds out Joan was stringing him along."

JOAN

I wanted to take Quentin home and give him a very big, very personal thank-you. He'd saved me. Like Sir Galahad, he'd come to my rescue. The whole time I had sat in that dreary holding room with the shoplifters and prostitutes and husband-sluggers, I'd just held on to his last words, that he knew someone who could get me out. And even though it had taken hours, it would have seemed so much longer if I hadn't known he was in my corner.

My nerves were buzzing, and my hormones had gone into overdrive as we drove through the quiet streets toward my house. I wanted to take him inside and release all my pent-up emotions on him. It would do me a world of good, and I was pretty sure he'd like it too. But Ronnie would be there. And maybe Pearl. Hopefully Pearl.

I'd called Ronnie once from Central Lockup, but at a time that I calculated he'd be gone. I'd left some vague reason to cover my long absence. Though I wanted to call Pearl, for her sake as well as mine, I'd been too afraid her caller I.D. would reveal where I was.

But as Quentin and I pulled up to the house with most of the lights still burning, I realized that I couldn't keep today hidden from my children. Barracuda Woman would make sure the whole world knew.

My heart welled with gratitude as I turned to Quentin. "Thank you doesn't begin to express my feelings—"

He leaned over and kissed me.

With a little groan of relief I kissed him back, putting every fiber of my two-years-without-sex body into it. He pulled me to him and I went, despite the seat belt and the center console. I would have bruises tomorrow from the cup-holder digging into my left hip. But those bruises would go away a lot faster than the bruises this day had inflicted on my soul.

Then again, Quentin was doing a pretty good job of healing those too.

When we finally broke apart, he leaned his head back against the headrest and chuckled. "Don't take this the wrong way, Joan, but *damn*, am I glad you got arrested."

"Glad?"

He cupped my cheek with his right hand. "Yes, glad. When I first laid eyes on you, you seemed way, way out of my league." He made a wry face.

"I'm not," I piped in. Ooh, what a bold hussy I'd become!

"Yeah, well, that's because you don't see yourself like the rest of the world sees you—smart, gorgeous, classy as hell." He gestured with his hand. "Just look at this house."

His thumb slid over my lower lip, a slow, sultry caress. "But when you called me from jail, that changed things. It took you down a peg."

I stared into those scrumptious eyes of his. "So you're saying you don't respect me anymore?" I teased.

Smiling, he shook his head. "It just put you within reach, that's all. It made you human."

I smiled back at him. "I'm very human, Quentin." *And very, very horny.*

He seemed to read my X-rated thoughts, because he leaned forward and kissed me again. And again. Until I was afraid I would leave a wet spot on the seat of his car.

"You'd better go inside," he whispered against my ear.

I arched my neck so he could access it better with those very talented lips of his. "Why don't you come in with me?"

He shifted back, leaving my greedy neck wanting more. "You've had a rough day, Joan. As tempting as your offer is, I don't think this is the right time."

"If you're worried about my son—"

"I'm worried about you."

"Me?"

We stared at each other across the dark interior of his car.

"Here's the thing," he said. "I don't particularly want gratitude in bed with us."

In bed. With us. So he *did* want to have sex with me. Hooray!

Then the meaning of the rest of his words struck me. He wasn't the kind of man who took advantage of a vulnerable woman, and he thought my gratitude for today made me vulnerable.

In contrast to Ed and Dennis, who sought out women's vulnerabilities as a way to get them in the sack, Quentin really was Sir Galahad.

I sat back in the seat and gazed through the windshield, smiling and filled with this amazing sense of well being. Not since… When? When was the last time I'd felt this special, the focus of someone else's total attention?

"What?" Quentin asked, touching the corner of my smile.

I closed my eyes and let that smile heat all the way through me. "This was one of the worst days of my life. And yet, it's turned out to be one of the very best. Because of you."

I felt the rise of tears, but I blinked them back and turned my head toward him. "Thank you, Quentin."

"My pleasure," he replied in this low, husky voice that gave all sorts of meaning to the word "pleasure." We sat there, just looking at each other, and though we were both eager to take the next step in our relationship, we knew it wouldn't happen tonight. But we had plenty of time.

"Would you like to have dinner tomorrow night?" he asked.

"I was hoping you'd ask."

"Seven o'clock?"

"Seven it is." Nineteen and a half hours till I saw him again. I opened the door and got out. The sooner he left, the sooner he'd be back.

"Arrested? You mean, like, to Central Lockup?" Ronnie asked, this incredulous look on his face.

"She rammed me with her car. Deliberately. So I slugged her. But since *she* was the one bleeding, *I* got arrested."

"Whoa." He stared at me from across the breakfast counter as if he'd never really seen me before. Like I was this alien mother-creature. "You slugged her?" Then he grinned. "Way to go, Mom! But how'd you get out of jail? Wait a minute. You mean that message you left for me was bogus?"

"I didn't want you coming down to that place. Besides, a friend bailed me out."

"I'm glad of that. Hey, I forgot. There was a message for you from Dad."

I rolled my eyes. "I bet there was. But tell me, was there a message from Pearl?"

"Not for you. But she did call me."

Thank God! "Where is she?"

"She didn't say where she's staying. But she sounded

okay. I think she's lonesome. She doesn't know what to do."

"She could come home."

"But only if she abides by your curfew, right?"

I bristled. "You manage to."

He patted his injured leg. "What else am I gonna do? But seriously, Mom, Pearl's okay. She's just really pissed at Dad."

I wiped the kitchen counter restlessly with a dishcloth. "It feels more like she's angry with me."

"Don't worry. She'll get over it. Especially when she hears about what Barb did to you. And that you punched her out." He laughed. "So tell me, what's it like in jail?"

After giving him the abbreviated version, I fell into bed and slept like the proverbial rock. I woke up groggy. Punch-drunk. Ha, ha. But by nine I was at Oasis with Liz and Nita. We were there more to talk, though, than to exercise. Even Nita.

"So why'd the bitch ram you in the first place?" Nita asked.

"I don't know. I keep racking my brain, but I can't figure it out."

"Something must have set her off," Liz said.

I gripped the stationary bike handles and stared at the speedometer, keeping to a steady ten miles per hour. "She was ranting about me being jealous of them, of me trying to ruin them."

"Well, in a way you are," Liz pointed out. "Not jealous. But you are trying to ruin them. The Payback Club and all that."

"True. But she doesn't know about that. Besides, you haven't exactly scored with Ed."

She wrinkled her nose in dismay. "Don't remind me. The thing is, our plan wasn't for me to sleep with him, just to make her think I was. Maybe she saw me with him in the park or something, and then she saw you and me together and figured it out."

"There's something else," Nita said, "She may be married to him, but she knows he cheated on his first wife. It's always got to be in the back of her mind that he could be cheating on her."

And of course, he had been, only not with Liz. But I didn't say that out loud. "Whatever her reason, she used that sixty-thousand dollar car of hers like it was a twenty-dollar sledgehammer."

"Sixty-thousand dollars?" Nita exclaimed. "Damn, what does the woman drive?"

"The most expensive thing Ed would buy her. A Mercedes. You know, the little sporty kind."

"Wow," Liz said. "I love those."

I sighed. "Yeah. Me too."

Nita put her hand on my arm. "Is it white?"

"Yeah, it is. Why?" At her look of consternation, I slowed my pedaling. "Why?"

"She knows about me and Teddie."

I stiffened. I wasn't entirely over being P.O.'d at her for that.

"Why do you think that?" Liz asked.

"Because last week a little white Mercedes followed me home. At least it tried to. I got spooked and managed to shake it by driving through an apartment parking lot off Edenborn." She made a face. "I thought it was some drunk guy, or some horny old man. You know?"

"Where were you coming from?" I asked.

She hesitated, then averted her eyes. "A date with you know who. My last one," she added.

Despite my distaste for this subject, everything was beginning to make sense. "But why would she necessarily connect you to me?"

Nita shrugged and met my gaze. "I don't know. Maybe she asked at Ed's gym and they told her I worked here too? No, wait. I have an Oasis parking sticker in my Jeep's back window. And a bumper sticker too. Does she know that you come here to work out?"

"She might. But do you really think she'd get the connection?"

"Maybe," Liz said. "Like Nita said, the woman married a man who's a known cheater. How could she ever be sure of him except by constantly checking up on him? Plus, she couldn't be too happy about the legal action you're taking against Ed. Put all that suspicion and resentment together and what do you get? A big crash scene on Magazine Street."

Could she be right? "She did seem really out of control," I said. "Maybe that's what she meant by me *ruining* their lives."

"Sex and money. That's a powerful combination." Nita pursed her lips. "I think Liz is onto something."

Liz laughed. "Ironic, isn't it? I was supposed to be the one to wreck Ed's marriage, but Nita ended up doing it."

"And I get all the blame. Or credit." I started to smile. "Maybe this payback stuff is beginning to work out. But enough about me. What's going on with you, Liz? How's Cora Lee working out?"

"Cora Lee is fine. She's an easy guest."

"But?" I prompted when she didn't go on.

She looked up at me and I saw the shimmer of tears in her eyes. "Dennis left a message on my machine. He wants me to come back to the salon."

"No. You can't!"

She shook her head. "I know that, Joan. I could never go back to that man. Never. But he also said that if I don't come back, he's selling the place."

I left the gym with a plan. But I didn't want to say anything to Liz just yet. After a quick stop I headed to Shear Delight, but it was closed. A sign in the window said Stylists Wanted. In smaller print it said Chairs For Rent. So Dennis was going for the quick cash, lowbrow version of a salon, renting chairs out to beauticians. First he stole Liz's salon; now he was running it into the ground.

I dialed the number on the sign—Dennis's cell phone, as it turned out. "Hi, Dennis. This is Joan Hoffman. What's with the salon being closed?"

"You there now?" he asked.

"Right out front. I was hoping for a quick blow out. What's going on?"

"Staffing problems. Hold on, I'll let you in."

"You're here?" I turned to the window and saw him come in from the back room.

He waved. "Sure am."

No way was I going into the salon alone with that man. But there he was, flipping the latch and waving me in.

"No, no. I need a stylist, Dennis. I have a big meeting this afternoon."

"Why?" His eyes ran over me, oily and disgusting. "You already look great."

I suppressed a shudder. "Thanks. But this is important. A big investment meeting." I made a regretful face. "I guess I'll have to beg Dr. Phil to squeeze me in."

"Dr. Phil? You left the high-and-mighty Dr. Phil for us?"

I shrugged. "He can be a little stuffy, you know? But I'm sure I can find another stylist." I turned to go. "Let me know if you reopen."

"Wait. Wait a minute." He caught me by the arm. "Tell me about this investment meeting."

Bingo. I smiled regretfully and waved my hand at him. "Sorry, but I'm not sharing this deal with anyone."

The sunlight flashed off the diamonds of my tennis bracelet. I'd deliberately worn every bit of sparkle I had. As I'd hoped, Dennis noticed.

"You got it all wrong, Joan." He gave me a smarmy smile. As if I could ever be taken in by the likes of him. "What I was thinking," he went on, "was that you might want to invest in a hair salon."

Gotcha!

I acted surprised by the idea. "You mean, Shear Delight?"

"Yeah. Sure. Why not? With my set up and your connections, we could give ol' Dr. Phil a real headache."

"Maybe." I dragged out the word. "But I'm not really looking for a business partner." I paused and looked at the shop as if studying it. "If you decide to sell outright, though, I might consider it. Maybe," I reiterated, backing away. "I can't promise anything, though, especially if my afternoon meeting goes the way I want. Bye now."

"Joan, wait." He hurried after me. "I had no clue you might want to buy the place outright. What sort of money are you talking about?"

I had to swallow my Cheshire cat smile before I turned back to him. "That's hard to say. It depends on a lot of things—debt, inventory, the terms of your lease."

"I got no debt," he said.

Of course not. Liz got stuck with all the debt. "Really? Well, then, why don't you put a proposal together and we'll talk."

"But what about your meeting this afternoon?"

I tilted my head to the side and gave him a long, steady look. "I guess you'd better work fast, then."

As I walked away, I punched my new attorney's number into the phone. "I was wondering," I said when Andrea came on the line. "How fast can you put together a lien on a business operating in New Orleans? No, not for me. For a friend of mine."

CHAPTER 14

LIZ

The truth is, Cora Lee is a very nice woman. Girl, really. She's only two years older than Joan's daughter. Anyway, she's very nice, and judging from how lovey-dovey and sweet she was to Pumpkin and Kitty Little, I could tell she was going to make a very good mom.

The thing is, kids need dads too.

I knew what Joan and Nita would say about the crazy idea that had been haunting me the last two days: that I was nuts; that Cora Lee was better off without him; that he would be an even worse dad than he was a husband. It was all true. Yet I still felt like I had to give it one last try.

So I called Dennis.

Considering how sweet and cajoling he'd been the last time he'd called—not counting when he'd called drunk and I'd hung up on him—I expected him to at least be nice.

"Too late," he said before I could even explain why I was calling. "You had your chance to come back, babe, but you blew it. Now I've got a buyer for the shop—big bucks—and I'm moving on. To Austin. Texas," he added, as if I was too stupid to know Austin was in Texas.

"But what about Cora Lee?" I blurted out.

"Cora Lee? Didn't I tell you she was nothing to me? Didn't I? But no, you just wouldn't listen. You had to go and ruin everything, and now it's too late for you."

God, he was such an egotistical idiot! "Cora Lee is pregnant, Dennis. With your child."

"So? I told her the same thing I told you." He paused. "Anyway, how do you know about that?"

I ignored his question. "You need to do the right thing by her, Dennis. And by your baby—"

"If she wants money to get rid of it, I'll help her. Otherwise, she's on her own."

How had I *ever* loved this man? Still, I kept on. "I think you should marry her, Dennis, and give your child a decent home."

I heard him laughing. Really laughing, like I'd just made some hysterical joke. Then he hung up.

I shouldn't have been so shocked by his behavior. After all, he'd lied to me, cheated on me, and stolen from me. But abandoning his pregnant girlfriend and practically ordering her to get rid of their baby, like it was a hunk of phlegm she just needed to cough out...

Hanging up the phone, I shook my head, as much in sorrow as in disgust.

I jerked when the phone immediately rang. Had he changed his mind? Excited, I grabbed the phone, but I wasn't really surprised when it turned out to be Joan.

"I did a bad thing," she began. "At least your disgusting ex-husband is going to think it was bad."

"Dennis? What did you do?"

"I'm negotiating to buy the salon from him."

My mouth sagged open in shock. "You're the buyer he was just bragging to me about?"

"I'm the one. But I'm only buying it if you want me to."

"You bet I want you to! But wait. He was happy as a clam about it. He said you were paying big bucks."

She laughed. "You have to give it to the boy, he is an optimist. But here's the thing. According to my attorney, you can place a lien on the business in the amount of all the loans you took out to start it up. He can't sell the business without paying off the liens first—or else lowering the price to account for the lien amount."

"So he won't get the big bucks, as he puts it?"

"That's about right."

"Oh, my goodness, Joan. You're an absolute genius! That's so purely diabolical!"

"Why, thank you. I thought so too. Anyway, as far as the salon goes, you and I can decide to be partners in the business, or else you can buy me out as soon as you're able to."

"I'd love for you to be my partner. Or maybe over time Cora Lee might want to buy you out."

"Cora Lee? Come on, Liz. Don't you think you're overdoing it with this girl?"

I sat down on the couch and crossed my legs beneath me. "I can see why you might think that. But look at it this way. She opened my eyes to Dennis's true nature. I'm glad he and I are getting divorced. I really am. All he does for me now is make my skin crawl."

"I'm glad to hear that. As for Cora Lee... Well, I'll have

to reserve judgment on her. Meanwhile, I think our budding partnership calls for a celebration. How about you and me and maybe Nita—even Cora Lee—how about we all get together for drinks or dinner? Something fun."

"You mean no more sneaking around, pretending we don't know each other?"

She snorted. "It's kind of a moot point, don't you think?"

"Okay, then. How about tonight?"

"No. Tonight I'm going out with Quentin."

I sighed. "Gosh, I hope I meet a nice guy like him someday."

"You will." Then she giggled. "I tell myself not to expect anything from this, to just relax and enjoy it as long as it lasts. But it's hard not to spin it into some fairy-tale romance. You know?"

"You deserve one," I said.

"You deserve one too. You know, Mr. Right is going to come along when you least expect him."

JOAN

I had two uneventful days. Well, "uneventful" is a relative term. Pearl came home, announced she had a job selling ads for *Gambit,* an alternative weekly newspaper, and moved her stuff out. I didn't ask how she was getting around town without a car. We have good public transportation in New Orleans, but I doubt Pearl has ever been on one of the buses. For my peace of mind, I decided to leave her cell phone service on.

Ronnie graduated from crutches to a cane. His doctor was pleased with his progress and in two weeks he said Ronnie would be ready to drive. Three, tops. Ronnie went out with Suzanne again. Not a date, he said. But I noticed that they talked on the phone at least three times a day.

I didn't hear word one from Ed or the Barracuda. I guess she didn't know yet that the charges against me had been dropped. I'd love to see her face when she found out. I did hear from my new attorney, however, that Ed had been served the papers for the property settlement as well as a demand letter that he reimburse my account and the children's for all the funds he'd taken out.

Dennis had also received the lien notice. I hadn't spoken to him, but he'd called me three times. I was letting him sweat.

As for Quentin, we'd had dinner one night, and met for a quick lunch the next. Tonight the girls were coming over for dinner and drinks. But this afternoon I was treating myself to a shopping trip for new lingerie. After a whole day without seeing Quentin, I'd decided that the time had come. Our next date would be our fourth—our fifth if you counted the night he arranged to get me out of jail.

We had plans for tomorrow night, and I decided I needed something very red and very sexy.

Ronnie left the house around six, going out with one of his old high school friends. Liz and Cora Lee showed up promptly at seven, and Nita showed up ten minutes later.

"I brought brownies," she said, staring around the house. "Impressive place you have here. I'm thinking I should have brought crème brûlée or something fancy like that."

"Give me a break," I said, shaking my head. I'd forgiven Nita her mistake with Ed—with Teddie. But I wasn't as comfortable with her as I used to be. Maybe tonight would get me there. "Come on into the kitchen."

Liz was tossing a salad of wild greens, almonds and strawberry slices. Cora Lee had poured a jar of nuts into a bowl. Nothing particularly domestic about her. Then again, I hadn't been much of a cook when I'd married Ed. Maybe I needed to cut her a little slack, too.

I'd made one of my specialties, a ham and spinach quiche, and bought a half-gallon of Jamocha Almond Fudge ice cream. Nita would probably fuss about the calories. But how could she? She'd brought brownies.

"Okay, I've got a bottle of Valpolicello for those who want red, and Chardonnay for those who want white."

Liz looked up. "No wine for Cora Lee."

I waggled a bottle of sparkling white grape juice at her. "I already thought of that."

"Something's missing," Nita said. "We need music."

"Stereo's in that armoire." I pointed to a pecan wood piece I'd bought right after I'd gotten married. "Turn on the C speakers too. They're for the patio, which is where I thought we'd eat."

I was thinking soft rock or adult pop. I figured she wouldn't go for classical. I had at least a hundred CD's for her to choose from. But Nita tuned in to a hip-hop station—at least I think it was hip-hop. It had a heavy rhythm to it.

She grinned and shook her hair, which she'd worn down for a change. "Let's dance."

Cora Lee slid down from her stool. "Ooh, yeah. I love to dance."

"Me too," Liz said, putting the salad bowl into the Sub-Zero. "It's good exercise and so much more fun than working out. Sorry, Nita," she added with a shrug.

"Hey, I'd rather dance than exercise too. But I can't get paid for dancing—except maybe on Bourbon Street."

"You'd probably be good at it," Cora Lee said. Coming out of someone else's mouth that might have been interpreted as insulting. But I was beginning to see what Liz saw: Cora Lee was too sweet and artless for me to hold a grudge against.

"Come on," Nita said, pulling us into the sunroom. "Booty call. Everybody's dancing."

I know how to waltz, how to jitterbug, how to Cajun dance and even how to tango. Ed and I had learned for our twentieth wedding anniversary party. But I'd never shaken my "booty" like Nita was shaking hers.

She obviously read my mind. "Just pretend Quentin is here." She grinned and circled her hips in time with the sultry beat. "Think of it as using your body to show him what you're capable of in bed."

Liz and Cora Lee both burst out laughing. Then they started mimicking her moves.

"Ooh, Quentin," Liz cooed, thrusting her hips back and forth. "Do me, baby. Do me!"

My face turned tomato-red. "Y'all are awful."

Cora Lee caught me by the hands and pulled me to join them. "You can do it."

I blew out a big breath. "Okay, but first—" I grabbed my wineglass and took a quick, fortifying swallow. I was a

German girl drinking Italian wine being taught by a Latina *chica* how to dance to African-American music. Only in New Orleans.

We danced until we were sweaty. When the phone rang I took the call in the parlor.

"Joan, is that you?"

It was my elderly neighbor, Mrs. DeMontluzin, and she sounded worried.

"Is something wrong?" I asked. "Should I come over?"

"No, no. Nothing like that. It's just that, well, you'll think I'm just a silly old worry wart."

"Not at all. What is it?"

"Well, you see, I heard this music coming from your patio and, well, it's not what you usually listen to. And it's louder than you normally play it."

"And it disturbed you. I'm so sorry. I forgot that I told my friend to turn on the outside speakers."

"It's not really *too* loud. I just worried, well, that someone had broken in or something terrible like that."

"But why—" I broke off when it hit me. Nita had Hip Hop playing. Black music. So Mrs. DeMontluzin had assumed some black kids had broken into my house, turned up the music and were now ransacking the place—overlooking the fact that most thieves tried to come and go as quietly as they could.

I assured her that all was well and hung up. If poor Mrs. DeMontluzin was worried about my new choices in music, she was going to have a cow when she saw my new choice in men. I grinned at myself in the mirror over the mantel. I was really beginning to like this crazy new me. Rejoining the girls in the sunroom I asked, "Is everybody ready to eat?"

With Pavarotti's favorite Italian opera pieces on the stereo, we had dinner out on the patio. I pride myself on my garden. By day it's pretty and serene. But at night it's positively magical.

I'd lit at least two dozen candles on the table and in strategic spots among the azaleas and holly fern. The pond had glowing solar balls floating in it, and the two live oaks at the back of the garden were subtly up-lit. The fountain gurgled and the night-blooming jasmine filled the air with sweetness. Perfect.

We'd started off just right with the dancing and laughter. Now the food and the night mellowed us out. I'd just gotten up to turn on the coffeemaker, and Nita and Liz were picking up the dishes when I heard the front door chime.

"Maybe Mrs. DeMontluzin decided to come over and join in the fun," I joked as I headed inside. Instead, I saw two men through the cut glass of the French doors.

Strangers.

No way was I opening the door. "Who is it?"

When they both reached inside their sports jackets I took a fearful step back. But they held out badges, not guns. "Police," one of them said. "We're here to speak to Joan Hoffman."

Oh, shit. Barracuda Woman must have sicced them on me again. Did I have to let them in?

But what if it's about one of the kids? What if one of them is hurt?

I jerked the door open. "What's wrong?"

"We're not sure," the taller of the two said. "We were hoping you could tell us."

"My kids. Are they okay?"

"This isn't about your children," the other one answered.

"I'm Detective Norris," the first one said. "This is Detective Henning. Can we come in?"

First came overwhelming relief. Then came anger. "If this is about that—" I almost said bitch "—that *woman*, then no, you may not come in. I have dinner guests, and I refuse to let her ruin one more minute of my life. I went to jail. I got out. I'll see her in court and nowhere else."

The sandy-haired one—Detective Norris—raised his brows. "This is about Edward St. Romaine. Your ex-husband."

That drew me up. "About Ed? What about Ed?"

"May we come in?"

My hand tightened on the doorknob. Oh, how I wanted to slam the door in their faces. But of course, I didn't. What good would it do? "Don't tell me he's pressing charges against me too."

Detective Norris stared patiently at me. With a frustrated sigh I waved them into the front parlor, but inside I was shaking. I did not want to go back to jail. I hadn't done anything wrong. But I knew that wouldn't save me. "So what's this all about?"

"When was the last time you saw your ex-husband?"

"Saw Ed? That would be…at my daughter's graduation about two weeks ago."

"You were married to him how long?"

"Twenty-four years. Almost."

"And when were you divorced?"

I crossed my arms. "Officially about a year and a half. We separated six months before that. What is this all about?"

"How would you characterize your relationship now?" Detective Norris asked, ignoring my question.

"Rotten." When they just waited I went on. "I'm suing him because he stole money from my retirement account as well as from both of our children's trust funds."

The swarthy guy scribbled something in his notepad.

"And when was the last time you had any communication with him? Phone calls. Messages. E-mails."

I was beginning to get an uneasy feeling about this. "I'm not sure. Is Ed all right?"

Detective Norris studied me with this hard, measuring stare. "Your ex-husband has been reported missing."

"Missing?" I started to laugh. "It's more likely he ran out on that vicious wife of his."

When the detectives only stared at me, my humor fled. Ed really was missing? I felt a leap of fear in my chest. He was a liar, a thief and a bastard. But I didn't want anything truly awful to happen to him. "Have you talked to his wife?"

"She was our first stop."

"And she, of course, pointed the finger at me."

The swarthy guy's lips twitched, like he wanted to laugh but knew he shouldn't. Detective Norris didn't so much as blink. It was enough to make even a rational person lose it, and I'd quit being rational four days ago, in the 3200 block of Magazine Street.

"I think you should know that my ex-husband's wife is

on a vendetta to do me in. She deliberately smashed her car into mine. I don't know exactly what her problem is, but when I tried to defend myself from her, I was the one who got arrested—"

"Joan? Is everything okay?" Nita came into the foyer with Liz and Cora Lee trailing behind her.

"I'm fine, Nita. These gentlemen were just leaving."

Of course Detective Norris didn't budge. "Nita?" he asked. "Nita Alvarez?"

Nita drew up in the archway, this wary look on her face. All of a sudden I knew this was not just some aggravating police harassment created out of Barracuda Woman's evil brain.

"Are you Nita Alvarez?" the detective repeated, fixing his laser eyes on her.

Nita took a deep breath and lifted her chin. "Yes."

He glanced from her to me. "Isn't this convenient. You're next on my list of people to question."

"Question about what?"

"Ed's missing," I said, wanting to disrupt his hard-ass act. "Detective Norris thinks I have something to do with it."

"Detective Norris?" Liz piped up. "Is that you, Keith?"

She sidled past Nita to stand next to me. "Keith Norris from McMain High School, class of eighty-five?"

It felt good to see him thrown off center. He wrinkled his brow at her, but she gave him a huge smile. "It's me, Liz O'Connor. From Mr. Gagliano's chemistry class."

He glanced down at his note pad, then up at her, obviously flummoxed. "Liz Savoie?"

She held her arms out to her sides and smiled. "That's me."

CHAPTER 15

LIZ

What a weird night!

It started out with so much fun, just us girls having a great time dancing, laughing and eating dinner in Joan's beautiful courtyard. We were all mellowing out with good food and lots of wine. Well, none for Cora Lee. But she was having a great time too. I really like her, and I could tell Joan and Nita were coming around too.

Then Keith shows up. Detective Keith Norris.

He recognized me. I know he did, even though he acted all cool and cop-like.

"Liz O'*Connor* Savoie," he said. He looked back at his notebook with his forehead creased. "You're on this list too."

Then he got even more businesslike than before. "We need to question all three of you. Separately."

"Why?" Joan demanded to know, her fists planted on her hips. She'd gone into Garden District matron mode, haughty and sure of herself. "Are you charging us with anything?"

He didn't answer. "Ms. Alvarez, wait in there." He

pointed to the front parlor. "Ms. Hoffman, we're finished with you for now. You can go back to your dinner."

"Back to my dinner? You've ruined my dinner. Now you're grilling my guests—no pun intended," she bit out. "This is my house and you can't order me around in it."

He gave her this long, even look. "Fine. Ms. Alvarez, Mrs. Savoie, it looks like we'll be questioning you down at the Second District Police Headquarters instead. If you could get your purses."

"Wait! No," Joan said. She looked ferocious, but also scared. "You don't have to do that. I'll go in the back."

"Thank you," he said, as cool and polite as if her temper didn't mean anything to him one way or the other. As if he was made of Teflon.

I frowned at him as Joan and Cora Lee left. "As I recall, you used to be a nice guy."

The other cop raised his brows. "I'll go question Ms. Alvarez."

Then it was just me and Keith.

"Okay," he said, still not looking directly at me. That's when I realized he wasn't so cocky as he'd been before. Mr. All Business Policeman. He hadn't expected to run into someone he knew. I'd made him nervous.

Back at McMain he'd been a big man on campus: shortstop on the baseball team, a star on the track team. And smart too, with good grades. He'd dated the head cheerleader, Amy Curtis, all senior year, and they were pretty much the top couple at school. Compared to them I'd been a nobody. A late bloomer.

But I think maybe that he'd noticed I'd bloomed.

He cleared his throat. "So. How long have you known Joan Hoffman?"

I gave him an incredulous look. He was sadly mistaken if he thought we were going straight from hello to police interrogation. I sat down on a pretty burgundy settee under the stairs. Don't ask me what made me so bold. Maybe the two and a half glasses of wine I'd had. Whatever, I stretched one arm across the back of the settee, crossed my legs, and smiled up at him.

"Hello, Keith, how are you? I guess I don't have to ask what you've been doing the past twenty-something years. As for me," I went on when he just stared at me. "I'm a hair stylist now. I love what I do." I paused. "Do you?"

He swatted his little black notepad against his leg a couple of times. "Yeah."

"Harassing people?" Just imagine how much attitude I would have had if I'd been drinking vodka.

His brows drew together. "Putting criminals behind bars."

"Joan Hoffman is no criminal."

"Maybe. All I know is that her ex-husband is missing and we're trying to find him. When's the last time *you* saw him?"

Uh-oh. I looked down at my hands and worked at keeping them relaxed on my lap. Should I admit I knew Ed or deny it?

I looked back at him. "I met Joan's ex-husband in a bar. Through Larry Foucher."

"Larry Foucher." He wrote that down. "Who's he, your boyfriend?"

"Larry? No. We just had a drink. He was there with a couple of people from his office, and Ed St. Romaine was one of them."

"And this bar was…?"

"Mr. B's."

He scribbled that down. "And this happened, when?"

"Um, let's see. About two weeks ago."

"And you haven't seen Ed St. Romaine since or communicated with him in any other way?"

Another uh oh. But it was better to stay as close to the truth as I could. I didn't want to be caught in a lie, especially by Keith. "I did see him after that in Audubon Park. He was jogging and so was I. But we just said hello and kept going. That's all."

He'd been watching me closely. Now his gaze fell to my lap, to my hands which had somehow gotten all knotted together. I tried to relax them. "So, what's this all about?" I asked. "One thing I can tell you, Joan is not the type to hurt anybody. Even her ex-husband."

"She slugged the new Mrs. St. Romaine."

"That's different," I said. "She was provoked. And besides, she was defending herself."

He didn't reply for a minute. Then, "You never did say how long you've known Ms. Hoffman."

"Two months." *More like one.*

"And Nita Alvarez?"

"The same."

"You all met at Oasis Body Works?"

He knew that? I nodded. "That's right."

He walked toward the stairs, like he was thinking. Then

he swung back. Even under his sports coat I could see he was still in good shape. "Do you belong to a gym?" I asked. "I never worked out until recently. I thought I'd hate it—and at first I did. But now I like it."

"You and Ms. Hoffman have gotten friendly pretty fast," he said, ignoring my prattle. "Why is that?"

Okay, he wanted to play tough guy? I could be tough too. "We've both been treated badly by our husbands. A lot of women have. So we bonded. I might add that my ex is alive and well, and as awful to his latest girlfriend as he was to me."

Finally he looked at me. Not with that I'll-eventually-uncover-all-your-evil-deeds detective glare. This time he looked at me like someone who's just run into somebody from the old days is supposed to look: curious, approachable. Maybe even friendly.

So of course I took that as a signal to plunge right in. "Do you have an ex too?"

I got the barest hint of a smile. "Yeah. I do."

I smiled right back. "Has she gone missing?"

This time I got a real smile, the one that had made me and every other girl at McMain imagine him dumping good old Amy for us.

"No. She's remarried and living out in Kenner with her engineer husband and a bunch of kids."

"Yours, mine, and ours?"

He shrugged. "We had one, he had one, and they've had two more."

As always, the thought of a family full of kids softened me up. "That sounds nice. Kids should have brothers and sisters."

"You have any kids?"

I shook my head. "And no brothers and sisters either. So no nieces and nephews."

"What keeps you in New Orleans?"

"It's my home. The only place I've ever lived, and I love it. Why do you stay?"

"My son."

"Does that mean you'd leave if it wasn't for him?"

Before he could answer, Joan marched into the foyer. "How much longer is this interrogation going to take?"

Immediately the detective mask came down over his face. "Just wrapping up."

The other detective was finished too, because Nita walked stiffly from the parlor, paused to look at me and Joan, then abruptly headed back toward the kitchen.

"We may have more questions," Keith said. "I suggest none of you leave town."

Joan rolled her eyes at me, and followed them out the door. "Aren't you going to tell me what's going on?" she asked. "You obviously think something's happened to Ed. What?"

"It's an ongoing investigation," he replied. "We don't know anything yet."

"But what am I supposed to tell my children about their father?"

Keith stared at her. "The truth." Then, with only a swift glance at me, they left.

JOAN

I was furious after the detectives left. Livid at the implication that I'd had anything to do with Ed's disappearance, and worried about where in the world he could be. Nita was mad too, but also scared, as if she was somehow in trouble with the police for sleeping with Ed. Cora Lee was oblivious, which I found annoying even though I knew she'd never met Ed.

But it was Liz's reaction that bothered me the most. She didn't seem upset by any of it. I banged coffee cups onto saucers, then sloshed P.J.'s Hazelnut Decaf into four cups. Nita ranted about that Detective Henning smirking at her all the while he was questioning her about how well she knew Ed.

Meanwhile, Liz just perched on a stool, her elbows braced on the granite counter, her chin resting on her crossed hands, with this dreamy, faraway look in her eyes.

I shoved a cup of coffee at her. "Is your friendship with that detective going to help us? Make them look closer at Barracuda Woman instead of us?"

She blinked and refocused on me. "Gosh. I don't know. But honestly, does it matter? I mean, we didn't do anything to Ed, so we don't really have anything to worry about."

Nita snorted. "I guess you never heard of cops pinning a crime on an innocent person before?"

I slid a cup to Nita. "We already know how vicious Barracuda Woman can be. I wouldn't put it past her to do away with her own husband just to frame me."

"And me," Nita muttered. "She knows I slept with him. God, I hate married men who fool around!"

Amen, sister. I stared at Liz. "I'm guessing you had a schoolgirl crush on Detective Norris, right?"

She smiled and gave a sheepish shrug. "Practically every girl in the whole school did."

"I hope you didn't tell him about the Payback Club."

"Of course not," she exclaimed.

When Nita made a funny little noise, we all turned to her. She took a nervous sip of her coffee, then put it down. "Actually, I did sort of mention to Detective Henning—"

"No!" I groaned. "Why would you do that? It makes us look even more guilty."

"I was trying to show him that we only wanted to break up their current relationships."

Liz's eyes got big. "Relationships plural? You mean, you told them about our plot against Dennis, too?"

"I didn't mean to!" Nita turned a pleading palm up to us. "I just wanted him to see that we weren't plotting to hurt either of your exes. I wanted him to understand that and to realize that Barracuda Woman knew about me and Ed, and about me being your friend. Don't you see? She's the one with the motive, the one most likely to have done him in. She's the wronged wife. This time," she added.

Liz looked at me. "She's probably right. I mean, what would be your motivation for hurting Ed at this late date?"

I nodded. They had a point. It was better for the detectives to know everything. "So we end up looking more like a group of desperate housewives than real criminals," I said. "But there's one thing we're overlooking. If we had nothing to do with Ed's disappearance, then who did? Like you said, Nita, it's probably the Barracuda. But what did she do to him?" A shudder of fear snaked through me. "And where the hell is he?"

After they left I called Pearl—in vain. She must still be too angry with me to answer my calls. So I curled up on the couch in the front parlor and waited for Ronnie to get home. In the meantime I worried about Ed, imagining a million awful scenarios.

What if Barracuda Woman had run his car off the road somewhere and killed him? Maybe that's why she crashed into me, to cover up the earlier damage to her car.

Or maybe she'd killed him and dumped his body way back in the swamps. That forlorn area along I-59 is famous for that. Then she could have dumped his car someplace and called the cops. I wouldn't put it past her. And even if the cops found his car, it wouldn't be odd for his wife's fingerprints to be all over it.

I tried to remind myself that Ed was only missing, that he wasn't necessarily dead—or even hurt. But I guess I'd seen one too many episodes of *CSI*, because I pictured all sorts of macabre scenes, with the upshot always being Ed dead, my children fatherless, and me feeling guilty for ever having wished he would get what he deserved.

The truth was, Ed had gotten exactly what he deserved the day he married the Barracuda.

As I waited for Ronnie to get home, dabbing at my teary eyes, reliving all the best parts of our marriage, I prayed and bargained with God. And I promised that if Ed could just be found okay, I would never wish anything bad on him again.

Ronnie looked very pleased with himself when he hobbled in through the back door just after 3:00 a.m., until he spied me. "Mom. Look, I'm sorry I'm so late," he began. "But—"

"Your father's missing." I stood up. I hadn't meant to blurt it out so abruptly.

He paused. "What do you mean, missing? Barb can't find him?"

I shook my head. "This is serious. He's really missing, and the police are involved. Two detectives came here tonight and questioned me about when I last saw him. All kinds of stuff. They want to talk to you and Pearl too."

His eyes got really big. "He's *really* missing? Have you talked to Pearl yet?"

"She won't answer her phone."

He whipped out his cell phone and in twenty seconds had her on the line. "Yeah, missing," he reiterated. "The cops want to talk to us too."

He looked up at me. "Should we go down to the police station now?"

"Let me call them," I said. "Find out where your sister is."

That's how at four in the morning the three of us happened to be sitting at the Second District police station on Magazine Street. We picked up Pearl at a shabby, shotgun camelback on Annunciation Street near Washington Avenue. I could tell she'd been crying. I gave her a big hug when she came down the front steps, whether she wanted one or not. But she hugged me back, my little girl, scared to death for her father.

At the station the three of us sat together, holding hands. To my surprise, Liz's not-so-friendly Detective Norris appeared to question them. Didn't he ever go home to sleep? He took them separately to a small room. I hated that. Did he think they were going to lie to him? That they were somehow involved?

When he finished with them, I confronted him. "Look.

You have to tell us what's going on. I mean, surely you have some theory. Who was the last person to see Ed? Where was he at the time? Is his car missing too? And how long has he been gone?"

I thought he wasn't going to answer, and I swear I was ready to slug him just like I'd slugged Barracuda Woman. "It's that bitch he's married to, isn't it? She's done something to him. She's vicious that way."

"Sit down, Ms. Hoffman."

I wanted to scream that I didn't feel like sitting down. But the man just stared at me and waited until I sat.

"Okay, this is what we know. He was last seen leaving his office the day before yesterday at about five-thirty. He was supposed to have dinner with a client that night, but he never showed. Then he didn't show up at work the next morning. He wasn't reported missing by his secretary until that afternoon. Yesterday afternoon."

"So he's been missing for almost two days?" Ronnie said, his young voice trembling.

"Oh, my God," Pearl cried, squeezing my hand so tight it hurt. "Two whole days?"

"What does his wife have to say?" I bit out the words.

He pursed his lips. "Mrs. St. Romaine has been up in Chicago on business. She flew out of New Orleans several hours before her husband was last seen."

So she hadn't done it? I didn't believe that. "I don't care where she was. She's involved. That is one vindictive bitch."

"Maybe," he said in this too-pleasant voice. "Or it could be that she's being set up."

227

"By who?" I asked. Then I realized that he meant *me*.

"*You're* the one he threw over for a younger woman, Ms. Hoffman. *You're* the one who plotted with your friends to get even with him—which you conveniently failed to mention."

"I believe Nita explained that to your partner."

"And you're the one suing him for the return of money you claim he owes you."

"Which I can't get if he's dead!"

"Your friend Nita admitted to having an affair with him, just like you planned."

"Mom?" Pearl shook my arm. "What's he talking about?"

"Your son is the one who busted him," Detective Norris went on, hammering each point like one more nail in my coffin. "Your daughter despises the new wife so much she didn't want her at her graduation ceremony." He paused and gave us a cool look. "Until we get to the bottom of his disappearance, everyone's a suspect."

"Even Liz?" I hissed.

He cocked his head. "At the moment she doesn't seem to have much motive. But if she's hiding anything, she could be considered an accessory. The same applies to your children."

That's when it finally struck me how deadly serious this whole thing was. Ed was really missing, and I really was the prime suspect.

The only good thing about the whole nightmare was that Pearl came home with Ronnie and me. The sun was just turning the horizon a pale lavender-gray beneath a thin layer of clouds. I made us grits and scrambled eggs, though I didn't have much appetite. But it was Southern comfort food, and I sure needed comforting.

So did Pearl, because instead of sleeping in her own bed, she put on an oversized shirt and crawled into bed with me.

As I lay there and listened to her steady breathing, I felt a rush of emotion. Barracuda Woman might have wrecked our family, but today it seemed like she'd thrown us back together.

But was it really her? I wondered as I gave in to my exhaustion. If she really had been in Chicago the whole time, that meant she'd have to have hired someone else to hurt Ed. Though she was a cold-hearted bitch, I wasn't as sure about her being foolhardy too.

But if not Barracuda Woman, then who?

CHAPTER 16

LIZ

By eight-thirty the next morning I was at Oasis. Cora Lee came along too. We found Nita in the locker room. "Okay, girls," I said. "We've got to help Joan out of this mess."

"What about me?" Nita said. "Those cops think I'm in on it too."

"Too? What do you mean 'too'? Joan didn't do anything to Ed."

Nita pressed her fingers against her temples. "I know, I know. That's not what I meant. It's just that—oh, damn. Okay." She took a deep breath. "The thing is, I was arrested once. For battery. It was kind of like Joan's deal with Ed's new wife, except that I really *was* guilty. Even though I got a suspended sentence, and it was seven years ago, I'm sure those detectives knew about it before they even questioned me."

"Battery?" I said. "Who did you hit?"

She shook her head in dismay. "Who else? An ex-boyfriend's new girlfriend. So naturally those cops are gonna think I'm involved in this, especially since I dated Ed. And it looks even worse because Joan and I are friends. God, they must have thought they hit the jackpot last night when they found us all there together!"

"I know it looks bad," I agreed. "But since neither of you are guilty of this, all we have to do is find out who really is."

"What do you mean 'we'?" Nita threw her hands up in the air. "How are we supposed to find out anything?"

"Calm down," I said. "Just calm down. I was thinking. It seems like Keith—Detective Norris—already knew that the three of us had met each other here."

"He did?" Nita asked. "But how?"

"Somebody must have told him. I'm figuring it's either Ed's wife or someone who works here."

"You're right," Nita said. "Maybe I should nose around and find out who ratted us out."

"That's a good idea. As for me…" I lifted my chin with more confidence than I felt. "I'm going to call Keith."

They wanted to listen in on the conversation, but that would have made me too self-conscious. As it was, my palms were positively soggy and my heart was slamming in my chest when I pulled out the card he'd given me. *You're not calling the man for a date*, I told myself as I stared at the card. This was his police number used for police business. And this was definitely police business. Finding the truth about what happened to Ed was what we all wanted.

I punched in his number, then stood at the back window that looked out onto Oasis's zen garden, mainly used for yoga and tai chi classes.

"Norris here," he answered in this no-nonsense voice.

"Hi, Keith. This is Liz. Liz Savoie."

I heard this ominous silence. Then, "Hello, Liz."

"I...um...well." If my phone had come with a cord, I would have been twisting it around my fingers. "I was hoping you had some new information about Joan's ex-husband."

Another pause. "I spoke to her kids last night. All I can tell you is that we're pursuing several leads."

Several? As in Joan, Nita and me? "So are we," I blurted out.

"Stay out of it, Liz. You're a civilian and—"

"But Joan is our friend. We're not going to sit by and let her take the blame for something she didn't do."

"How do you know she's not involved?"

"I just know."

"How?"

"I just do!" Then I realized where his suspicious cop's brain was going with this. "If you're implying that maybe I know where Ed is, Keith, you're barking up the wrong tree. I don't know where he is, or who's involved with his disappearance. But I know it isn't Joan."

"You sure that's not just wishful thinking?"

Ooh, I wanted to reach through the phone and choke him. "Call it a hunch, okay? Don't cops get hunches?"

"Yeah. But we're trained investigators."

"Really? Well, I've been cutting people's hair my whole life, listening to other people's bull. I'm guessing you've never been to an old fashioned beauty parlor, have you?"

"I go to a barber."

"Well, maybe as part of your investigation you ought to come into my salon and let me cut your hair. You'll see then that it's a big gossip mill, a nonstop Catholic confessional full of ugly truths, ugly lies and everything in between."

He chuckled. "So no one has anything good to say?"

I actually made him chuckle! All my frustrations and nervousness melted like a Plum Street snow cone spilled onto an August sidewalk.

I laughed too, feeling like a seventeen-year-old flirting with the coolest guy at school. "It's not all bad. There's lots of good stuff in there too. Lots of joking and laughing. My point is, you can't be a really good hair stylist without learning how to read people pretty well, sort of like being their therapist."

"And you're a good hair stylist?"

"I don't want to brag, but yes, I am. If you need proof though, just make an appointment with me and see for yourself."

I held my breath, waiting for his response to that. Unless he was an idiot—and I knew he wasn't—he had to know I was interested in more than just cutting his hair.

"Maybe I'll take you up on that," he finally said. "After this investigation is over."

"Fair enough." I was grinning like he'd just invited me to the senior prom.

"Meanwhile, keep your nose out of this, Liz." His voice was back to all business.

"That's going to be hard," I said. "Joan is my friend. I may not have known her very long, but I know she's a good person. Even though her ex-husband treated her horribly, she didn't do anything to hurt him."

"That may be. But somebody is involved in his disappearance. The longer he's gone, the more likely something bad has gone down. And whoever's in on this, I guarantee, they don't want to be found out. That's why I can't have you and your friends snooping around. It could be really dangerous."

A little shiver ran up my spine. I hadn't thought about that. But I shook off my fear. "Why, Keith, I didn't know you cared," I said, trying to keep things light. He didn't buy it.

"I'm not joking, Liz. We don't know who or what we're dealing with here. St. Romaine could have just skipped town. Or he could be dead."

Dead. I swallowed hard.

"You don't want to be in the middle of a murder investigation," he went on. "Trust me on this."

"But…but I kind of already am in the middle, aren't I?"

When he didn't answer I pressed my point. "I'm already in it because of our Payback Club. I know Nita told your partner about it. I'm in it, so I'm probably a suspect too. That means I've got every right to try to get to the truth and exonerate myself."

"Look, I understand why you feel that way. But consider this. If there's a bad guy involved—and there probably is— do you and your friends want to be caught in the cross fire? I'm talking literally here, Liz. *Real* cross fire."

Real cross fire, as in real guns. I could feel my adrenaline beginning to pump. But I made myself focus on his words, not on my rising panic. "You know more about this that you're telling me."

"What I know is that we've got a missing man, plus love, hate and money on the line. Do you know how many crimes start with those three ingredients?"

Now he was really beginning to scare me. He really believed Joan was involved. But since I knew she wasn't, that meant it had to be the Barracuda. Before I could respond he said, "Hold on." I heard some muffled voices, then, "...found his car?"

Keith came back to me. "Look, I have to go. But remember what I said, Liz. Stay out of this."

Believe me, at that moment I wanted to. But there was no way I could abandon Joan.

"Well?" Nita asked, after I'd hung up. "Did he tell you anything new?"

I shook my head. "Not really. Except..." I looked up at her. "Right at the end somebody came up to him. They said something about finding his car."

"His car? You mean Ed's?"

"I don't know. I mean it could've been another case. But somehow I don't think so."

"True. But they're focused on this case, so it probably is Ed's car."

I called Joan. She answered on the second ring, but I could tell she'd been asleep.

"They found his car?" she asked after I filled her in.

"I'm not absolutely certain. But I think, maybe."

"Did they say where?" she asked.

"No. Maybe you ought to call Keith. I mean, Detective Norris."

After I hung up, Nita and I just stared at each other. I

shook my head. "She's going to call Keith. In the meantime there's got to be something else we can do."

Cora Lee was standing in front of a full-length mirror smoothing her knit dress over her stomach and studying her still-slender profile. "Do you think those cops questioned the people where Joan's ex-husband works?" she asked.

I shoved my phone back into my purse. "I'm sure they must have. Didn't they say Ed's secretary was the one who first reported him missing?"

"Maybe you could talk to her too," Cora Lee suggested.

"That would be cute," Nita said. "I can hear you now. 'Hi. I'm Ed's ex-wife's good friend. So, what do you know about his disappearance that you haven't told the cops?'"

"Or," I said, as inspiration struck me. "I could call Ed's friend, Larry Foucher."

"The one that hit on you at Mr. B's?" Nita asked, her dark eyes beginning to sparkle with excitement.

"The very same."

JOAN

Maybe I should have called Detective Norris. But I was too terrified of what he might tell me to dial his number. What if Ed was dead? Never mind that I was the prime suspect. I still had enough faith in the judicial system to believe I would eventually be cleared. Eventually.

But what if Ed *was* dead?

I'd spent too many years loving him, building a life with him and a family to ever want him dead. I might never want him as my husband again. I might even want revenge on him through our Payback Club. But Ed would always be the father of my children. Always. He was the only person in the world who loved them as much as I did, even if he didn't always show it.

I definitely wanted Ed to get his comeuppance. But I didn't want him dead.

I sat on the side of my bed with my back to Pearl who was still sleeping, and pressed a hand to my chest. Ed could not be dead. I'd know it if he was. I'd feel it.

Then logic took over for sentiment. Maybe I'd feel it; maybe not. One thing I knew, Detective Norris would eventually be in touch about Ed's car. For now I wasn't saying anything about it to the kids.

I'd gone downstairs and was making coffee when the phone rang again. The police?

I grabbed for it, my heart hammering with dread. It was Dennis Savoie.

"Hey, there, Joanie. Where ya been?"

Joanie? I rolled my eyes. "I've been kind of busy, Dennis. Snowed under, in fact."

"Not the investment deal you were talking about."

"The very one," I lied.

"Hey. What about my offer to sell you half of the salon?"

"I'm not sold on that idea, Dennis."

"But it's a money maker. You know that location. Magazine Street is hot these days. It's the best spot in town."

"Maybe." I decided it was time to go for it. "Look, Dennis, why don't we quit beating around the bush? How much do you want for the place? All of it? No partnership deals. And before you quote me some ridiculous amount

237

of money, remember I'll need to see your books, and I'll want to see a profit and loss statement with projections for the rest of this year and into the next."

"Geez, Joan. You know we've only been open a couple of months. We don't have that much of a track record."

"Another thing," I said, ignoring his whining. "Are there any encumbrances on the business? Outstanding debt? Loans?"

"I told you before I don't have any loans on the place."

"Great. What about outstanding invoices? Liens? Stuff like that?"

There was a moment of hesitation, just enough to let me know he'd received the lien papers I'd helped Liz file against him.

"Like every start-up business, I've had a few problems. But they're no biggie."

"No biggie? Somebody's got a claim against you for something?" When he didn't answer, I added, "How much?"

He let out a disgusted sigh. "It's not a set amount. It's stupid, a pain in my ass is all."

"So what is it, Dennis? Give it to me straight, or this whole conversation is over."

"All right, all right. I just found out that this former business associate of mine has filed a lien on the shop. But that only matters if I try to sell it off. That's why the idea of a partnership between us is so perfect."

Did he think I was an idiot?

"How much is the lien for?"

"Uh, I'm not sure. Thirty or forty thousand, as I recall."

Forty-six thousand five hundred, you sleazeball!

But I kept my cool. "I don't know, Dennis. Forty thousand is a big chunk of change." I could practically hear him squirming.

"She'll settle for less. A lot less. Besides, like I said, she's got nothing on us unless we decide to sell."

"So you say. But like I keep telling *you*, I don't want a business partner. I'm doing fine on my own."

I heard this long silence before he said, "What if…what if I offered to sell the place to you outright?"

Now we were getting somewhere. I walked out onto the patio. "I don't know, Dennis. I'm not going to lie. I am interested. But there's no way I'm shelling out big bucks to take on somebody else's debt. Who's this person with the lien, this old business partner?"

"She's my ex-wife," he added in a voice that made her sound like some vampire sucking his blood. He was such a leech!

I started to laugh. "So what she wants is probably a lot more than money, right? She wants blood. Okay," I said, making my voice as hard-nosed and business-like as I could. "Here's my offer. Ten thousand to buy out your lease and take on your thirty- or forty-thousand dollar debt."

"What? No way!"

"Think about it, Dennis. You're actually getting fifty thousand."

"How do you figure that?"

"Ten thousand in your pocket, forty thousand worth of a clean conscience."

"My conscience is already clean," he muttered. "No. I'd need at least seventy-five thousand."

"Less the forty thousand, that's thirty-five upfront." I paused, just to make him sweat. "Nope. Too much. The place isn't even open anymore. Look, I have to go."

"Wait. Just wait a minute. Okay, how about you give me twenty-five thousand and I give you the shop."

"Fifteen's my max." I was really impressing myself.

"Twenty."

"Fifteen."

I could hear him breathing hard. He was not a happy camper. I went in for the kill. "You know what? Why don't you just sleep on it, Dennis? I have another call coming in so—"

"I'll take the fifteen."

"You will?"

The idiot had to be desperate for money if he'd walk away from the salon for that. Then again, you had to work to make a profit in a salon, and he obviously didn't want to do that. "Okay, then," I said. "It's a deal. I'll have my attorney draw up the papers. I'll be in touch." I hung up, waited a couple of seconds, and then dialed Liz's number.

"You'll never guess who I'm meeting for drinks," Liz said before I could even say hello.

"Not the good detective."

She giggled. "Don't I wish. But no, this is actually better. I'll give you a hint. We're meeting at Mr. B's Bistro."

My heart leaped with hope. Ed?

But just as fast I knew better. "At Mr. B's?" I searched my mind. "Not Larry Foucher?"

"Yes, Larry Foucher. I wanted so bad to pump him on the phone for all the office poop on Ed's disappearance.

But I didn't want to be too obvious. So we're meeting today at six."

"That's a brilliant idea, Liz! You are the best."

She laughed. "I don't know about that. I mean, I might not learn anything new."

"Yes, but at least we'll know whatever they told the police."

"Did Keith tell you anything about the car they found?"

"I didn't call him."

"Why not?"

I sighed and stared at my toenails. I needed a pedicure, and bad. "I guess I'm just afraid of what he might tell me. I don't want it to be Ed's car, Liz. I really don't. I mean, sometimes I absolutely hate the man. But I don't want him dead, or even hurt."

"I know, honey. I know. I'm sure Keith will call you once they know anything."

I snorted. "Sure he will. Cops always share their information with their primary suspect. But listen, I called you for another reason. Guess what I just bought?"

"What?" Then she let out a squeal. "Not Shear Delight?"

"Yes, Shear Delight. We are now partners, my dear."

"Oh, my goodness, Joan! I'll never be able to thank you enough. Never." Then she sobered. "I hope you didn't let Dennis gouge you on the price."

"Actually, I'm rather pleased with how hard-nosed I was. He's walking away with only fifteen thousand dollars—by the way, he did get the lien papers. So I figure with your forty-six thousand and my fifteen, I'm a twenty-five percent partner. Does that seem fair?"

"Yes. Of course. Wait," she said. "If the loans get repaid out of the shop's profits, then it's only fair that you be a fifty/fifty partner."

"I guess that's true. Or you could buy me out over time and own the place yourself, free and clear."

She laughed for joy. "I don't care how we work it out. I'm just so happy to have my shop back. How soon do you think until everything is settled and we can get in?"

"He seems pretty anxious to get his hands on some money. So I'm thinking soon. I'll call my attorney and have her draw up the papers."

"You know, I'll never be able to repay you for this, Joan."

"Well, maybe you can promise to do my hair for free."

"You'd better believe it. But what about Dr. Phil?"

I ran a hand through my short, spiky hair, then laughed. "I like the way you do it better. In fact, there are a lot of things about my life that I like better now than I ever did before."

"Me too," she said. "And having you for a friend is one of them."

Don't ask me why that brought tears to my eyes. But despite how messy my life was, in a weird way I actually felt more in control than I had in ages. I had my job, my kids, and I'd just out-negotiated a used car salesman. "I'm so happy we're friends, Liz. And partners too."

"Well, as your partner, I guess I'd better consult with you before we hire anyone."

"Hire whoever you want. You can be the managing partner, I'll be the silent partner."

"Okay then. As soon as we hang up I'm hiring Cora Lee."

Cora Lee. As I hung up I shook my head in amazement. Who would ever have imagined such a scenario? The only thing more unlikely would me hanging out with the Barracuda. I laughed out loud; then I called Quentin.

"I have a proposition for you," I said, as nervous as when I was sixteen and asked Jimmy Northrup out for Sadie Hawkins Day.

"A proposition?" he said in this smooth basso voice that struck a major chord on my turn-me-on meter. "That sounds promising."

"I'd like to take you to dinner, someplace really special, like Emeril's or Galatoire's." I took a deep breath. "Dessert afterward at my place."

He chuckled. "Do I get to choose the dessert?"

My face was hot. When had I become so bold? "Of course. But there's one catch."

"A catch?"

"We can't see each other for a while."

"What?"

"Let me explain. You see, I found out yesterday that my ex-husband is missing. We don't know exactly what's going on, but the police have already questioned me, my friends and my children."

"Damn, woman. When did all this happen?"

"We're not sure. It looks like he's been missing three days or so. And of course since my run-in with Barracuda Woman I'm their prime suspect."

"You gotta be kidding!"

"I wish I was. Anyway, I don't want to drag you into this, Quentin. That's why I think we shouldn't see each other for a while. But the minute this mess is cleared up, we have a date. Okay?"

"Okay. Fine. But Joan, how are you holding up? I mean, you might be divorced, but he was your husband for a long time."

How ironic that the new man in my life was the one who made me cry over the old one. I found a tissue and dabbed at my leaky eyes. "I don't know. Okay, I guess. But I'm so scared for him. I don't want him hurt, and I sure don't want him dead. Ed can be such a jerk sometimes. A lot of the time. But he's still Pearl and Ronnie's father."

Then, like an absolute fool, I really started sobbing. It didn't help that Quentin was so nice about it. I might not have been back on the dating scene for long, but I knew you weren't ever supposed to cry on your new guy's shoulder about your ex.

When I finally caught my breath I apologized. "I wouldn't blame you if you changed your phone number after this."

He laughed. "As long as you aren't crying because you secretly want him back."

"God, no!"

"Look, Joan. You sound pretty shaky. How about I come over, maybe take you out for coffee or something?"

"I'd love it. But really, I think you need to keep your distance from me until this is over with."

He sighed. "Okay then. But I'm doing it under protest. Meanwhile, I'll be dreaming about dessert."

Oh. My. God. I was damp in all kinds of places when we hung up. Dessert. He was going to be mine and I was going to be his. That meant he would be seeing this forty-six-year-old body naked. And that meant I would be living at the gym between now and then. I might not be able to make my breasts stand up at attention ever again, but I could work on my thighs and my tummy and my underarms.

I was packing my gym bag when the phone rang. This time it was Andrea Purvis, my new attorney. "What's this I hear about Ed St. Romaine being missing?" she said, skipping any greeting.

"How did you hear?"

"A friend at the *Times-Picayune*."

"It's going to be in the paper?"

"Tomorrow. Front page."

"Good lord." I sank down on a chair. "You probably know as much as I do, Andrea. The police came last night to question me, but they didn't reveal much of anything."

"And of course, as his ex, you're a suspect."

"Right. But I don't know a thing about it. I was totally shocked."

"Yeah. Just don't panic if they keep you high on their list, Joan. And if at any point you feel like you need an attorney, call me. You hear? Day or night, call me."

"Thank you, I will. Meanwhile I'm just trying to figure out what's going on."

"You know," she said. "I've discovered some interesting things about Ed, things that could be related to his disappearance."

I gripped the phone tighter. "What do you mean, interesting?"

"Well, I've been assembling information on him, mostly financial stuff for the property settlement. It turns out he has an awful lot of debt. And hardly any assets."

"No. How can that be? Ed has always made a great living. And even though he and Barracuda Woman are living awfully high, she's got a pretty good job too."

"Then why did he make that illegal mortgage on your house without your knowledge?"

I shook my head. "I don't know."

"And why are his bank accounts nil, his credit cards maxed out and the loan value of his retirement accounts tapped out?"

After we hung up I just stared blankly at the wall. I was scared now. Really scared for Ed. None of this made sense and every new bit of information painted a grimmer picture.

I heard the doorbell chime, but for a minute I was too paralyzed to move. It chimed again and Ronnie called, "I'll get it." I hadn't known he was awake.

Whoever it was, I hoped they would go away.

But what if it was about Ed?

I charged into the hall, then skidded to a halt beside the stairs. In the foyer Detective Norris looked past Ronnie to me. Behind him a group of uniformed policemen stood like an invading army.

Ronnie looked mad, but also scared. "Mom?" he said turning to me. "They say they have a search warrant."

CHAPTER 17

LIZ

I tried to remember everything Joan had told me about attracting rich, eligible lawyers. I wore my retro Diane von Furstenberg wrap-dress that really makes my boobs look good. I got a pedicure, a manicure and a facial at the salon where I worked, and the new guy, Andrew, did my hair in this soft, swingy style. I felt really good about myself as I walked down Royal Street, though I knew I'd have blisters tomorrow from my stiletto heels—Jimmy Choos from the Junior League Thrift Store. But it was worth it.

Larry was waiting at the bar, so I tried to put as much sultry into my walk as I could without looking like a Decatur Street hooker. It must have worked, because I turned a lot of heads. He was grinning like a circus clown when I stopped in front of him.

"Wow. You're even prettier than I remembered."

"Why, thank you."

"Here. Let's get a table." He took my elbow and escorted me to a table in the window with a reserved flag on it. Very classy.

"I was really excited when you called me," he said after

he'd seated me. He kept smoothing his tie down, and he had a faint blush on his face. Poor thing. Despite his law degree, big law firm, and fancy salary, at heart he was still a geeky high school boy.

I smiled at him, trying to put him at ease. He was mine for the taking. If only I felt even a tenth of the attraction for him that I felt for Keith Norris, I could be the rich lawyer's wife, living in a big house in the Garden District or Old Metairie or Lake Vista. But I just wasn't interested.

Only I couldn't let him know that.

I demurely lowered my eyelashes, trying to remember all of Scarlett O'Hara's tricks. "Well, I usually don't call guys." That was true. "But you were so nice." I tilted my head, raised my eyes back to his, and smiled. "I decided to take a chance."

He beamed back at me like he was a two-hundred-watt bulb. "I'm so glad you did. You know, I tried to call you, but I must have written your number down wrong."

"You didn't write it wrong," I confessed. "I gave you the wrong number on purpose. I always do that to guys I don't know well. As a safety precaution," I added.

"Oh." His eager expression fell. "Yeah. That's probably a good idea," he conceded.

"But I liked you. That's why I called."

This time he went red to his ears and grinned. "Good."

We ordered drinks. An apple martini for him, a frozen daiquiri for me, and for a while we chatted and drank. Actually, I hardly drank anything. He kept ordering martinis. I think he was nervous. He was really a sweet guy. Clueless with women, but he was trying as hard as he knew how. I felt just awful for leading him on, especially when he asked me to go to the Greek Festival with him on Saturday.

"Gee, I'd love to. I really would. But I'm going out of town to visit my mother that weekend."

"Oh. Tha's too bad."

Aha. He was slurring his words. Time to make my move. "So, Larry, how are your friends that I met that last time here with you?"

"Which friends? Oh, you mean from work?" He let out a snort. "They're not my friends. I just work with 'em."

"Really? They seemed awfully nice. Ed somebody and Doyle and that other woman."

This time he laughed out loud.

"What's so funny?"

Putting his elbows on the table, he leaned toward me. "C'n you keep a secret?"

"Ooh." I giggled and leaned toward him. "I love secrets." Notice, I didn't promise anything.

He glanced around, then lowered his voice. "Looks like good ol' Ed has run off with the company till."

"What?" I sat back in utter shock. That was *not* what I'd expected. "No way."

"Yes, way. He's been missing three days."

"Oh, my goodness. Have y'all reported him to the police?"

He rolled his eyes. "The cops know he's missing. But as for the money…" He sat back, shaking his head. "The partners don't want that gettin' out. Bad PR they say. Makes the firm look shtupid. Stupid," he corrected himself.

I wanted so bad to jump up, run out of there, and call Joan. Ed wasn't just stealing from her and their kids. He was stealing from his own law firm. Was he crazy?

But I couldn't leave Larry just yet. It would look way too suspicious. There was nothing to do but order him another martini and pump him for more information.

I leaned forward and tried to look sincere. "I hope it's not too much money."

He snorted. "I hear it's a lot."

"They won't have to lay off people, will they?" I put my hand on his arm. "You job won't be affected, will it?"

"Mine? Naw." He put his hand over mine. "I'm one of the top billing lawyers in the firm, Lizzie. Didya know that? 'M up for partner, but I don't know. If all this stink gets out, I don't know if I wanna be 'sociated with a bunch of losers."

Lizzie. "I see what you mean." I pulled my hand free and picked up my glass.

"D'you want another?"

"Thanks, but not yet. I'm afraid I'm a lightweight when it comes to drinking. The liquor goes straight to my head." I giggled for effect. "But tell me, how did Ed get away with it? I mean, he seems like such a straight-up guy. Who finally figured it out?"

"Doyle." Larry belched. "'Scuse me." He belched again. "Doyle's the one who noticed it."

Doyle Carmadelle. Wasn't he also Joan's first divorce lawyer?

"Good ol' Doyle," Larry went on. "'Course, if he'd been paying attention none of this would've happened in the first place."

"What do you mean?"

"He's the managing partner, in charge of the moolah. He should've caught on to Ed's con a long time ago."

"I don't know," I said, twisting my glass in a wet circle. "When you trust somebody, it's hard to believe they could lie to you. Lie and cheat and steal." I was thinking of Dennis, of course. But it didn't make me feel any better to know that Ed was even worse than him. Wasn't there one husband in the whole world who could be trusted?

I watched Larry throw back one more martini. I guess he thought he looked sophisticated and that I was impressed. But a drunk is a drunk, whether he's swigging cheap apple wine or pricey apple martinis. I picked up my purse, pushed back my chair, and stood. "I suppose I'd better get going."

"Wait, wait." Larry stood up, stumbled, and would have fallen if I hadn't braced him.

He squeezed my shoulder. "You smell so good, Lizzie. Like a flower garden."

"Why, thank you." I waved to the waiter, asked him to call a cab, then together we got Larry to a seat in the entry. "Thanks, Larry." I kissed him on the cheek. "I enjoyed it." Boy, did I ever.

"I'll call you," he said. "You and me. We can go on a date. Okay? Anywhere you say."

"That sounds nice." Then, Jimmy Choos notwithstanding, I practically sprinted to my car. I started to punch in Joan's number. Then I stopped. Did Keith know about any of this? Because if he didn't, I wanted to be the one to tell him.

JOAN

Detective Norris and his team of uniformed thugs wouldn't reveal what they were searching for, but it didn't take me long to figure out. They pawed through everything, drawers, closets, cabinets, file folders. But they only took things related to money. Bank statements. Investment account statements. Old tax files. Insurance policies. They even took my Hunk of Crap and Ronnie's laptop.

Ronnie and Pearl sat with me in the front parlor while the police did their work. Ronnie was livid with fury. "Who in the hell do they think they are?"

But Pearl was pale with fear. "This is about Daddy, isn't it?" I could feel her trembling. "If they're searching our house, they think he's dead."

"I don't know what's going on, sweetheart," I tried to reassure her. I was as worried as she was, but a part of me was suspicious. If Ed were dead, why would they care about our financial records? So did this mean they thought he was alive? Was all that underhanded stuff he'd done with my money and the kids' and that fraudulent mortgage on the house somehow related to his disappearance? Could he have taken the money and run?

But that didn't make sense.

I watched Detective Norris come down the stairs. His phone rang and he answered it. Then he paused four steps up and his eyes honed in on me. "Really?" I heard him say. Then his jaw tightened. "Damn it, Liz. I told you to stay out of this."

Liz?

He turned away from me and I couldn't hear the rest of their conversation, but it was brief. I stood up, determined to ask him what was going on. But as soon as he hung up and turned my way, my phone rang.

"That's Liz," he muttered, his face unreadable.

I grabbed my phone. "Liz. What in the world is going on?"

I stood there frozen as she blurted out everything Larry had revealed. A part of me was so relieved. This meant Ed wasn't dead. He might have pulled a fast one on everybody and skipped town with the money, but he wasn't dead.

But another part of me wanted to cry. How had this happened? When had Ed—my Ed—become so obsessed with money that he would steal from everyone he loved, and then abandon them? I knew he loved his children, and he'd loved being a partner at one of the premier law firms in town. I'd even accepted that he somehow loved his new wife.

"Do they think Barracuda Woman is involved with his scheme?" I asked.

"Shoot. I forgot to ask him that. But didn't Keith say they'd already talked to her?"

"Yes." I glanced up to find the good detective watching me. No doubt eavesdropping. "You know he's here right now."

"You mean Keith? Where? At your house?"

"That's right. He brought a search warrant."

"Oh, my! I'm coming over right now."

"Why? To see him or to help me?" I was too upset to

stop myself from being catty. But Liz ignored my bad temper.

"To help you *and* to see him. He owes me because I called him with Larry's information before I called you. Surely he'll realize now that none of this involves you."

"Maybe."

After I hung up I took the kids into the garden, as far away as we could get from the police crawling all over our house. I told them what Liz had discovered.

To my surprise, this time Pearl didn't cry. She sat down on the glider next to the fountain and just stared at me. But I knew her, and from the crease between her eyes and the jut of her chin, she was getting angrier and angrier by the second.

"Why didn't he just tell us he needed money from our trust funds?" Ronnie asked. "He's my dad. I would've given it to him."

"Because he knows I would have objected to it," I said.

Pearl stood up. "It doesn't matter why he did it. He stole our money, Mom's money, and money from his own law firm." She shook her head. "I wonder if he stole any money from that bitch he married."

I'd wondered that myself.

Ronnie ran an agitated hand through his hair. "What will happen to him when he's caught?"

"I don't know." I shook my head. "I guess it depends on whether anyone presses charges."

"Are you going to?" he asked me.

"Actually, I'd already started legal proceedings against him to get our money back."

"I'm pressing charges," Pearl vowed. "After all the crap he's put us through—the divorce, his new wife. My graduation. He *had* to do things *his* way, and too bad for us. Well, I say, what goes around comes around. This time it's too bad for *him*."

"But Pearl, he's our dad—"

"You know what?" I interjected. "We don't have to think about that right now." I walked up to Pearl and smoothed a tangle of hair from her cheek. "First he needs to be found. Then we'll see about the rest."

Pearl met my gaze, and I watched as her fierce anger faded into disillusion, and then sorrow. She put her arms around my waist, and I hugged her tight. "It will all turn out okay eventually. Meanwhile we just have to hang tough. We have to hang tough together."

Against my shoulder I felt her head nod, and something in my heart turned over. My baby girl was back, my darling daughter who'd been so torn up by her Dad's defection that she'd struck out at all of us, had returned to the circle of my love. I reached an arm to Ronnie and he joined us in a group hug.

That's how Liz found us.

"Oh, isn't that sweet," she cooed, smiling with delight. "I bet ya'll haven't done that in a while."

"We'll be doing it a lot more," I said. "Whether they like it or not. So. How about I make us a big Southern breakfast?"

"Mom," Pearl said. "It's dinnertime."

"So? I'm in need of comfort food about now. Bacon and eggs and grits sounds perfect for dinner."

"Oh, yeah," Ronnie said. "I want my grits with cheese."

"I like mine with lots of butter," Liz said. "But don't tell Nita."

"We ought to call her," I said. "Get her over here too."

"Wait," Pearl said. "Isn't she the one that was, like, dating Dad *after* he married Barracuda Woman?"

"Yes," I admitted. "But she didn't know he was my ex, or that he was married."

"Man, this is so messed up," Ronnie said.

Liz pulled me to the side. "Can I ask Keith to stay too?"

"Are you serious?" Then I rolled my eyes. "If you must. But he won't stay. He's a by-the-book cop. The fact that you may have broken the case open for him won't mean anything to him."

"He's just doing his job, Joan. Really, he's not so bad."

"Maybe. But I don't want you getting hurt, honey. And in the end I'm afraid he'll hurt you."

"I'm a lot stronger than I used to be," she replied. "And a lot smarter too. After all," she added with a saucy grin, "I was smart enough to pick you for a friend."

"Smarter than me," I had to concede.

"Where did you two meet?" Pearl asked.

"At the Oasis," Liz and I responded in unison.

Pearl gave me a wry smile. "Well, I guess you better call Nita then. That's where you met her too, right?"

"Right."

Nita showed up ten minutes later, just as NOPD's finest were leaving. "I made a list of what we've taken," Detective Norris said.

I took it from him. "I need my computer in order to run my business. How long will you have it?"

"I can't give you a definitive date. But as soon as we've finished with it, we'll return it to you."

That was a big help. Still, I detected a less suspicious attitude on his part. Thanks to Liz's information I guess I wasn't so high up on his suspect list. I heaved a sigh. "I'm making breakfast for everyone. You're welcome to join us."

His eyes cut to Liz, then back to me. "Thanks," he muttered. "But I have work to do."

I watched him leave without looking at anyone else. But that fast I knew. He liked Liz. That meant even when this investigation was over with, if I was going to stay Liz's friend—and I was—then I would just have to accept Detective Keith Norris too.

Okay. Once I was exonerated of any wrongdoing in this case, I could do that.

I turned back to the kitchen where my two kids and my two best friends were starting to pull out plates and pans and a box of grits. This was nice, me and the people I most cared about.

But two people were missing.

"Liz, why don't you call Cora Lee and see if she's hungry."

"That's a good idea."

"And since some of the pressure seems to be easing off me as a suspect, what do you think about me calling Quentin?"

CHAPTER 18

LIZ

I overslept the next morning—maybe because we'd stayed up till almost two, eating, laughing, and generally blowing off steam. Cora Lee had come, but by ten o'clock she'd fallen asleep on the front parlor settee. She might not look pregnant yet, but she sure had all the symptoms.

Quentin had come over too. It was the first time Pearl had met him, and I braced myself for an explosion. But to my surprise she took his good-looking, youthful blackness in stride. The truth is, Quentin is so studly I bet Pearl would have dated him if he'd asked her first. But knowing he'd bailed her mother out of jail, and seeing how Joan's face lit up when he arrived, must have set Pearl straight.

I was glad, because up to now Pearl had come across as a rich, spoiled brat, not someone I thought I ever could like. But this crisis with her father must have put everything back into perspective for her, because she, her mom and Ronnie seemed like the perfect example of a loving family. Exactly what I wanted to have.

Anyway, we cooked and ate and dissected Ed's disappearance every which way we could. Then Joan told everyone about our new partnership in Shear Delight, and we all toasted with orange juice.

If only Keith had been there too.

We didn't leave Joan's house until almost two o'clock, but I was too keyed up to fall asleep until nearly four. That's why I overslept and was late to my first appointment—9:00 a.m., highlights and a cut—and looked like a wild-haired, puffy-eyed mess when I arrived. I worked like a fiend to make up for my goof-up, because Archibald is a stickler for punctuality. Not that it really mattered if he got mad at me. I planned to give him notice today. But I guess I hate to disappoint anyone.

It was almost noon before I caught him alone. "Something really wonderful has happened for me," I began. "I'm buying my old salon back."

"Buying it back?" Then his eyes narrowed. "Does that mean you're quitting on me?"

"Well, yes. I'm sorry, Archie—"

"After all I've done for you?"

"I don't mean I'm leaving today. You know I would never leave you in the lurch. I'll be happy to stay on until you can find someone—"

"No, no!" He threw his hands up in the air. "If you don't want to work for me, fine! I'm sure as hell not going to keep my competition employed!"

And that fast I was out of a job. Not that I was sorry. I just hoped the deal with Joan and Dennis happened soon.

"My attorney's drawing up the papers as we speak," she told me when I called her to tell her what had happened.

"I'm supposed to get them tomorrow. Then all I have to do is write him the check and get the keys."

"And you can do that? Write him a check for that much money and get us in the shop that fast?"

I heard her laugh. "We can do it, Liz. You and I. So maybe you should just relax today and tomorrow, because once we're in the shop, I hope you'll be very, very busy."

She was so optimistic, the knots of tension in my back began to ease. "You better believe we'll be busy. You know, when I drove by the shop it was closed. Maybe I should call Mai and Marc to see if he laid them off. I hope they haven't already found new jobs."

"Good idea. But wait until Dennis has signed on the dotted line."

"Oh, yeah. We don't want him to get wind of this."

"Right. On another, less pleasant topic," Joan said. "Did you happen to see the paper this morning?"

"No. Something about Ed?"

She read the important parts to me, and though there weren't a lot of details, it managed to sound pretty scary. "How are you doing with all this?" I asked.

"It's funny. I've sort of decided not to let any of it get to me. I suppose that means I'm kind of numb."

"Well, just hang in there, I guess. This can't last forever."

After we hung up I ran out to buy the *Times-Picayune*. I'd just finished reading the entire article about Ed and the tangled web that surrounded him, when who should knock on my door but Keith? Thank goodness I'd fixed my hair and makeup at the salon.

"I have a few questions for you," he said, all stiff and coplike.

I just smiled at him—once I was over my shock. After all, if he only had a few questions, he could have just called.

"Sure." I held the door open. "Come on in."

He followed me to the kitchen, glancing around, like he was trying to figure me out from the appearance of my apartment. Was that just an automatic cop thing, or was he really interested in me? "Would you like some iced tea?"

"No thanks."

I poured us each a glass anyway and sliced fresh lemon wedges for it. He didn't say anything; neither did I. Was he jockeying for time? I know I was.

"So." I set a glass and napkin in front of him, then sat across the kitchen table from him. "What questions?"

He cleared his throat and flipped open his little notebook. "In the course of our investigation we've learned that Joan Hoffman is buying your old salon back from your husband."

"Ex-husband," I said. "It'll be official next month."

He stared at me. "Ex-husband," he said. "But she *is* buying the business, correct?"

"Yes. But how could you know that?"

"It's what I do, Liz. Find out things about people."

"Oh. Well, did you know that she and I are going in as partners? Co-owners?"

"Yes, I heard that. But for now you work at a place called Archibald's?"

"Wrong." I replied, pleased that there were some things he didn't know. "I quit. Today." Then I smiled at him, filled with nothing but good feelings about my future. "Joan and I are hoping to have Shear Delight reopened within a week or so."

"That sounds good."

I nodded. I couldn't think of anything else to say, especially with those vivid blue eyes of his studying me so intently. Something was clicking between us, but he didn't exactly seem happy about it.

Finally he cleared his throat. "Thanks for the tip about St. Romaine's law firm. Once we confronted the managing partners they came clean about their financial losses."

"Why didn't they say anything about it the first time you questioned them?"

He shrugged one shoulder "Who knows why lawyers do any of the things they do? They said they didn't want the bad press. I guess they'd rather lose money than lose face."

I twirled my glass in a circle on the Formica tabletop. "That's kind of what Larry said too. Only now they'll lose both. Unless you can find Ed and the money, right?"

"Maybe. Even if we find him, the money could be long gone."

We both lifted our glasses and drank. I was nervous having him in my apartment, but a good kind of nervous, especially since I didn't think he was here just because of Ed St. Romaine. "Do you ever see any of the old gang from McMain?"

He shook his head. "Not too much. I see Jake Loew now and again—he's a Jefferson Parish cop. And I went to the twentieth reunion a couple of years back."

"I went to mine too. I graduated the year after you."

"Yeah, I know."

"You know?" I said. "More investigation stuff?"

He gave me this odd look. "I remember you from high school, Liz. You used to date Bill somebody. He was in my homeroom."

He remembered me and the guy I dated? "Wow," I said, trying to cover my goofy excitement over that. But I couldn't keep down the humongous grin on my face. "I haven't thought of Billy Gehle in years. I wonder whatever happened to him?"

Keith didn't smile back. It was like a cloud had passed over his face. "If you want to look him up again now that you're single, you can probably find him on the Internet."

"Who, Billy? I'm curious about him," I said. "But not that curious."

And that fast the sun was out again. "Good," he said, just as Pumpkin jumped onto his lap.

It probably sounds really flaky and woo-woo New Age. But when Pumpkin jumped onto Keith's lap and Keith started scratching him behind the ears, that was like the final stamp of approval. I leaned forward. "When will this investigation officially be over?"

I could tell by the glint in his eyes that he knew what I really was asking. "When St. Romaine is located."

"So you're saying we can't date until you find Ed St. Romaine?" I could not believe I was being so bold! But I went on. "That doesn't seem fair."

Slowly he grinned. "If you promise not to stick your nose in the case anymore, I guess we could consider your part in the investigation done."

It was my turn to grin. "Good."

"But there is one thing," he said.

"What?" My heart was beating so fast I thought I would faint.

"It may be kind of old fashioned, but I still like being the one to do the asking."

My stomach did this funny little fluttery thing, and I could not stop smiling. "Okay. I can live with that."

"Good. So." He planted his palms on the table and stood. "I'd better get going." But he paused and gave me this long, steady look. His face didn't smile, but his eyes did. "I'll be in touch."

JOAN

It was around midmorning that the phone calls had begun.

"I read about Ed in the paper."

"My dearest Joan. I've been meaning to call you, and then I saw the paper. How are you holding up?"

"We've missed you at the Bon Temps Luncheon. And oh, your poor children must be positively traumatized."

"He's obviously gone off the deep end," another viciously curious acquaintance said. "I bet you're glad now that you're divorced from him."

I quit answering the phone at ten twenty-two. If it was this bad just because Ed was missing, how much worse and more mean-spirited would it become when the paper revealed the next chapter in Ed's sordid tale, about all the money he'd stolen from us and his firm? I knew that had to be coming next, because the last call I received was from Channel 26, and even now Channel 4 was setting up on the sidewalk in front of the house.

Ronnie peered past the window sheers, scowling. "Man, I don't want them to film me walking with a cane."

"What's the matter, afraid you'll look lame?" Pearl asked as she ate a banana. "Get it? Lame?"

"Ha, ha," he said. "That was funny. Not."

She shrugged and lifted a corner of the curtains to look outside. "Just don't go outside, then."

"But I need to go to the gym. Suzanne is picking me up at eleven for swim therapy. What's she gonna think when she sees all this crap?"

"I'll bring you to the spa," I told him. "Call Suzanne and let her know, then get in the car in the garage and I'll take you."

"Well, I'm going out through the front gate," Pearl announced. "And I'm telling everyone that Barracuda Woman is the real problem."

Ronnie snorted. "Lawsuit city. You should know that. You're a lawyer's kid."

"You can't sue someone for telling the truth."

"Sure you can," he said, bracing himself on the open refrigerator door while he rummaged around inside. "Especially if you don't have any morals—"

"Like Barracuda Woman," we all said in unison.

"I know you're angry, Pearl," I said after we quit laughing. "But it would be better for everyone if we just stay quiet and at most say that we don't know where he is and that we're worried about him."

"But I'm not worried," she said. "I'm pissed. Daddy's

missing because he wants to be missing. I don't think anything bad has happened to him at all."

That's what I thought too until Detective Norris showed up. By then the kids were gone, the television cameras had left, and I was on the phone with a client, trying to explain why I couldn't e-mail her a draft of her newsletter without letting on that the police had my computer.

From the grim look on his face I knew it wasn't good news. "I'll get right to it, Ms. Hoffman. We've recovered your ex-husband's car. The lab went over it and found two bullet holes—"

"What!"

"—and bloodstains on the front seat."

My knees turned to Jell-O and I had to sit down on the bench in the foyer. "Is it...*his* blood?"

"The lab is checking on that. Do you own a gun?"

"No! No, I've never owned a gun in my whole life. Or even touched one. Wait. I did try skeet shooting once when we were on a cruise. Does that count?"

He ignored me, which was actually kind, because I was babbling. "How about your children?" he went on.

"Of course not!" I jumped up and glowered at him. "They have no reason to hurt their father and I can't believe you'd ever think they would!"

"We're looking at everyone, Ms. Hoffman."

"I know. But...but I thought the new theory was that he'd skipped town with money from the firm."

"We can't ignore the bullet holes in his car." He paused. "Also, it turns out that the money started disappearing from the law firm's coffers several years ago. While you two were still married."

I stared at him, not believing my ears. "Are you implying that I'm involved with that too? Get real. *He* divorced *me*. If I'd had any inkling about this, I'd have damned sure used it against him in our divorce proceedings!"

"Maybe. But I'm told Dreyfous, Landry, and McCoy is considering suing you for a return of at least a portion of that money."

He landed that bombshell on me, then left, mission accomplished. As soon as I could breathe again, I snatched up the phone and punched in Doyle Carmadelle's number. Doyle, of course, wasn't there. At least not to me.

"Fine," I bit out to his secretary, whom I'd known for years but who now acted like I was a stranger. "Tell Doyle that I have some information for him. Something he'll be very eager to know about."

I was lying, of course. But I figured he wouldn't call me any other way. Then I called Andrea Purvis.

"Whew," she exclaimed once I filled her in. "You really get around, don't you? This is the most fun I've had in a divorce case in ages."

I sat down cross-legged on the couch in the TV room. "It doesn't feel fun to me."

"I guess not. Look, Dreyfous, Landry, McCoy is probably just blowing smoke. And even if they come after you, it'll be long after this missing Ed business is cleared up."

"But what if it's never cleared up? We thought he'd run off with the money. But if somebody shot him…" I felt awful worrying about being sued while Ed could be dead somewhere.

"Are the cops pursuing any leads?"

"Not that they've mentioned to me. I seem to be the only one they want to crucify."

"Were you ever in Ed's car?"

"No. It's new."

"Good. No fingerprints. And can you account for your time the day Ed went missing?"

"Probably."

"I suggest you recreate that day on paper. Everywhere you went and who can verify it."

I could do that. But it made me sick to think it was necessary. "I don't have anything to do with this, Andrea. I swear."

"I know that, Joan. I just want the cops to know it too." She paused. "How are you holding up with all this?"

I shook my head. "Okay, I guess. Mostly I'm in shock."

"The best way to deal with that is to go on with your daily routine. Work, play, whatever. And speaking of work," she added. "My secretary is faxing you the contract for purchasing that salon as we speak. Glance over it and get back to me on any changes."

It was a relief to have something positive to do. Once I had the papers I called Dennis first, then Liz.

"He's meeting me at the salon at four," I told her. "I'm bringing him a cashier's check, he's bringing the keys, and we'll sign the papers. It should take all of three minutes."

"I wish I could be there to gloat," she said. "I want him to know I got back what he stole from me."

"We can do that," I said. "Once he signs the papers, I'll call you. You might want to bring Cora Lee too."

CHAPTER 19

LIZ

Cora Lee and I sat in my car around the corner from Shear Delight, waiting anxiously for Joan's call. We had all decided to dress for Dennis.

Joan's accessory was money, and she wore almost every real jewel she owned: lots of rings, three bracelets on one arm, her Rolex on the other, a triple strand of pearls, and a pair of gorgeous diamond-and-pearl earrings that were never meant to be worn during daylight hours. Her hair was big; her skirt was short; and we made her double the amount of perfume she usually wore. Picture Candice Bergen feeling just a little bit slutty.

Cora Lee's accessory was youth. She wore a cute halter sundress that hid the overnight thickening of her waistline. She didn't need a push-up bra to emphasize her breasts, which were already getting bigger thanks to Junior. We made her up like a dewy fresh teenager, all rosy cheeks, pouty lips, and shiny, swingy hair. I swear, the girl would have been carded at any bar in town. Well, at any respectable bar.

As for me, I was at a loss until Joan asked me how I thought of myself these days. "Who were you before Dennis, during the years between your first divorce and the time you met him?"

"I…I don't know," I admitted, and it shamed me. "I was just this hair stylist who worked hard and was good at what she did."

"Did you date a lot?"

I shook my head. "A little, but they usually turned out to be losers and…I guess I figured I was a flop with guys. Bad judgment. So I worked. I was all about the work and saving money for a shop of my own. It wasn't until I hit my thirties that I realized I was running out of time to have a family. So I started dating again, and eventually I met Dennis."

"So you were a businesswoman," Joan said.

"Yeah. I guess I was."

"A tycoon in the making." She grinned.

I laughed. "Right."

"So let's dress you as one. Ms. Entrepreneur Extraordinaire."

That's how once more I came to be wearing my navy blue suit and cream blouse with the plunging neckline. But this time I put my hair up in a sleek chignon. I wore sky-high pumps with man-eater pointed toes, and Joan loaned me a red sharkskin briefcase that matched the blood-red manicure Cora Lee had given me.

But none of that changed the fact that I was sweating bullets in the air-conditioned chill of my car. You see, as much as I hated everything Dennis had done to me, I still wasn't sure I hated *him*.

I try not to hate anyone. Bad karma.

But I hadn't seen him face-to-face in months. What if he looked at me with those soulful eyes and gave me that crooked, one-sided grin of his? He'd seduced me on our first date with that grin. He'd won my heart with that grin, and won a million arguments between us with it too.

Could I resist it now?

I took Cora Lee's hand and stared earnestly at her. "Are you scared?"

She nodded. "The man does have his charms."

"I know. But he's a selfish, self-centered bastard."

"Yeah. And a sneaky, lying one too."

My phone rang and we both jumped. I fumbled with it, dropped it on the floor before finally snapping it open.

"I guess he's not answering," I heard Joan say. That was our cue for "the deal is done."

I hung up and looked at Cora Lee. "Okay. It's show time."

All the lights were on in the shop, and Dennis was sprawled back in Chair Three, his back to the door. When the entry bell tinkled he barked, "We're closed," without bothering to look up.

"No, we're not," I retorted.

His head jerked around first. Then when he saw me *and* Cora Lee, he spun the chair around and just gaped, eyes wide and mouth open like he couldn't believe it was us.

It felt amazingly good to see him at a loss for words. But even more satisfying was the fact that he didn't move me. He didn't. I didn't feel love or hate, or even pity. Something else seemed to flood my insides, something sweet and satisfying that chased all those other emotions away.

Not the taste of victory so much as the taste of…self-confidence.

I breathed in deeply and smiled. "We're definitely open for business, aren't we, Cora Lee?"

"That's right," she agreed, standing tall with one hand resting possessively over her stomach.

I waltzed right past Dennis like he was as inconsequential as a roach crawling across the floor. I set my sexy red briefcase on the counter and flipped it open. "I have the partnership papers right here," I said to Joan.

"Great. Where do I sign?"

Dennis still didn't say a word until she pulled out a pen, one of those expensive ones inlaid with enamel and gold. Then he lurched up from the chair and glared at us.

"Wait just one damn minute," he growled. "What in the hell is going on here?"

Joan shrugged. "I should think it's obvious. I bought your business, now I'm taking on a partner."

"A partner? But what about me? I told you we could be partners, only you said—" He broke off as the truth finally dawned on him. He pointed at Joan. "You plotted against me." His accusing finger swung to include me and Cora Lee. "You betrayed me."

"*We* betrayed *you?*" I scoffed. Then I started laughing. I didn't have to force it. The whole situation suddenly struck me as hilarious, like some goofy sitcom where the man is too stupid to figure out that he's been had.

Once I started laughing I couldn't stop. His face got dark with rage, which started Joan laughing too, and then Cora Lee too.

"Don't spend all that money in one place, Dennis," Cora Lee managed to say between guffaws. "You're gonna need it for child support."

"Child support? No way!"

"Better get a job, Daddy," Joan taunted him. "This time you messed with the wrong women."

I won't repeat the awful cursing that erupted from his mouth. Every foul word I'd ever heard, plus some I could only guess the meaning of. How had I ever loved this man?

But that didn't matter. I wasn't going to dwell on the past. I took Joan's pen and with a flourish signed my name. "There." I smiled at her, my dear, wonderful friend. "We're officially partners now, and as managing partner, my first act is to hire Cora Lee." I stuck out my hand, which Cora Lee shook.

"I accept," she said, shooting a smug look at Dennis.

"Screw you!" Dennis shouted as he strode for the door. "Screw all three of you!"

"Don't you just wish," Joan flung at his back.

He had no response to that except to slam the door so hard it vibrated. For a moment silence reigned. Then Cora Lee turned to me, a very serious look on her face. "I can start work immediately. But I wonder, are you planning to offer health benefits?"

JOAN

The scene with Dennis could not have been more satisfying. Like the ending to *The First Wives Club* or that Dolly Parton movie *9 to 5*. But it left me exhausted. Maybe it was just the culmination of a long, emotionally draining week. Anyway, though it was only six-thirty when I got home, I was too wiped out to anticipate anything more strenuous than ordering a pizza, putting on my nightgown, and sticking a movie in the DVD player. *Thelma and Louise* this time, though I always turn it off before the final scene.

I must have dozed off, because when the phone rang I jerked, and in a moment of confusion, couldn't find the phone next to the bed.

Finally I grabbed the receiver, pointed the remote control at the TV to lower it, and said, "Hello."

I heard noises, crackling interference and the sound of—what?—Birds? Crickets? "Hello? Who's there?"

"Joan?"

My heart stopped. "Ed?"

"Joan," he repeated. Then I could swear I heard him sob. "Joan!"

"Ed. Is that you? Oh, my God, where are you? Everybody's been frantic looking for you."

"Joan," he repeated again in this hoarse, emotional voice that was his and yet not his. "You have to help me."

I had the phone receiver pressed so tight to my ear it hurt. "Of course, Ed. Of course. Where are you? I'll come get you."

"No, no. You can't do that." He paused, and the background noises took over again. It sounded like he was outside somewhere. "I have a plan," he said. "Just bring me a car and my passport."

His passport? My heart hurt for him. "I don't have your passport, Ed. And anyway, the police know everything."

"What?"

"They've been here, Ed. To the house. They questioned me, and the kids too." Now that I was getting over my initial shock, I started to get mad. "I know you don't give a damn about me. But how could you do this to your children? How could you?"

"You don't understand. It's not the police. It's Doyle."

"Doyle? He's talked to the police too."

"He has?"

That was the clearest he'd sounded so far. "At first Doyle and the other people at your firm didn't tell the police the whole truth. About the missing money. But then Liz talked to Larry and figured it out and—"

"Liz?"

The line went dead.

"Damn it!" I stared at the phone, then hung it up. "Call back, Ed. Call back."

He did. "Look, my battery's almost dead."

"Tell me where you are. I'll come get you."

"No. It's too dangerous."

"I'll go with you to the police, Ed. For the kids' sake, I'll stand by you and help any way I can."

He started crying again. "I'm sorry, Joan. I'm so sorry. I've been such an ass."

It felt so good, so satisfying, hearing him admit that. He *had* been an ass, and the past two years had been hideous. But the previous twenty-five defined the bulk of my life, and they still meant a lot to me. "Look, Ed. Just tell me where you are."

"It's too dangerous," he repeated. "If they find me, they'll kill me. They will!"

"Kill you? Who? What do you mean?" Then I remembered the two gunshots in his car. And the blood. Suddenly I felt cold. "You're not talking about the police, are you?"

"Just drive your car down to Verdunville. There's this boat ramp. Leave the car in the parking lot there. And hide the keys on top of the driver's front tire."

"Verdunville?"

"It's just past Morgan City. Take Highway 90."

"No, Ed. This doesn't make any sense. I think—"

"Just do it, Joan. Please. My phone's dying on me. Just do it, okay? If you ever loved me, just do this one last thing—"

Then he was gone.

I sat there for ten minutes, trying to reach his cell phone, then when that didn't work, debating what I should do.

"Damn it, Ed!" I shouted at my useless telephone. I was back to being scared for him, but I was furious too.

Downstairs I heard Ronnie's voice, and a woman's. Fueled by pumping adrenaline, I threw on a pair of jeans and a sleeveless teal shell. Then I hurried down to the kitchen.

Ronnie looked up. "Hey, Mom. You remember Suzanne?"

Of all times for him to have company! I managed a smile. "I've seen you swimming laps, but we've never been introduced."

She was pretty and definitely older than Ronnie, and they both walked with a similar sort of limp. But though his eventually would disappear, hers was permanent. That didn't seem to bother Ronnie, though. As I watched him pull out bread and cheese and roast beef and tomatoes, it was obvious to me that he was smitten.

"Dagwoods are my specialty," he boasted to her. "Can I make you one, Mom?"

"Um, no." I wanted desperately to tell him about his father's call, but now was not the time. "I'm on my way out."

He gave me a skeptical once-over from my uncombed hair and bare face to my shoeless feet. "You are?"

"Don't be a smart aleck. Watch out for him, Suzanne, he's got a sassy mouth and a bad attitude." *And a big heart.* I smiled at them both, remembering when Ed and I had been this new to each other. How could things have gone so wrong?

Upstairs again, I threw on some lipstick, found a pair of sandals and called Liz.

"Thank God he's alive!" she exclaimed after I'd described our aborted conversation.

"Yes, but he's terrified. I told him I'd pick him up, but he said it was too dangerous."

"Too dangerous?"

"That's what he said. Instead he wants me to leave a car for him down in Verdunville."

"Where's that?"

"Somewhere down in the swamps past Morgan City."

"Are you going to do it?"

Several beats of silence went by. "I think I might. Not to leave the car for him, though. But to talk to him."

"But, Joan. He said it wasn't safe."

"Yeah, that's what he said. But you know, Ed's been acting really weird for a while now. First Barracuda Woman. Then our divorce. Then came that eyelift, and all this money stuff. I'm beginning to think he's lost it, Liz. Gone crazy. Obviously his wife isn't going to help him. Why else would he have called me? I have to at least try to help him, if only for the kids' sake. So yes, I'm going to drive down there, park the car where he said, and wait until he shows up. What else can I do?"

I knew what she was going to tell me before she said it. "You could call Keith."

"I could. And eventually I will. But first I want to go down there and see Ed for myself."

"Well, then, I'm going with you."

I should have said no. But the truth is, I was relieved to have some company. I didn't want to tell the kids about their dad. Not just yet. That's why when I went downstairs, I told Ronnie I was taking a drive with a friend down to Morgan City. Better to stay as close to the truth as I could. "I won't be back till tomorrow."

"Is this friend named Quentin?" he asked, shooting a grin at Suzanne. "Quentin is her boyfriend."

"Not with Quentin," I said. But I felt a blush on my cheeks. My night with Quentin was coming, just as soon as this mess with Ed was behind me. "I'm going with my friend, Liz."

"Cool. Have fun. Wait, did you say Morgan City?"

"Yes. Why?"

"I just remembered that Dad said something about a fishing trip out of Morgan City."

My heart speeded up. "When was that?"

"I don't know. They went a couple of months ago."

"Not the trip. When did he tell you about it?"

"I don't know. Last week? We were at the gym—one of the times we were working out together." He gave me a curious look. "Is something going on I should know about?"

"No," I lied. "Liz's mother lives down there." I gave them a bland smile, but my mind was whirling. Ten minutes later I picked up Liz and we were on our way.

Highway 90 is dark at night and lonely, especially to two urban girls used to street lighting and lots of traffic, day and night. By the time we drove through Boutte and past Raceland and Morgan City, then made two wrong turns and had to backtrack seven miles, it was almost eleven o'clock when we reached the marina. It was more of a simple boat ramp than a full-scale marina.

"I guess we won't be opening the shop tomorrow," Liz said in a hushed voice as we pulled into the deserted shell parking area. I parked the car, then turned off the motor and the lights.

"We should have given Cora Lee a key to open up," I said in the same nervous whisper.

A car went by on the narrow local road behind us.

"I wonder where he is," Liz murmured.

"I don't know." There wasn't much around us. A small wood-framed office with peeling paint and a buckled metal roof sat next to a wooden bulkhead with two rusty gas pumps. A concrete boat ramp sloped into the dark water, and a few boats were tied up to the left at a short

U-shaped wooden dock. One light burned outside the office; another burned at the dock. Beyond them Six Mile Lake and the marshes stretched dark and ominous.

Was Ed somewhere nearby watching us?

"Maybe he's on one of those boats," Liz murmured.

"Or maybe he's in a boat out on the water somewhere."

"Does he own a boat?"

"Not that I know of. Ed was never a hunting and fishing kind of guy. Not when we were married. But Ronnie told me that Ed referred to a fishing trip down here."

We waited fifteen minutes. It seemed like five hours.

"Maybe he knows we're in the car and he won't come out until we leave," Liz said.

"Leave and go where?"

A thousand crickets filled the night with sound, and somewhere a frog sang his mating call. But still it seemed ominously quiet. "I still think we should call Keith," Liz muttered.

I have to admit that the longer we sat in this dark, lonely place, the better turning this whole thing over to the hard-faced detective sounded. "I plan to call him, Liz. I just want to see Ed with my own eyes, you know? To make sure he's not hurt, and maybe find out who he thinks is out to get him."

"What if Ed never shows up?"

I didn't answer her, but that thought was already torturing me. What if Ed didn't show up? Then again, what if he did show up, refused to listen to me and took my car?

I glanced at my watch. "It's eleven-thirty. If he doesn't show up by midnight, I'll call Detective Norris. I'm not telling him where we are, though, just that Ed's alive and we're trying to find him."

"Fair enough." She unscrewed her water bottle and took a long swallow. "I have to go to the bathroom."

"No, you don't. You just think you have to go because there's no bathroom available."

"No, Joan. I really have to go."

"Well." I gestured to the great mosquito-infested outdoors. "Pick your spot. There's no one here to see you."

"Except maybe Ed."

I sighed. "Do you want me to go with you?"

"Yes. But not till you call Keith."

"Good grief, what does he have to do with it?"

I could barely make out her face in the inky blackness of the swampy night. But what I saw was utterly serious. "I'm not getting out of this car until some law enforcement officer knows where I am. In case we get grabbed," she added in exasperation.

"Do you want me to call him now?"

"I can wait till midnight," she conceded in a small, pained voice.

Precisely at midnight I dialed the detective's number. He answered on the second ring. "Don't you ever sleep?" I asked.

"No," he answered. "Do you?"

"Not as much as I used to."

"So what's up that has you calling me at midnight?"

I glanced at Liz. "Ed called me today." I explained everything—his fear and desperation, and his need for my car—basically, everything except where he told us to leave the vehicle.

"So you're somewhere down in the swamps, sitting alone in the dark, waiting for your crazy ex-husband to show up—and maybe the thugs that are chasing him, too."

"I'm not alone. Liz is right here with me." *So there, Mr. Stick-Up-Your-Butt.*

He muttered something, but all I could make out were the words *women* and *idiots.*

"So your really think there are thugs after him?" I asked.

"Damned straight. That's why you need to start your car right now and drive back home the same way you came."

Boy, did I want to do just that. "Can you trace this call? Can you tell where I'm calling from?"

"Me personally? No. But with a little help from the communications guys I can locate you according to the closest tower your cell phone is connecting through." He paused. "What's the matter, afraid those thugs will jump you and Liz? That you'll both be alligator bait long before we can find you? Is that what you want, Ms. Hoffman?"

He was a belligerent so-and-so, but he'd managed to read my mind. "All I want is Ed found and this whole mess over with."

"That's all we want too." He paused a moment. "Could you put Liz on the line?"

I handed the phone to her. "He wants to talk to you. Don't tell him where we are."

"Hi, Keith," she said with a nervous giggle. "Well, not too scared."

I stared out the side window, trying to give them their space.

She laughed again. "Well, I see water. And boats—"

"And Ed." I straightened up. "I see Ed!"

"What?" she said.

I pointed to a figure on the dock. A man stood just beyond the reach of the single light bulb.

"Is it really Ed?" Liz asked.

"I'm not sure."

Then I heard a gunshot.

Liz screamed and dropped the phone. I screamed and ducked and accidentally hit the horn.

The man on the dock disappeared. Then all hell really broke loose.

CHAPTER 20

JOAN

We went from pitch black to baseball-diamond bright, from all alone in this God-forsaken swamp to suddenly surrounded by a dozen cops—every one of whom had a gun. It was like we'd stumbled onto some giant stage set, only it was all too real.

"Oh, my God!" Liz cried. She'd slid down in her seat at the first shot, and wedged herself on the car floor. "Where did they all come from?"

I was scrunched down near the floor too, but not so far that I couldn't see the dock. What had happened to Ed?

"Police!" a man yelled. "Drop the gun. Drop it now!"

"Police? Keith?" Liz's head popped up.

She was right. I recognized his voice. But how could he possibly be here?

Frantically I scanned the flood-lit scene. "Over there." I pointed to the marina office.

Sure enough, Detective Norris came out crouching, his gun trained on some big guy who looked as pissed as hell. But not pissed enough to take on this many cops. The goon dropped his gun, then fell to his knees, his hands clasped behind his head. He'd obviously done this before.

Keith's partner cuffed him while Keith, still crouching low, ran toward the dock. A trio of uniformed cops stood near the water's edge. Had they found Ed?

For an achingly long minute the officers conferred with Keith. When the detective turned and stared over at my car, my heart sank like a lead fishing weight. The most horrible scenario raced through my head: they'd found Ed, only he was dead, shot by that first bullet.

Then two of the cops turned their flashlights on the water, and my hopes rose. Maybe Ed had jumped in the water to avoid the bullets. Maybe he was still alive.

Then again, he could have been shot and fallen in the water, or drowned in it. Maybe they were looking for his body.

A panic attack set in, full force. I could hardly breathe. I had to get out of the car, so I shoved the door open.

Liz grabbed my arm. "Don't go out there."

"I have to find Ed."

"They'll find him, Joan. Anyway, he brought this all on himself."

"I know he did. But..." How could I articulate my careening emotions? "He's the father of my children, and we had a good life together. For a long time it was good, Liz." Our eyes held. "This was never the kind of payback I had in mind."

She let me go and I ran toward the dock. I should have worn tennis shoes, not jeweled sandals.

When Keith saw me, he scowled and waved me off. "Get out of here. Now!"

No way. "Where's Ed?"

"Wait in the car. Deputy!" He grabbed a uniformed officer and pointed him at me. "Put her in her car."

"Ed!" I shrieked into the night. " Ed! Where are you? No! Let me go!" I said, trying to dodge the cop.

"Joan?"

Everyone froze at the shaky call that came from somewhere beneath our feet. He was under the dock!

"Ed?" It was him, I knew it! "Ed, where are you? Are you hurt?"

"Joan. You came."

Splashing beneath the wooden dock brought all the flashlights out again—and the guns.

"Don't shoot him!" I screamed. "He's unarmed." I paused. "You are unarmed, aren't you?"

"Yes." He let out a muffled curse. "But I've been shot."

He looked just awful when he swam out from beneath the dock, like an old man who could barely keep his head above water. No one wanted to jump in to help him, but one of the cops did toss him a life ring.

"Help me," Ed moaned, clinging to it.

"If you're bleeding," Detective Norris retorted, "you'd better get out of there before the gators catch your scent."

That got him going. In less than ten seconds he was at the dock and two officers hauled him up.

When Liz came up beside me, the cop holding me let me go. "Is he all right?" she asked.

"I think so. But he's in a world of trouble." Sure enough, despite Ed's bloodstained arm, he was frisked, cuffed, and read his rights.

"I hope we're not in trouble too," Liz murmured.

Good old Detective Norris obviously heard that, because he turned his hard gaze on the two of us. "You're damned right you're in trouble."

"For what?" I said, sounding a lot braver than I felt. I'd only been arrested once but I knew I didn't want to relive the experience. "Ed called me scared and crying, desperate for help. Then I called you to let you know."

"Yeah. But you didn't call me until three hours later when you got here and got scared too. Am I right?"

"Maybe. But I *did* call you. I wasn't trying to hide anything. I just didn't want you to scare him off— Wait a minute." In all the shooting and excitement I'd overlooked Detective Norris's very convenient appearance here. "You couldn't have gotten here that fast after I called." My mouth dropped open it hit me. "You followed us, didn't you?"

"But there was no one behind us," Liz said, shaking her head. "Remember? I kept looking back to see."

When Detective Norris looked at Liz his cop-face softened a little. "We were already here."

"Already here?" I said. "But how did you know?"

"He's a detective, Joan." Liz stared at him with shining eyes. "That's what he does."

I know everybody was operating on megadoses of adrenaline, but I could swear Liz's blatantly admiring remark made the big, bad detective blush.

It took another hour for the cops to process the scene. I didn't get to talk to Ed at all. But I watched from a distance as an EMT checked his shoulder. It seemed like the bullet had only grazed him. Thank God. He bled a lot, and he might need stitches, the EMT later told me. But he'd recover. At least from the bullet.

But why had that man been shooting at him in the first place?

When another pair of cops emerged from a stand of trees beyond the marina office with another guy in custody, it only deepened the mystery. Two thugs had been after Ed. But why?

We got no answers that night, even though Detective Norris questioned Liz and me about how we'd spent every minute of the past few days.

"For someone not involved in any of this, it sure seems like your Payback Club paid off," he said once he closed his little notebook.

"Beginner's luck," I retorted. At this point I was way too exhausted to care if I irritated him or not.

His brows arched, but Liz piped up. "Now, Keith. It's obvious Joan was only trying to help Ed for old times' sake. Remember, *he* called *her*."

"Yeah, I know."

Something about the casual way he said, "I know" caught my attention. "You know? You mean, you knew he'd called me even before I told you about it? Oh, my God!" All of a sudden I understood. "You got here before us for the same reason you 'know' Ed called me— you had my phone tapped, didn't you?"

He didn't bother to deny it, but only shrugged. "It was strictly legal. By the book."

"Did you listen to other conversations she had?" Liz asked. "Like with me?"

He nodded. "That's how I knew the two of you were partnering in that salon of yours."

"Why, you sneaky thing," she exclaimed. "How long has her phone been tapped?"

Quite frankly, I didn't care. I was so relieved this ordeal was over, I didn't care if he'd had a water glass pressed to my bedroom door. "All I want to know is, can you untap it tomorrow?"

"Sure," he said. "No problem."

"Fine. Come on, Liz. Let's go home." I looked at the detective. "We can leave, can't we?"

"Are you two okay to drive?"

"Probably." Then I paused. "What will happen to Ed?"

He glanced at the police car where Ed now sat, bandaged and handcuffed. Miserable. "He'll be booked on a variety of fraud charges here in St. Mary's Parish. They'll probably bring him to a hospital in Morgan City tonight. Then he'll be extradited back to New Orleans."

"Can he be bailed out of jail?"

He gave me a hard look. "I wouldn't suggest doing that, Ms. Hoffman."

"Don't worry, *I'm* not bailing him out." A part of me wanted to, but that was his new wife's job. If he still had a new wife.

"Good. Chances are a judge will consider him a flight risk. Then again, he's an attorney, so he probably knows a judge or two." That last came out with a sarcastic edge.

"Come on, Joan." Liz took my arm. "Let's go home. I'll drive while you call your kids."

LIZ

I tried not to eavesdrop while Joan talked to Ronnie and Pearl, but it's hard when you're in the same car.

"Yes, he's fine, honey.

"No, baby. Don't go to Central Lockup. He'll be booked in a jail down here tonight. I don't know when he'll be back in New Orleans.

"There are consequences for bad behavior, sweetheart. He'll probably have to go to jail for fraud."

Honey. Baby. Sweetheart. Those were the words that got to me. Who did I have in my life to use such endearments on? Pumpkin was the only one. Joan had her children. Cora Lee would soon have her baby. But I had no one. And at thirty-nine, I might already be too old.

My cell phone rang. Probably Cora Lee worried about us.

But it was Keith. It's funny how fast his voice banished my poor-pitiful-me blues. "Hi. Already checking up on us?"

"No. Yeah. Where are you?"

"We just passed the exit to Thibodeaux. Have you left the marina yet?"

"Just about to." He paused and I held my breath. *Please, please, please let him ask me out.*

"I have a question for you."

Damn. Another question. All my hopes deflated.

"That guy that spilled his guts to you," he went on.

"Larry?"

"Yeah. Larry Foucher." He paused. "You dating him?"

Up, up, up my spirits soared. "No. I was just pumping Larry for information."

"You do that a lot, lead guys on for what you can get out of them?"

I caught my breath. Is that what he thought of me? "When my best friend is a suspect in a crime she didn't commit, yes. I do. But if you're wondering if my interest in you was just because of this case, Keith, well, just ask me out on a date and you'll have your answer."

I could hardly breathe, and beside me I knew Joan was listening. "You told me you like to do the asking," I said into the yawning silence. "And anyway, I'm kind of an old-fashioned girl myself. So if you're interested, go ahead. Ask."

"Okay," he said. "How about dinner. Tomorrow night?"

"Yes." The word popped out without the least bit of dignity or pride. "Yes," I repeated, grinning at Joan like a village idiot. "But—"

"But?" he interrupted in a clipped voice

"But by 'tomorrow night' do you mean tonight coming up? It's already two in the morning, so actually tonight would be today."

He laughed and I just melted at the sound. "Today is Thursday," he said. "Tomorrow is Friday, and that's the night I'm talking about."

"Friday. Great. Yes."

I couldn't stop smiling, and it didn't help that Joan was grinning back at me. "You're crazy to go out with him," she told me after I finally hung up with Keith. "That man is one hard case."

"Maybe. But he's a straight-up, hard-working Boy Scout—"

"The exact opposite of Dennis," she finished for me.

We drove another hour, through Des Allemands, Paradis and Boutte. Joan called Nita to fill her in, and also woke up Cora Lee. We were approaching the Mississippi River Bridge and I thought maybe Joan had dozed off when she said, "This Payback Club of ours, it didn't exactly turn out the way I expected."

"No. But honestly, for me it's even better than I imagined. I mean, I have my shop and a new partner—and a new best friend."

She smiled over at me. "And we did wreck Dennis's new relationship."

"Yeah. Only I sure didn't expect to get Cora Lee and her baby as roommates—and to be glad about it."

We laughed together. "And then there's the handsome detective," she added in a suggestive tone.

"Yes, there is Keith. But you're not doing so bad at payback either. I'm guessing that Barracuda Woman is going to dump Ed, if she hasn't done it already."

"Yes. But in a way… It almost doesn't matter. I never thought I'd say this, but I'd rather Ed be happy with that horrible woman, than be locked away in prison."

"The two have nothing to do with each other," I said. "He's not going to prison because he married her. He's going because he's a thief."

"I know," she murmured. "But still."

We didn't get home until almost four. I hoped Cora Lee would wake up, because I was still too keyed up to sleep and I needed someone to talk to. But she was conked out, and even Pumpkin didn't stir when I slid into bed. I lay there in the dark, replaying every one of my conversations with Keith, and somewhere along the way I must have fallen asleep, because I ended up having this wildly erotic dream about him. Something that involved handcuffs and the back seat of a police cruiser.

Then that dream morphed into another one with each of us pushing a double baby carriage. Four babies. Even I wasn't that greedy!

JOAN

I woke up to the delicious smell of fresh coffee. "Sorry to get you up," Pearl said, sitting down on my bed. "But it's almost one o'clock, Mom, and I have to leave for work soon and I just had to talk to you."

"Yeah," Ronnie said, sitting on the other side of the bed. "Plus you've got like a hundred messages including two from Andrea Purvis and three from Quentin."

Quentin? That chased the cobwebs out of my head.

I pushed upright, squinting against the bright daylight. Almost one, Pearl had said. Why was I—

It came back in a startling rush, everything that had happened last night, and everything that had led up to it. "It wasn't a dream," I said.

Pearl rolled her eyes. "You mean "nightmare" don't you?"

I let loose a long sigh. "Yes. It was that."

"Here." Ronnie handed me a mug.

"Thanks. Wait, how did you get up the stairs?"

He grinned and flexed his injured leg. "It's the next phase of my rehabilitation, going up and down stairs."

"Oh, honey." I reached out and squeezed his hand. "That's so good." Then I put down the coffee and reached for Pearl's hand too, and for a moment we were connected, just like when they were little and used to climb in bed with Ed and me on weekend mornings.

Pearl must have been remembering the same thing too, because she squeezed back, a very young, sorrowful expression on her face. "He ruined everything."

"Your dad messed up, Pearl. But the only life he really ruined is his own. We're all going to be fine. All of us."

"I'm never going to forgive him," she vowed. "Never."

"I used to feel the same way, honey. I wanted so badly to get even with him. But now… Now I mainly feel sorry for him."

"What about all the money he took from us?" she asked.

"Believe me, I'm going to do everything I can to get it back. But I'm not going to let any of what's happened rule my life. And you shouldn't either."

"Grandma called this morning," Ronnie put in. "She saw the newspaper." He tossed it to me. "She was pretty upset. You'd better call her."

I grimaced. Sure enough, the front page had a picture of Ed—not a mug shot, thank God. The accompanying article focused on his disappearance and the money fiasco with his firm. It also mentioned the lawsuit I'd filed to get back the money he'd taken from me and the kids. But though it mentioned he'd been captured, there were no details about last night's events.

Still, how had the reporters even found out about it in time to get it in today's edition?

"Well," I said, pushing the paper aside. "I guess I'd better get up and face the day. What's left of it. But first…" I gathered them to me in a family hug. "I love you two. More than anything. And so does your dad, despite the bad decisions he's made. Try to remember that, okay?"

Ronnie nodded, too choked up to speak. Pearl's face was wet. "I love him too," she sobbed. "But I'm still mad at him."

It was a start.

Pearl left for work, dropping Ronnie off at Oasis on the way. Downstairs I faced a flurry of little yellow notes. Not only did I have the messages Ronnie had mentioned, there were numbers from a reporter from the *Times-Picayune* and every major news station in town, as well as someone from the AP newswire service.

It was going to be a long day. Which meant that I might as well start it off right. I picked up the phone and dialed. "Hello, Quentin."

"At last," he said in that low rumbly voice that sends tremors straight down to my belly. "Are you all right? When your kids wouldn't let me talk to you I got worried. But they said you were just wiped out."

"I'm fine. Fine. I was just so exhausted I guess they wanted to let me sleep."

"Then you probably haven't heard the latest."

"The latest?"

"Yeah. It turns out that one of the other attorneys at your ex's law firm was in on the scam. Do you know a Doyle Carmadelle?"

"Of course. What sort of scam—and how do you know all this?"

"My sister's best friend works in the newsroom for Channel 6. Now that your ex is in custody, he's spilling his guts. It turns out he and this Carmadelle guy were skimming money from the firm. But they started to get nervous about being caught."

I sat down hard on the stairs, unwilling to believe what I was hearing, but knowing in my heart it must be true. "I bet it started when I told Doyle about that fraudulent mortgage Ed took out. And then when I filed that lawsuit against Ed to get my money back."

"Yeah, that *would* do it. Anyway, when he started getting scared that the whole plot was going to cave in on him, Carmadelle got the bright idea to kill your ex and then blame everything on him."

"You mean Doyle hired those men? No." And yet it all made such perfect sense. Oh, poor Ed. How could he have been so stupid?

"I don't know," Quentin said. "To add insult to injury, I hear your ex's new wife has already filed divorce papers."

I laughed at that. "Big surprise." But really, I was sad for Ed and the way he'd ruined his life. Then the doorbell rang, and I jumped up. "Oh dear. Someone's at the door. It's probably someone with the press, though." I hesitated in the hall, then turned my back to the foyer. "The hell with them."

"I don't know, Joan. You'd better get it."

"Why? I'd rather talk to you."

"Well, that's nice to hear. I take it our date is finally on?"

I grinned at myself in the parlor mirror. Life could throw

all kind of left turns at me, but let Quentin say something like that, and all was right with the world. "Is tonight too soon?" I asked.

"Tonight is perfect," he said. "How does seven sound?"

Ooh, yummy! "Fine," I said. *More than fine.* But somehow I managed to hide how my insides were jumping for joy. That gave me five hours to get ready. But first I had to make reservations for dinner someplace really cozy, and to make sure the kids had plans away from the house. How was I going to arrange that?

The doorbell chimed again.

"Whoever that is sounds pretty insistent," he said.

"I don't care."

"Just answer the door, Joan. And if you don't want to talk to them, send them packing."

"Oh, all right. Hold on."

The bell sounded again, just as I jerked it open. "What do you...want?" I trailed off when I spied Mr. Tall, Dark and Handsome. Quentin.

"To see you," he said into the phone. Then he walked in, we both hung up and our date began.

Artist-in-Residence Fellowship–
Call for applications

She always dreamed of studying art in Paris,
but as a wife and mother she has had
other things to do. Finally, Anna is taking
a chance on her own.

What Happens in Paris

(STAYS IN PARIS?)

Nancy Robards Thompson

Mothers, sisters and other passengers

Novelist Maggie Dufrane's mama is the Mississippi queen of drama. When her sister Jean drops a shocker on the family, Mama thinks it's the best gossip she's heard all year. But it's up to reliable Maggie-the-family-chauffeur to fix things…again.

Driving Me Crazy

PEGGY WEBB

A woman determined to walk her own path

Joining a gym was the last thing
Janine ever expected to do. But with
each step on that treadmill, a new
world of possibilities was opening up!

TREADING LIGHTLY
ELISE LANIER

What happens when new friends get together and dig into the past?

Ex's and Oh's
Sandra Steffen

A story about secrets, surprises
and relationships.

Sometimes the craziness of living
the perfect suburban life is enough
to make a woman wonder…

Who makes up these rules, Anyway?

BY
STEVI MITTMAN

Available February 2006
TheNextNovel.com

Since when did life ever tell you where you were going?

Sometimes you just have to dip your oar into the water and start to paddle.

THE
SUNSHINE
COAST
NEWS

KATE AUSTIN

HN32TALL

Available February 2006
TheNextNovel.com